COURAGE

Lauren H Salisbury

Copyright © 2018 Lauren H Salisbury

Proofreader: Tia Silverthorne Bach of Indie Books Gone Wild (http://ibgw.net)

Cover design: K. Locke of Logos Creative Studio (https://logoscreativestudio.com/)

All rights reserved. No part of this publication may be reproduced, distributed, or transmitted in any form or by any means without the prior written permission of the publisher, except in the case of brief quotations embodied in critical reviews and certain other non-commercial uses permitted by copyright law. For permissions contact:

www.laurenhsalisbury.com/contact

ISBN: 9781976944611

For my husband, Dave, who inspired and encouraged me to follow my dream of writing – and then did the majority of the cooking while I sat at my laptop.

ACKNOWLEDGEMENTS

There are so many people without whom this novel would never have made it into print. If I miss anyone out of this list, I can only say that I am extremely sorry and I promise to remember to include them the next time round. Here goes nothing, then.

Thank you especially to Marion Rossiter, my alpha reader, but also to David Salisbury and Katie Crews. You valiantly read the early versions of Courage and argued through each and every sticking point until it was good enough to let other people read. I will always appreciate your enthusiasm once you discovered I could actually write a half-decent story. Each of you helped more than you realised, and you made the perfect team to keep me going.

Thank you also to my beta-readers: Jo Trickey, Bill Jenkins, and Colin Wilkinson. Your feedback helped me to tweak the manuscript until I had enough confidence in it to publish. You also made me think in a lot more depth about the details and issues I wanted to portray.

My deepest gratitude goes to Angela Silverthorne and Tia Silverthorne Bach. You were both answers to prayer, and I cannot stress enough how thankful I am for your input and support. Angela, you not only beta-read the manuscript and gave great feedback, but you also provided encouragement and advice that I desperately needed at the time. I will always value the friendship you offered. Tia, your generous proofreading help has given Courage the polish it needed to be ready for publication. I promise to follow your lead and pay it forward when the time comes.

Special mention has to go to Kent Locke, who designed the cover for Courage (which I love) and provided miraculous value for money. Thank you for your kindness and patience. You'll get more coffee eventually.

Thanks also have to go to my nieces, who helped invent names and titles, and, along with Eliana's class, prayed for the success of the book.

Lastly, full credit has to go to my Father in heaven and my saviour, Jesus Christ. You gave me the idea and the words to write this novel, and I can only pray that I've done them justice. Thank you for leading me every day; without you, I would be lost.

CAST OF CHARACTERS

Humans
Gilla	human slave on U'du
Amina (Ami)	Gilla's work friend
Aronin (Aro)	leader of the Resistance
Benn	senior medic
Damaya (Dee)	Gilla's best friend
Elias	Gilla's husband and Resistance leader
Gerom	Damaya's son and Mirami's rival
Menali (Nali)	Gilla's friend and Mirami's teacher
Mirami (kiddo)	Gilla's daughter
Than	Gilla's brother and member of the Resistance
Willan	Resistance leader

Esarelians on the cruiser
Ashal	Ra'hon (ruler) of Esarelian Empire, Reemah's father
Lorith	Na'hor (ultimate commander of military)
Nishaf	chief scientific advisor to Ashal
Reemah	Ra'hos (princess)
Selah	Reemah's friend
Sunath	chief trade and commerce advisor to Ashal
Velay	half-Oeal, Reemah's best friend

Esarelians on U'du
Lamesh	guard, second to Risoth
Risoth	Head Guard on U'du

Others
Jat	Baketag guard on U'du

Chapter 1

Day: 9   Month: 06   Year: 6428
Location: Planet U'Du, main slave settlement

Gilla wished her pregnancy could be over already; her back ached, her feet were sore, and her bump kept getting in the way of fusing the wiring in place. She wiped her forearm across her brow and took a moment to stretch her protesting muscles. The life-pods they were calibrating for the new space cruiser stood before her in an endless line of arduous labour. Glinting in the light of a hundred globes spread evenly over the cavernous ceiling of the building, the black metal of each pod was smooth and cool to the touch. As far as Gilla was concerned, the beauty of their design and form was offset by the effort necessary to manufacture each one.

The majority of the structure she toiled within comprised a large open space sectioned into six main areas. These extended into the distance to her right, with the adjoining prep rooms and storage bays beyond. It was only one of a dozen such buildings in her sector where each specialised workforce was made to complete a separate component of the Esarelian construction. Gilla's area contained six long rows of life-pods at various stages of assembly, with human slaves scurrying round each like the worker ants their masters took them for. Easily replaceable, yet highly skilled, their lives were lived on a perpetual knife edge.

Gilla and her friends were lucky the assignments for their building focused on circuitry and systems testing. Hauling the sometimes cumbersome and heavy parts into place for fusing was worse. With such physically intensive and often dangerous tasks, accidents were common and fatalities shrugged off as inconsequential by their guards.

Even at this distance, she could hear the din of activity from within those buildings. The rattle of pulleys, the clangs and screeches of metal coming to rest on metal, and the hiss and pops of fusion created a clashing symphony of industry that echoed and multiplied through the enormous rooms and far beyond. Gilla pitied those inside. Only their ear buds blocked the worst of the noise and prevented them from becoming deaf.

Gilla looked along the row of work stations and winced as Damaya threw her fusion wand on the floor and also stood back. They were nearly at the end of their shift and were not likely to finish their quota. At this rate, they would be receiving reduced rations again, the punishment for incomplete work. It made Gilla cringe to think of the penalty affecting all three members of her crew rather than just herself. Not that they minded; they had all been through similar situations, through pregnancy or illness, at some point over their years together.

Overcome with fatigue, Gilla swayed and put an arm out to steady herself. Damaya rushed over, snatching a canteen of water from the floor and thrusting it into her hands. "Here, drink something. Do you need to rest? Argh! You shouldn't be here in your condition."

Gilla put a protective hand over her swollen abdomen. "I'm all right, really. I just have a twinge in my back from bending to reach the AS panel. Besides, it's not like I have a choice to be here; I've still got a month and a half to go."

Harrumphing in response, Damaya moved behind Gilla and rubbed small circles on her lower back but made no further comment. The rules governing their labour as slaves were clear, but their lives could be worse. They weren't DNA-tagged or tracked, and Gilla *would* get one month of maternity leave once her baby was born, though she knew that was due to logistics rather than compassion, and there would be no exceptions before the event.

However, Gilla and the rest of her people were not free. They worked every single one of the twenty-two days each month, fifteen months a year, and were forced to rely on the Esarelians for everything, from the food they ate to the clothing on their backs. Most importantly, they couldn't travel off-world, a liberty every other species in the Empire took for granted. She hated having no control over her life.

Amina, the third member of their crew, slid a stool across the floor in their direction and turned back to her work. Though her countenance showed concern for Gilla's predicament, Amina wouldn't leave her station and join them. Gilla understood and accepted this. Besides, she figured that at least one of them should attempt to keep up their tally of completed pods. She called out a soft, "Thanks," and received a jerky nod in reply.

Damaya eased Gilla onto the stool and pushed the canteen more firmly into her hands. Relishing the temporary reprieve from back pain that was much more than the twinge she admitted to, Gilla swigged the slightly sour-tasting water. She flinched as a vice-like hand gripped her upper arm and yanked her back to her feet.

"Back to work! Your shift doesn't finish for another half cycle."

When Jat shoved her towards her unfinished life-pod, she stumbled and lost her balance. Damaya caught her as she began to fall, holding on until Gilla was steady on her feet again. Her friend glared impotently at the Baketag guard who always managed to catch them unawares. His two forward-facing eyes stared coldly back at her, and Gilla shivered at the barely restrained violence shining in them.

It was rare to see one of the four-eyed, four-armed Baketags outside the military units of their own kind. The few that left usually did so unwillingly and with a black mark against their honour. However, she could well understand why the Esarelians had employed this particular deserter to keep the workers on U'du in line. He made even the bravest, strongest of them think twice about disobeying. Before Damaya could say anything to set him off, Gilla tugged her friend a couple of steps away and turned her back to her work station.

Damaya reluctantly picked up her wand and resumed fusing the automated systems panel before her, muttering under her breath. Gilla heaved a sigh of relief and, giving one last glance to the retreating guard, returned to her own work. Before she could think better of it, she half whispered along the line, "Thanks for the back rub, Dee. You know I love that you care, but try not to get in any more trouble if you can help it."

"Huh! She can't help herself," Amina said.

"I can when I need to, Ami." Gilla couldn't help but notice that Damaya spoke at a normal volume and looked across to see the naturally mischievous spark back in her brown eyes. They turned serious as she continued, "Are you sure you're all right, though, Gilla?"

"Yes, Gilla, are you sure? I hate to agree with Trouble over here, but you do look like you're struggling. We can cover for you if you need us to."

Gilla warmed at the concern from her friends and their willingness to risk punishment for her. It gave her a burst of renewed strength. Shaking her head, she determined she'd finish the shift.

"Well, all right then. Let's get these done and get out of here." Damaya pounced and slashed, looking like she was attacking the life-pod instead of building it and making Gilla giggle under her breath. Amina took one look at their crazy friend and continued working in stony silence.

From out of nowhere, Jat growled, "No more talking either!"

Anticipating the need to head Damaya off, yet again, Gilla replied as meekly as possible, "Yes, sir!" She tucked her head down and ignored the low-pitched grumbles from her friend for the last quarter cycle of their shift.

In a small prep room attached to the manufacturing building, Gilla stared at her warped reflection in the cleansing cubicle. Warm brown eyes, bracketed by a few thin lines and set in an oval face, stared back at her. They were framed by thick wavy hair with one or two grey strands mixed through the dark-brown locks. Marks of age came early to those under the Esarelian rule, and she could hardly believe she was only thirty. Shifting her focus down, she studied the usually trim, average height figure that was currently nearly twice its normal width. Her gaze softened as she wondered what her baby would look like. She hoped for the strong limbs, half-cocked smile, and unusual hazel eyes of her husband but would be happy with any colouring if she could just deliver a healthy child.

Pulling herself from her reverie, she stepped out and re-braided her hair before donning the ubiquitous jumpsuit. Blue, it designated her position as a worker in the manufacturing sector and was as utilitarian as everything else provided by the Esarelians for slaves kept planet-side.

"So who do you think is worse, creepy Lamesh or scary Jat? My vote's for Lamesh. I know most people would pick Jat just because he's lethal enough to put an entire squad of warriors to shame, and he never makes a sound until he's ready to pounce, but Lamesh makes me feel like I really need to scrub my skin whenever he gets near. Besides, the Esarelians in general suck the life out of every other species around them, so the worst individual's got to be one of them, right?"

Damaya could never be kept down for long. Her cheerful, feisty nature was one of the things that had drawn Gilla to her friend when they were little girls playing together in the school-wing of the Nursery. Knowing from experience that no answer was expected or required, Gilla bent to slip on her shoes and turned to see Damaya's head propped above the privacy screen. As usual, sections of her light brown, curly hair stuck out at odd angles from the bandana that she claimed kept it under control. Her eyes held a natural spark that spoke of her perpetual cheer, and a huge grin finished the impish look. Damaya slung her arm around Gilla's shoulders and manoeuvred them through the crowds of shift change and out into the glaring sunlight.

Outside, the slightly spongy ground radiated its customary heat, and the humidity in the air from the nearby lake made Gilla's jumpsuit stick to her body. She knew the sun would be reflecting off the water at the other side of the settlement in blinding flashes that danced as the surf rippled along the grey-pebbled shore. The peaceful scene was in stark contrast to the constant drudgery of those who were forced to live along its banks. Still, it was better than being out in the wilderness beyond the slave settlement, where the slightest breeze across the unending grey landscape kicked up dust that clogged pores and windpipes.

From the entrance to her building, she could just make out through a haze of heat the jagged peaks of distant mountains bordering the vast plain she called home. Not even the purple plant life trailing the lake and coloured by the precious water pierced the monotony out there. She didn't think darkening shades, as the slaves dug deeper into the crust of the planet and away from the bleaching effects of the sun, counted as a change in scenery.

Charged with finding new routes to the water hidden underground, their efforts had already enabled the Esarelians to build three satellite settlements around small pumping stations out beyond the rock strewn wilds. The pitiable wretches chosen as searchers laboured in isolated locations, under the full sun and without break or aid, to excavate by hand the dark rock interior. Even the thought of that work detail made Gilla thankful for the blue of manufacturing. Shuddering, she turned her attention back to the path and Damaya's rambling monologue.

Waiting for them around the corner, with a tall, willowy frame radiating tension and light-brown eyes flashing fire, stood Amina. Her anger was palpable and directed entirely towards Damaya. "Are you *trying* to get us punished? What was that in there? You keep going about, thinking you can act out whenever you want and not suffer any consequences whatsoever, but you're wrong. We're *slaves*, Damaya! Slaves! They can do whatever they want to us and we'd better not complain about it or it'll get a whole lot worse. If you're going to do anything stupid or against the rules in future, just leave me out of it, you hear?" By the time she finished, she was poking Damaya in the chest and glaring down at her, breathing heavily through flared nostrils.

Gilla stepped between them and rested a conciliatory hand on the older woman's arm. "Whoa. Calm down, Ami. It's all right. No one got in trouble, and it was my fault today, anyway. I was the one who stopped working first. We know what they can do, and it won't happen again, will it, Dee?"

Damaya merely shook her head, as if temporarily stunned into silence by the force of Amina's feelings. Gilla rubbed the arm she was holding until Amina's face relaxed and then crumbled in defeat.

"I'm sorry. I just can't afford to... after what happened... it's just not worth riling them up." She shook her head before strengthening her voice. "I would've covered for you, though, if you were having problems with the baby." She walked away with a gait somewhere between a stomp and slump, her tight brown bun bobbing behind as if agreeing with her assessment.

Damaya started to follow after her, presumably to protest her innocence, possibly to apologise. Whatever her intent, Gilla stopped her and nudged her in the direction of home instead. "Just leave her to cool down."

"What's her problem, anyway?"

"You know what her problem is." Gilla gave her a pointed look.

At that, Damaya sighed. "Yeah, I know. I feel for her, I really do. I have no idea what I'd do in her situation. But she can't stay like this forever or blame the rest of us for sticking up for ourselves."

"I think she's just scared of what else they can do. After all, she knows more than any of us..." Her voice drifted off. Neither of them wanted the reminder of what caused Amina's dark attitude. Gilla's hand instinctively found its way to her stomach and patted gently as if reassuring the child within that it was still safe, for the time being.

Her thoughts returned to her plans for the evening, and Gilla picked up the pace, determined to meet her daughter, Mirami, at the Nursery and get home before Elias had to leave for his shift in the uduin sector. They hadn't had much time together as a family lately, and enjoying a few hours of rest and catching up with each other's lives was important to her.

By the time she and Damaya reached the border between the work sectors and the slave settlement, Gilla's back was aching fiercely. It seemed to take forever to pass through the checkpoint. On the other side, the settlement stretched out before them like a discarded, jumbled pile of building blocks in a giant child's playroom. There were people everywhere. Rushing to or dragging themselves from exhausting shifts, few looked up from the ground beneath their feet. Their open shoes slapped and flapped in a soft applause that stirred little eddies in the dust. Any conversations were a muted mumble, no one wanting to stand out or draw attention to themselves more than was absolutely necessary.

Gilla lifted her chin in greeting to one of her old dormitory friends, who was passing hurriedly in the opposite direction. Dressed in green, the stocky woman was heading towards a shift in the processing sector, flash cooking and packaging compressed blocks of uduin ready for general distribution off-world. They had little opportunity to speak any more. Between working different shifts in different sectors and moving into their own shacks as they each married, finding time to connect was nearly impossible. The friendship was still there, however, and the other woman lifted her own chin in recognition, sharing a smile with Gilla and Damaya before moving past and out of sight.

The dormitories for single adults were built in meticulous rows on either side of a wide central pathway and formed a semi-regular grid. Outside these, the shacks for married couples and families fanned out in no discernible pattern, built wherever there was space whenever a new one was needed. The paths between them narrowed, twisted, and turned, branching off like weeds, so that it was easy to become lost if one didn't know the settlement well.

Slowly passing the stark dormitories, Gilla remembered what it was like to live in such close quarters with so many other women. Lifelong friendships, with bonds stronger than those between many relatives, were forged in those cramped melting pots of humanity. Unfortunately, disagreements were also amplified in such small spaces and emotions often ran high, boiling over in explosive fashion. Gilla definitely preferred the quiet, stable shack where her little family continued to grow.

She spotted a mother hugging a boy on the step of one of the dormitories, probably saying goodbye as the youngster joined the adult population for the first time. It was hard to watch a twelve-year-old leave home to become one more cog in the laborious machine of the settlement. That would be her and Mirami in a scant handful of years, and the prospect chilled Gilla, despite the heat of the afternoon.

The day she'd moved into a dormitory was still vividly clear in Gilla's mind. On reaching her twelfth birthday, she'd been classed as an adult by their Esarelian masters and forced to work full time. Issued with two blue jumpsuits, missing the brown training bands she'd previously worn, she'd been officially designated as a worker in the manufacturing sector and added to a shift roster that same morning. She'd also been forced to move out of her parents' shack and into one of the buildings used to house single female slaves.

Her whole family had accompanied her on the walk over to her new lodgings, even her little brother, Than. His distress at her leaving had shown in the way he'd clutched their mother's hand, something he'd long since decided was for babies. Her father, remaining stoic in the face of the inevitable, had carried her small bundle of possessions. She'd had nothing more than a blanket that held her water canteen; a spare jumpsuit, still in its wrappings; and a large pebble with bands of ash grey running through the charcoal-coloured rock that Than had presented to her as a birthday gift a few years earlier because it was "pwitty, like you."

When they reached the long rectangular bunkhouse, she'd wanted to run the other way, back to the safety of her home. Knowing that wasn't an option, she'd instead squared her shoulders, taken the bundle from her father, and plastered a cheerful smile on her face as she hugged each of them goodbye. She still recalled her mother whispering, "I'm proud of you," in her ear before pulling back from the embrace. Only the shaking of Gilla's knees had given away her nerves as she'd stepped forwards and inside, into her life as an adult.

That first night, after the globe had been turned off and with the unfamiliar sounds of strange women all around her, she'd wept silently into her sleeping mat. She'd longed to be snuggled between her mother and brother, their warmth and even breathing lulling her into rest. One of the older women had moved to Gilla's mat in the middle of the night and stroked her hair until sleep finally took her. The white-haired angel had looked out for Gilla through those first weeks until she'd become more comfortable with her surroundings and made friends her own age.

Shaking off the past, Gilla looked back at the dormitories around her. The buildings themselves were made from the ever-present grey rock. Rough-cut and basic, four walls with gaps where windows and doors should have been—if the Esarelians had spared the expense to provide them—were topped by slabs for a roof. Any basic furniture they contained, such as tables, stools, shutters and doors, was made by the slaves themselves from the deep-plum wood and lilac bark twine of the local garn trees. The one technological concession to their meagre existence was a single globe per household or dormitory. Some occasionally tried to add to their stark surroundings, but if discovered, the guards often removed additional items, so most learned to make do with what they were given.

The settlement's main prep rooms, containing banks of cleansing cubicles and waste units, were centrally located and unisex with standard half screens providing what privacy was deemed necessary. With a wave for Damaya to wait, Gilla waddled towards one of them, the baby jabbing her bladder in protest at her jiggling movements. She hurried. *He must be a boy*, she thought with wry amusement.

When she returned, her daughter, Mirami, was also waiting outside. Excitedly chattering about her day at the Nursery and the praise Menali had heaped on her for occupying the younger children with stories while they waited for their parents, Mirami distracted Gilla from her earlier thoughts before they turned bitter. She cleared her mind and replied enthusiastically to the seven-year-old. "That's great, Kiddo. You've always been good at telling stories."

"Maybe you'll be assigned to train in the Nursery next year," Damaya interjected. "Would you like that?"

"Oh yeah, that'd be great! I'm not sure I'd like the med-wing, but the school-wing would be good, and I'd love to work in the infant-wing. Auntie Menali lets me help with the babies sometimes after my lessons, and they're sooooooo cute." She clenched her small fists under her chin and wiggled, as if needing to emphasise her point more than eking four syllables out of a single-syllable word could.

The women laughed. Damaya ruffled Mirami's hair and replied, "Let's hope so then." To Gilla, she said, "I gotta go. I want to check on Gerom before I go home."

"He's going to realise you're doing that one of these days, you know. He's been in training for two years already… oh, forget it. You know what I think."

"Can't help it. Once a mother, always a mother. It's the rules." Damaya raised her hands and shrugged her shoulders in the universal helpless gesture. Winking, she turned and jogged away.

Mirami barrelled through the door of their small shack, calling for her father, before Gilla could remind her that Elias might still be resting before work. He appeared in the doorway to the single back room, where all three of them shared use of the sleeping mat, and his rumpled look lit up Gilla's heart. Flashing her an easy grin, he scooped up their young daughter and tickled her slender torso. Laughter filled the humble home along with desperate pleas to be released.

When Mirami was firmly settled back on solid ground and breathing normally, Elias stalked towards Gilla, the threat to repeat the activity with her as his next victim clear in his expression. She smoothly stepped behind the plum-coloured table with an admonition to behave. Turning towards the single cupboard on the wall, she asked how large a piece of the odourless, and tasteless, uduin he wanted to eat. She was carefully unwrapping their weekly rations and distributing part of the dense lavender block among the three eating bowls when his arms slid easily around her waist and his chin came to rest on her shoulder. He brushed a kiss across her cheek and quietly asked how her shift was.

Sensing her hesitance to admit the truth and unwillingness to lie, he saved her from answering by gently taking her hand and leading her to one of their roughly hand-crafted stools. It always amazed her that such a large, powerful man could hold her so delicately. He stood behind her in silent support for a moment and then slowly rubbed her shoulders and back until the aches and pains melted away. Finally, just before she turned into a puddle of rubberised bones on the floor, he squatted in front of her and gave his typical half smile.

"There's my beautiful wife," he purred.

Her breathy reply was almost automatic after so long together. "What would I do without you?"

"Find a sympathetic guard to con into giving you extra rations and easy shifts?"

"Do you ever stop kidding around?" She gave him a little shove, and he fell backwards, sprawling onto his back and filling the floor between her perch and the main door. There would be a dirty smudge left on his jumpsuit from the soft, rock floor, but she figured he deserved it. Their playful banter did her good, and she thanked God again for the family she'd been given. Together, they could endure anything.

Elias slid a look at Mirami, and Gilla took the cue to send her to bed so they could talk in private. Despite numerous protests, and after securing a promise of a song before sleep, she was soon tucked into the back room. Gilla watched as the miniature, if more delicate, version of her own looks relaxed in slumber. After waiting an extra minute, just to make sure Mirami was fully asleep, Gilla backed away and sank back onto the same stool as earlier. Elias gathered the other and, placing it next to her, sat down. The garn wood wobbled slightly and creaked in protest but held his weight. She took a deep breath in preparation. Whatever he needed to discuss would probably not be all good news.

He started slowly by saying, "Than attended his first leaders' meeting this month. He's finally growing up."

"Mm hmm." Her non-committal answer encouraged him to continue.

"You know we were hit badly by the last Selection, and we're still trying to recruit help. It's hard to find trustworthy, skilled people, but Than's doing well. Aro's also asked me to do some recon in case the guard shift patterns have been changed since our last raid. By the time we have the numbers to act again, we should have been able to gather all the information we need." He looked closely at her reaction, but her calm demeanour gave nothing away.

"What kind?" Her voice stayed steady, unlike her heartbeat.

"What kind of what?"

She drilled him with a look before slowly enunciating her next question. "What kind of reconnaissance?"

A slight tightening of his shoulders told her as much as she needed to know. It may be dangerous. She concentrated on maintaining deep, even breaths as he explained. "I've been watching and recording the guard rotations for the last few days, but it's not been enough to get the information we need. Two of the others are going to cover me so I can sneak into the main office and get the rotas while the guards are out at the next inspection."

He'd been a key figure in the resistance for many years, and there was only minimal risk involved in the task, but she couldn't help worrying. Maybe it was pregnancy hormones. "Be careful," she blurted. "I can't lose you."

"Don't worry, beautiful. I don't take any unnecessary risks. I love you and Mirami more than life itself... and this little one too." He pulled her gently into his lap, causing the stool to groan in protest, and then rested his hand protectively on her stomach. "But I need to do this, for all of us. We need our freedom. Trust me, Gilla. God will be with me."

Fixing his striking hazel eyes on hers, Elias let them convey the strength and depth of his feelings for her. Her fears settled. They were a team and she'd always fully supported him in his missions. A small smile tugged at the corner of her mouth as she voiced a familiar request. "Tell me what it'll be like."

A grin spread across Elias's face in the lopsided way that both calmed and excited her. He answered, as always, in a soft, lilting tone of reverence for their dream. "The planet will be green and blue, brown and white. There'll be tall trees and flowers everywhere in a rainbow of colours. No more ugly grey land and purple plants. Instead of stunted, prickly grass, there'll be soft moss to walk on. We'll build our home in a valley with a stream for the children to splash through after a long day of playing in the fields. They'll love it.

"Besides the main family room, there'll be private rooms for sleeping and for us to be alone occasionally. If we want, we could even have a full-sized cleansing cubicle attached to the back of the house. We'll have a large kitchen and a garden, where we can grow neat rows of fruit and vegetables in every variety. There'll be no more tasteless lumps of uduin to eat. The allotment will provide so much food that we'll be able to share it with neighbours at the local market.

"Going there will be fun. We'll root around for hidden gems among the stalls, and I'll even let you hold my hand all day long. The smells will tickle our taste buds, and Mirami will always be begging for treats from the others, even though her belly will be full to bursting."

A comfortable silence settled between them as Gilla relished the picture he painted. It was perfect. She sighed in contentment, enjoying the half cycle together before work demanded his attention once more.

"I really don't know what I'd do without you, Elias," she whispered as she snuggled more comfortably into his arms and enjoyed the fresh, clean scent of his skin.

"Neither do I, beautiful wife," he replied, kissing her forehead. "Neither do I."

∞

Elias had left Gilla and Mirami curled together in the back room of their shack, sound asleep. He hated leaving them and hoped their shifts aligned again soon so they could spend more time together. A few cycles each evening wasn't nearly enough with the wife and daughter he adored. Pretty soon there would be another little one to look after as well, and he wondered whether it would be a boy or girl. The thought made him smile, knowing he wouldn't care as long as the baby was healthy.

Taking the shortest route through the maze of shacks circling the settlement, Elias cut down a silent side alley and plunged into familiar shadows. He usually enjoyed the quiet solitude this section of his trek to the uduin sector gave him each day. It allowed him to think and pray, counting his blessings and asking God's continued protection for his growing family. He'd be swept up in the mass migration of humanity when he emerged into the crowded main thoroughfare and unable to stroll in peace as he did here.

A scuffling noise ahead belied the thought, and Elias examined the immediate area for a sign of its origin. Nothing moved. Whatever had caused it must have been farther afield. Cautiously rounding a slight bend in the twisted path, he ground to a halt as he spotted two forms semi-hidden between shacks farther down the alley. He could make out the tall, lean outline of a guard. The off-white skirt with a decorative belt of office and the plain headdress worn over his bio-suit gave Lamesh away. He was the only one who preferred full ceremonial clothes to the more practical jumpsuits or the skirt alone.

From where he stood, Elias could see that Lamesh was shoving a young slave girl along in front of him, down the narrow gap between shacks. The guard's back was shielding her from the view of those passing the end of the alley on one of the main passages. His positioning looked too deliberate, and an alarm began to ring in the back of Elias's mind. While rumour suggested that some women allowed Esarelian advances in return for additional comforts or lighter duties, Elias had never believed it. He was more predisposed to agree with Damaya's assessment of Lamesh, that the guard used his position to manipulate or force women to do his bidding. At first glance, this situation certainly supported the guard's reputation.

Elias scanned the young woman quickly. From Lamesh's tight grip on her arm and the look of fear on her face, she appeared an unwilling victim. Luckily, she also seemed to be, as yet, unharmed. Elias had no doubt that would change imminently, though, from the leer he could make out on Lamesh's elongated features and the intimidating stance the Esarelian had adopted.

There were no others in the immediate vicinity to observe whatever interlude Lamesh had planned with the frightened female. In fact, Elias doubted the pair was even aware of his presence. He could turn around and take a different path to his shift, stay out of the guard's business, and stay safe. Elias's conscience would never allow him to choose that option, however. If Gilla or Mirami were in such a dire situation, he'd want someone to come to their aid, and the thought of not doing the same for another never even entered his head.

Looking around, Elias assessed his options quickly. He needed to gain the girl's attention without warning Lamesh. Managing to catch her eye as she glanced frantically about her, Elias put a finger to his lips to caution silence. A flicker of his own eyes towards the end of the alley and back indicated that she should run as soon as Lamesh let go. Relieved that she had the presence of mind to keep from reacting too much to him, Elias moved on silent feet until he was only a few paces behind Lamesh.

Shuffling his feet slightly, Elias closed the gap between them. He knew what would result from his interference but was prepared to face it. He could handle the consequences, and whatever the girl would have faced if he'd not been here would have been much worse. With a silent prayer for success, he raised his hands and readied himself.

Elias staggered as if he'd tripped over a loose rock, or even his own feet, and ploughed into Lamesh's shoulder from behind. He grabbed the guard, ostensibly to steady himself, and wobbled again, throwing them both off balance for a moment. Lamesh stumbled forwards a pace before regaining his equilibrium, letting go of the girl to brace himself against the wall of the nearest shack.

By the time he cast furious, penetrating eyes on Elias, the girl had ducked under Lamesh's outstretched arm and was halfway to the main path and freedom. She looked back once and mouthed a "thank you" at Elias before disappearing around the corner. He knew she'd probably not find any assistance for him, even if she tried, and was strangely grateful that he'd have no punishment on his conscience but his own. With an internal sigh, he turned to face whatever it would be.

Elias held his hands out and hung his head in a humble pose, asking for pardon in a rush of words designed to keep the Esarelian's attention away from his fleeing victim. Dropping to his knees to add to the effect, Elias glanced up and saw the twisted pleasure it gave the guard to tower over his new prey.

Lamesh studied Elias as if he knew exactly what he'd done and why. Slowly and deliberately, Lamesh pulled the rod from his waist. He flipped a switch and a low buzzing accompanied the slight glow that appeared at the end of the weapon. The black metal of the contact nubs gleamed wickedly in the fading daylight, seemingly anxious for something to devour as Lamesh brought them relentlessly forward.

Elias tensed in anticipation but, as with his previous experiences with the rods, could never have been ready for the intense pain that radiated through his body when it briefly touched the exposed skin of his neck. Falling to the ground, he writhed in agony, and Lamesh leaned over to press the rod into his quivering flesh again.

His teeth clamped together, and his muscles pulled taut as the excruciating blast of disruptive energy coursed through him once more, jarring every cell in his body and stimulating the nerve endings with agony. There was no controlling the spasms that rocked him for the endless moments he endured while Lamesh inflicted his punishment.

Aeons later, the searing pain suddenly lifted, and Lamesh jerked to a stand. Elias couldn't see properly yet, but he heard Risoth's voice floating down from the far end of the alley.

"Lamesh, there you are. I need you with me, now."

There was a slight pause before Lamesh said, "I will be right there, Risoth."

Even Elias, in his prone and debilitated state, couldn't help but hear the sneer in Lamesh's pronunciation of his superior's name. However, he had more immediate concerns than a power play between the head guard and one of his seconds in command. Attempting to rise after a series of deep breaths, Elias had managed to prop himself up on one elbow when Lamesh's face came into view a mere hand's breadth from Elias's own.

"I will remember this, slave," he snarled and then was gone in a whirl of pale skirts that Elias barely registered as he slowly pulled himself to his feet.

A pain punishment would be no excuse for arriving late for his shift, and with that in mind, Elias took one tender step after another until he'd regulated his gait and worked the after effects of the rod from his system.

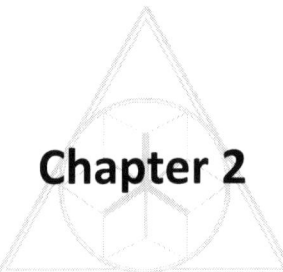

Chapter 2

Date: 311.428.127
Location: Esarelian Primary Space Cruiser, throne room

Beautifully carved from a single slab of obsidian, and cushioned with luxurious fabrics in shades of royal violet, the throne on which Ashal sat put him head and shoulders above the others present in the opulent room. He was wearing only a short, simply wrapped skirt and open sandals over his bio-suit. His full ceremonial robes felt too formal and confining when he was only meeting with his inner tier of three advisors, and the rest of the outfit was still on the stand in his private suite, much to the shame of his body servant.

Ashal was about to close the weekly meeting when Sunath, who represented the council of commerce and diplomacy, raised a finger for attention. Ashal hoped it would be a quick item, as he had other pressing concerns to attend to before he left to inspect the recently repaired space port. The malfunction caused by the latest human attack on their long-range transportation system had finally been rectified. As the Ra'hon, the ultimate leader, of the largest known Empire, Ashal needed to assure his people that they could resume travel between galaxies.

His race exceeded the height, strength, and speed of other known races thanks to their elongated limbs and dense muscle mass. However, their complete lack of body hair and thin, pale skin, courtesy of millennia aboard spacecraft after the depletion of their planet's natural resources, meant they were not entirely invulnerable. Without secondary transparent eyelids, their large eyes could easily be damaged by solar glare when planet-side, another reason most stayed aboard whenever possible. Their cold blood required constant heating, a task achieved in the frozen temperatures of space by the bio-suits worn almost as a second skin beneath their clothes and calibrated to each individual Esarelian. The nanotechnology in the suits also enhanced their natural longevity, releasing essential nutrients filtered from the manufactured light sources on-board. Furthermore, it diagnosed medical problems at an early stage, flagging them for repairs. The result was lifespans of up to a thousand years, after which point, and despite the scientists best efforts, the bio-tech had the opposite effect, speeding the degradation of cells and hastening death.

The existence of Ashal's inner tier of advisors was vital in ensuring those long lives were not spent in plots that could destroy their Empire. Holding his hand palm up, he indicated his permission for Sunath to speak.

"We need more workers, both on-board and at the mining colony on Pyteg. I would not normally bring this to your attention, as you know, but there are none available from the usual sources, and the need grows urgent."

"Why is that?" Ashal demanded. "Surely they cannot have used up that many since the last Selection." He grew weary of the near constant demands for a stronger, larger work force but knew that the progress on the new space cruiser would require many sacrifices. Besides, if he delegated these decisions to another, they would have an opportunity to snatch too much power for themselves. Ruling the Esarelians was a delicate balance, and one he would not throw away carelessly by showing his underbelly.

Sunath shrugged his massive shoulders and replied dismissively, "An entire contingent of workers was lost four days ago when they encountered a pocket of worms."

Ashal's second advisor and spokesman for the scientific council, Nishaf, sat forwards to make a suggestion. "Take them from the U'du colony. There are more than enough workers there; they breed like Lurinelian rodents. It has been done before and proven effectual each time."

"Will it impact the manufacturing of the space cruiser? I will not allow anything to impede progress and delay the grand launch. I grow weary of this craft and anticipate enjoying the design modifications I requested on the new model." Ashal could not wait to see it finished. Building a craft of the size and technological advancements he had envisioned would be one of the crowning achievements of his reign, something for future generations to look upon and acknowledge his lasting impact on the Empire. It was what all Esarelians ultimately aspired to—immortality through legacy.

It would also be the opportune time to make some much-needed changes to the throne room. He looked around him, taking in the large open space lit by myriad globes suspended in opulent clusters from the high, white ceiling. The new council table, as well as a selection of ornately carved danta wood chairs, would retract into the floor at the push of a button or his voice command. The projections above it would move around the room as needed, instead of remaining static above the centre of the table. Smaller versions for individual council members would remain in front of them for instant manipulation.

The design would be altogether more lavish, with expensive, rare wood replacing the metallic floor and some of the pristine white walls of the current room. He gazed over to the nearest panel, trying to decide whether to replace the rich, purple floor-length wall hangings framing each as well. He could have niches for moving holovids instead of the still holovis of the home planet, Esarel, artistically placed around the room.

Nishaf replied, breaking into his musings. "Not at all, Ra'hon. We can Select from the other sectors on the planet and leave that work force intact. If any concerns over the production rate arise, we can also lower the minimum age for assigning positions as necessary. In fact, that might be advisable regardless. Those humans," he sneered, rubbing the side of his neck absently with one long finger, "have far too much free time and would benefit from a stricter regime. I would think that their children cannot wait to begin their service to the Empire either, as would we all in their situation." He waved an elegantly manicured hand in the air for emphasis as he finished.

Ashal turned to Lorith, the final member of his inner tier, and narrowed his eyes. "You are very quiet on this matter," he stated, hoping to elicit a response.

Lorith shrugged.

Before Ashal could dig any deeper, the portal swung back and his daughter, Reemah, breezed into the room. Her smooth, soft voice, so reminiscent of her mother's, was very obviously mid-rant about the guard stationed outside not letting her through when she was expected. When she saw the inner tier, her words trailed off, she stumbled to a halt, and a small "oh" escaped her mouth. Waving off any transient discomfort at her predicament, she nodded a formal greeting and awaited her father's instructions. She was early.

"Reemah." Ashal assumed a flat tone in front of the others. "Wait for me in the antechamber." Her violet eyes, coloured thus by her royal heritage, flickered for a second and then matched his own neutral expression. Nodding again, she walked swiftly to the left-hand rear portal and out of sight to await his summons.

As she departed, Ashal returned his attention to the males before him. He noticed Nishaf's eyes track Reemah's movements across the room. In fact, the young advisor was barely concealing his interest. Ashal frowned as he quickly calculated the possible implications. His conclusions were not favourable and would need addressing sooner rather than later.

Lorith, on the other hand, ignored Reemah and spoke quietly with Sunath until the group was once more alone. Interestingly, he returned his attention to Ashal at the precise moment the portal closed behind her. Lorith had an uncanny awareness of his surroundings, which was one of the many reasons he was now Na'hor, supreme military commander of the Empire, and the final member of Ashal's inner tier at such a young age. Ashal again shook off his mental ruminations in order to conclude the meeting.

"Where were we?"

"The Selection?" Nishaf queried.

Not wanting the upstart to think he had gained any momentum, Ashal focused on Sunath and asked, "Will a small Selection be sufficient for your needs?"

"Yes," he agreed as his mouth twitched and his still-bright, blue eyes twinkled. Sunath had been a personal companion for many centuries and knew the workings of Ashal's mind as well as Ashal did himself. There were none he trusted more, although Lorith was getting close. "They make good workers, and I would rather use them in the mines than our own people, no matter where we find them. I will also assign several to this cruiser, as we need additional manual labour while we prepare for the changeover."

"Then you may proceed with another Selection. And lower the minimum age of workers on U'du. With the additional hands, our new cruiser may even be finished ahead of schedule. You are dismissed." Ashal began to rise, but his movement was arrested by the discreet clearing of a throat. He was running out of patience. "What is it, Nishaf?"

Nishaf's dark blue eyes darted to the door as he waited for the others to leave. His long, smooth face betrayed none of the inner thoughts Ashal knew continually churned around the male's cunning and ruthless mind. At only marginally over three hundred years, he had climbed quickly through the ranks of the Hon, the Esarelian leaders. Ashal was well aware of some of the vicious assassinations committed through the course of that journey and suspected others. As was their way, though, without incontrovertible proof or even allegation from injured parties, the deaths were simply and quickly ruled as foh'mahn, an elevation.

When Nishaf failed to speak, even after they had clearly been left alone, Ashal decided to hurry things along. "Well, what do you want?"

"Ra'hon…" Nishaf began carefully before clearing his throat again. His only defect, a slight scratch in his voice that accompanied a small neck scar, could have been removed easily by any trainee medic, but Nishaf kept them, bucking trends favouring physical perfection in all things. Sometimes, during tedious meetings when his mind wandered, Ashal amused himself by wondering why, conjuring fanciful reasons for the young male's insistence on remaining marred. This was not one of those times, and Ashal grew impatient.

"Stop using my title in private conversations. We both know who I am. Just get to the point, and quickly. I have to speak to Reemah."

"It is on that subject that I wish to speak, Ra… Ashal. I know she has recently displeased you, but your daughter has many fine qualities, long admired by those who have watched her…" He glanced up and away before continuing more confidently, as if he had practiced the speech many times. Ashal let him talk.

"She is becoming a fine Esarelian female and is a credit to you and our race. I am aware, however, as are most, of her penchant for disregarding any rules she deems an unnecessary burden. Older and, perhaps, wiser minds know these have been put in place simply to protect her, and I, as one such concerned individual, would offer my services in curbing her tendencies in this regard, leaving you free to attend to matters of state without the need to worry for her safety. I would be a calming influence on her, shall we say, exuberant nature.

"If you placed her in my care, it would also give us time to see if we suit in a more permanent manner. Reemah and I are of a similar age, a mere half century separating us, and are well suited in other regards. It would be a mate's privilege and honour to provide for her well-being and safeguard her good standing in the Hos. One day, I think she will come to realise that we—"

"I will stop you there." Nishaf's ingratiating tone was wearing thin, and Ashal had heard enough. "You misread my intentions in this matter and my mood. Leave me, now, before you say something we will both regret me having to address."

Nishaf immediately swept into a long, deep bow and backed away marginally. "Of course! I only wished to serve and to show my undying loyalty to your family. Perhaps, in time…"

"Reemah will choose her own mate, without pressure or guidance. I will not take that right away from any of royal blood." *No matter how she vexes me*, Ashal added to himself.

Wisely staying silent, Nishaf swept out of the room, leaving Ashal a moment of peace to decide how to approach the next delicate negotiation on his agenda. As if called by his thoughts, Reemah edged through the embossed metallic portal and cautiously approached. Nishaf had one thing correct, she really was an adult female now. Her long limbs moved gracefully, and the brilliant white jumpsuit she insisted on wearing instead of her ceremonial sheath showcased her slender figure, matching her skin tone and highlighting the sparkle in her eyes. The detached exterior Ashal maintained in public melted under the warmth of his favourite daughter's smile, until he remembered the reason for their meeting. He drew on his inherently unemotional reserve in order to proceed as planned and fixed his blank gaze on hers.

"Is all well, Father?"

"It is, child. Why don't you tell me what you know about a damaged fighter craft and a four-cycle period where my daughter was missing from the internal sensors?" he said, deliberately getting straight to the point rather than indulging in more pleasant conversation first.

"What did Nishaf want?" Her attempted deflection was a familiar tactic but not one he had time to tolerate at present.

"Nothing that will ever need to concern you. Now answer my question."

His stern tone did not affect her in the least. She knew her position with regards to his limited affection. "You already know what I was doing, or I wouldn't have been called in here for a dressing down. That is what this is, isn't it?"

"Not exactly." At that, for the first time since entering the throne room, an edge of true wariness entered her expression. "As we are both fully aware by now," Ashal continued, "a 'dressing down,' as you call it, has failed as an effective deterrent with you for some time. I will not have my first daughter causing havoc with the warriors by competing in arrow races. Those craft were developed for the purpose of combat situations, not for your personal entertainment. They are expensive, dangerous"—at this she rolled her eyes—"and for the express use of fighter pilots."

She began to defend her actions. "But—"

"So I have wiped your access to all craft. The primary technician assures me there is no way to bypass this particular block, and there will be no reconsideration until you have proven you are capable of discretion and discernment in your actual duties, which will begin at once. You're grounded."

Her mouth opened, but no words came out. He had never gone to this extreme with her before and had hoped he would never have to, that her natural rebelliousness would be tempered by maturity and her position as a Ra'hos, a member of the royal family. That day had not arrived soon enough, and he vowed he would never read another report of potentially life-threatening damage done to a craft his daughter had been flying.

Admittedly, the accident could not have been foreseen, and arrows were built to withstand battle damage. It had been an unfortunate coincidence that the latest rebel strike had caused a minor explosion as she passed close to the sub-space port. With her shield energy diverted to thrusters for more speed, an ingenious yet reckless move, the results had been almost catastrophic and had proved to him that he needed to act.

Knowing which battles she had no hope to win, Reemah slumped onto one of the vacant chairs and swirled her fingers in elaborate patterns across the table top. He watched as resignation settled over her features and then resolve hardened them.

"Very well," she murmured. "How long?"

"Until I see you are able, and ready, to act with responsibility, and not less than one full year." He studied her reaction closely, but aside from a small flinch at the time frame, she handled the news stoically. There might be hope she could be tamed yet.

She gathered herself and rose to approach his throne. "May I, Father?"

"Always, daughter. Come."

Covering his hand with hers, she kissed him lightly on the cheek before whispering, "I will try to make you proud, Father."

If only he could let her know how much she already did.

Chapter 3

Day: 17 Month: 05 Year: 6428
Location: Planet U'du, main slave settlement

"So, you've given up then!" Willan flung the accusation at the group and fell back against the wall in despair.

Aronin looked steadily around at those gathered in the secret underground room to gauge their reactions to this latest outburst. Willan was becoming more difficult to contain in his need to escape the dominion of the Esarelians. However, he did have a point. Aronin didn't want to see another generation endure hard labour and the fear of a Selection either. He spoke in his usual deep, resonant voice. "Of course not! All I said—"

"Then we need to take action. Elias got the info we needed, so let's use it before it's too late."

"He's right!" Than interjected his opinion before hunching back into the corner at a sharp look from his brother-in-law, Elias.

Aronin frowned. Young and impetuous, Than was also courageous, had great instincts, and was dedicated to freeing their people from the slavery they had endured for hundreds of years. This shadowing of the resistance leaders' meetings was a chance for Than to watch and learn, to prove his worth and start to work towards his own leadership role. Aronin wondered briefly if he had been given the opportunity too soon, before his own attention was once more drawn to the others around the makeshift garn wood table.

His trusted right-hand man and best friend, Dannon, was trying to calm everyone down, as was his way. "We must be cautious, Willan. Any strike we make will need to be thoroughly planned and based on *all* of the best intel we can get. We can't afford to fail."

He was right. They were in a precarious position and didn't want to precipitate another Selection. The last had severely depleted their numbers and was the main reason youngsters like Than were being given a chance at leadership positions within the resistance.

Elias jumped in, preventing Willan from further dissent. "Dan's right. We all want to escape and find somewhere we can live in peace. Our families deserve that, and I'm as dedicated to making it happen as any man here." He paused to let the truth of his words sink in. "But I'm *not* willing to throw my life away on a suicide mission. I've been on enough of those for one lifetime." He chuckled and continued, "We've got to be careful, and waiting until we can put together a solid plan with a good chance of success is the right move. We've trusted Aronin to lead us this far; trust him now, just a little bit longer."

The affirmation didn't surprise Aronin, as Elias's loyalty knew no bounds. Another top leader in the resistance, the large man was also a good friend. His support now buoyed Aronin but also reminded him of the great sense of responsibility he felt for them all.

Trying to focus on the matter at hand, Aronin cleared his throat. All eyes turned to him in expectation. "We still need to recruit more people before we can attempt another strike. Otherwise, the Esarelians will wipe us out before we can even get to a transport tub, never mind off the planet. I've been working on an idea that might just tip the balance in our favour, but I need to wait for news from my contact before I'm willing to risk our lives again. I'm sure God will guide us when the time is right to act."

"Yeah, right!" The vehemence behind Willan's statement made Aronin's dark brown eyes snap across to him. Aronin noticed a similar reaction from Elias, whose faith was probably the strongest of the group. Willan continued more defensively. "If He's even out there... I mean, come on. We might have a couple of original datablocs left in the Nursery, but the rest are just stories passed down through the generations. No one really knows what's true or not any more, and it's not like anyone's ever heard an answer to their prayers.

"The truth is, our forefathers travelled through half the known universe and saw no sign of any heaven, just a load of other lost species. If God *is* real and we're so special to Him, where is He? What's He doing while we suffer here? It makes no sense to put our trust in some unknown and unproven entity just because our ancestors back on Earth couldn't see for themselves what the universe is really like."

Elias responded before Aronin could. "Our ancestors put their trust in God to protect them and lead them to a new home world when Earth, well, the whole solar system, became uninhabitable. He led them—"

"Here! To become slaves to the Esarelians. We've been stuck here for who knows how long with no end in sight. Whoever that God was, He either stayed on Old Earth or gave up on them a long time ago. They would've been better off on their own, as are we. We need to put together a plan and execute it ourselves if we want to be free. We can't rely on some God no one's heard from in centuries." His frustration vented, the older man finally slumped onto an upturned crate and muttered unintelligibly to himself. He tugged occasionally on his scruffy beard, a match to his salt-and-pepper hair, with one wiry hand. An intuitive genius with anything technological or mechanical, Willan was more comfortable with scientific facts than with faith, or with people for that matter. He'd also been badly thrown by the latest failed strike, Aronin reminded himself.

Aronin gentled his voice as much as he was able and asked, "Have you completely lost faith, my friend?"

"No. Not in the cause," Willan whispered and then continued in a stronger voice. "I just want to concentrate on practical issues. What do we do while we wait for your precious contact?" His light-brown eyes pierced Aronin with a desperate need for a constructive focus.

At that moment, Than opened his mouth to speak up again. Before he could utter the first syllable, Elias clamped a hand on Than's shoulder. "Remember, you're here to watch and learn for now. Your time will come soon enough." Elias squeezed the shoulder in reassurance before letting go.

Shooting him a sullen look, Than opened his mouth again but then slowly closed it once more and grinned. Nothing kept him down for long. His fingers drummed his thigh in a continual effort to burn off excess energy, which was not nearly as distracting as his habitual pacing would have been. Fortunately, there wasn't enough room for that in the hand-dug, cramped headquarters. The lad really needed something to occupy him, and Aronin thought he had just the job in mind.

After outlining what he wanted their teams to accomplish before the next meeting in one month, Aronin looked around for assent. Dannon nodded first. The others followed, and the meeting broke up. One by one they climbed the uneven rungs into the shack above and melted silently into the cool night. As the vibrations of Than and Elias moving across the floor above brought trickles of dirt raining down, Aronin pulled the light globe from the wall and plunged the chamber into darkness. He would succeed, gaining freedom for his people whatever the personal cost. He also knew, without a shadow of a doubt, that God would aid them when the time came. He would have to.

Chapter 4

Day: 18   Month: 06   Year: 6428
Location: Planet U'Du, main slave settlement

Than and Elias pushed out through the main doors of the uduin building where they worked together. They spent endless hours each shift pumping water through one of the enormous vats of uduin. This kept the bases covered in moving liquid, while others controlled the precise levels of humidity needed to grow mass quantities of the vital organic material. It was back-breaking labour. The men were both strong from the constant stretch and flex of muscles each day, as were all who were forced into water circulation in their sector. With the third member of their crew, they were held accountable for the state of the uduin in their vat, and punishments for a below par yield were severe.

As always, Than left the building with a mixture of relief at his temporary escape and anger at the conditions they were forced to endure. The Esarelians could have used automated pumps to control the flow of water into each of the massive vats, but they didn't. They used slaves. Employing the same basic system from their home world, where uduin was first produced en masse thousands of years earlier, they forced humans to pump the water in by hand. After all, uduin was the Esarelians' most precious resource. It needed the best of care, and what could be better than the personal touch of over a thousand slaves in the primary settlement alone.

Technological advancements, it seemed, were reserved for easing the Esarelians' own lives, and they cared not for the burdens of those they owned. The only concession to modern capabilities was that the pipes bringing water into the buildings were enclosed metal, as opposed to the original open wooden troughs. Even this was only to preserve the quality of the water and not in any way to aid the humans struggling to keep up with demand.

Than snorted in disdain for his masters. He longed for a day when all the slaves would rise up and overthrow the relatively small, if physically superior and well-armed, contingent of guards set to oversee their gruelling daily schedules. If only that was all it would take to be free, the circulation workers in his sector alone, were they to unite, would have the strength to challenge the Esarelians.

Predominantly chosen for their large, muscular builds and given additional rations to build even more bulk, those uduin workers used to keep the flow of water level and constant were easy to identify, even without the mandatory red uniforms. They towered over their counterparts in the sector, whose role was to crop the plant-like creatures, and who were small and light enough to climb the rigging and reach the new growth. Pushing through the main entrance in a long stream of weary humanity, the rest of the men coming off shift slipped past Than and Elias like water around pebbles. The contrast in size between workers in red made Than think of a bizarre family of midgets and giants.

As he stretched his back and neck after the long shift, shaking off his fanciful thoughts, Than glanced across at his exhausted friend. "Feeling your age today, old man?"

"Watch it," Elias rumbled and swiped a huge paw in the direction of Than's head that he barely ducked in time to avoid. "I can still whip your scrawny behind."

Always willing to test his brother-in-law's resolve and release the constant restlessness he felt, Than leaped into a sparring stance in front of Elias and taunted, "Come on, then. Let's see it." He even threw in a beckoning hand gesture and cocky smirk for added emphasis.

Elias looked for a second as if he was truly considering the prospect but huffed a laugh instead and shoved Than aside. The same response as always, Than could mimic even the intonation of what Elias would say next perfectly by now. They spoke the words together. "I have somewhere better to be."

It was true. He did. Elias had been married to Than's sister for nearly ten years, and they were one of the most well-suited and happy couples Than knew. They made marriage look almost tempting. It didn't hurt that his niece was the most adorable creature on the planet. He might be biased, and have no comparative experience to draw on whatsoever, but he loved her surely as much as he would his own daughter and was extremely proud of the little girl.

Trudging together down the main path towards their respective homes, Than wished momentarily for a wife of his own to go home to. There was also an incentive in that marriage would come with the privacy of a shack instead of having to sleep amid the clouds of noxious gas and bone-rattling snores produced by some of the men in his dormitory. One day, he promised himself, he would have what his sister and the big guy had. Just as the thought crossed his mind, he spied a pretty smile flash from within a waterfall of silky, black hair, and he wondered if it might be that lucky day.

He slowed his pace and allowed Elias to drift ahead. Flashing a charmingly dimpled grin, Than zeroed in on the young woman in Nursery yellow. It took a while to saunter casually across the main thoroughfare in her direction, but he didn't want to appear too eager. Let them chase him had always been his motto with regards to the fairer sex; he knew he was a good catch. He shared his sister's athletic build underneath the defined muscles of his upper body. Shaggy thick brown hair, longer than most would wear it, fell across his forehead. Than had often been told it made him look more handsome that way. He'd also often been told to get it cut, but that was just Gilla. Shaking off the thought, he concentrated on the task at hand. How should he catch her attention?

With his head angled to show off his looks, he sidled up to her and said, "Hello gorgeous. Fancy a moonlit walk later?"

There was no response from the girl, who maintained a steady pace and failed to even glance in his direction. Not deterred in the least, Than decided to change tack, pursing his lips as he took a closer look at the beauty walking away from him. Maybe the best place to start would be by being useful. He noticed she carried a large bundle of brown material, presumably for the children she worked with in the Nursery, and inspiration struck. "Can I help you with that?"

She still ignored him. She must not have heard, so he moved closer to try again but became distracted by her hair. On closer inspection, it was a deep, rich brown that fell in soft waves about her face. He liked it. Raising his voice a little, he repeated the question. When she stopped suddenly and spun around, the pile of clothes she held nearly fell on the floor. He automatically reached out to steady it.

Deep brown eyes that matched her hair penetrated to his very core before her eyelids swept down and severed the moment. He stepped back. "I just thought you might..."

His words trailed off as he desperately searched the tumbleweed in his brain for something intelligent or witty, anything, to say to the stunning beauty before him. For the first time in his entire adult life when faced with a member of the opposite sex, he drew a blank.

As the pause in his sentence passed awkward and headed directly towards embarrassing, his attention snagged on Elias, who, almost out of sight, was approaching a crossing much farther down the path than Than would have judged possible in the time elapsed since he'd veered aside. A handful of spans beyond his brother-in-law, coming around the corner in a crisp, synchronised march, was a full squadron of guards led by Risoth, the head guard. Easily distinguished by his formal domed headdress with the thin purple band of office and long neck band, he was carrying a scanner and giving instructions to the guards behind him.

Between them, faces drawn and steps faltering, a group of dishevelled, shackled human men were prodded onward at the same brisk pace. The men wore mostly red but a few large greens were mixed in as well. Than's blood drained from his body as icy fingers crawled through his veins and squeezed his heart. The sight could mean only one thing—another Selection.

Than's mind scrambled. His natural instinct was to run as fast and as far as possible. No one knew what happened to those Selected, but it couldn't be good, and they never returned. How could he and Elias have missed the commotion such an event would usually create? Never mind that, the guards were almost upon Elias. There was nowhere for him to duck and hide and no way to outrun guards whose legs were half a span longer than a human's. They also carried rods, which had the capacity to stun, cause debilitating agony or kill if necessary. Than wouldn't leave him to face that alone, not while he had breath.

Figuring the odds, should Elias strike their interest, Than left the girl and began moving as casually as possible under the circumstances towards his brother-in-law. What would Elias do if they chose him? Would Than reach him in time to offer aid? What help could Than possibly give during a Selection? He berated himself silently for leaving Elias alone. Not one to pray often, he begged God to spare the other man, even at the cost of his own life.

A couple of heartbeats after Than first saw the Esarelians, others must have also noticed the squadron and reached the same conclusion regarding their sudden appearance. While those nearest the guards either stood rooted in place, slowed their pace, or attempted to backtrack subtly without notice, everyone farther afield could abandon discretion without fear of being caught. Shouts and cries finally went up around him as arms were pointed in the direction of the group and people moved away.

Slaves wearing all colours blurred into a splotchy rainbow around Than in their haste to escape the area. Anything being carried was dropped where individuals stood when they heard the warning and scattered across the ground as people forgot everything but the need to flee. Chaos reigned. In a circle of calm, like that at the centre of a hurricane, Than kept moving forwards, against the flow, his eyes locked on his brother-in-law.

Than checked their relative positions again and nearly fell. He was too late.

Risoth's assessing eyes fixed firmly on Elias, who was studiously avoiding eye contact with any in the group and had slowed as much as possible without drawing undue attention. Risoth swept the scanner down and up Elias's body once before his hand rose to point an extended finger squarely at Elias's chest. One word changed his life forever. "Him!"

What happened next felt at once both dreamlike and sluggish to Than. Elias's shocked expression morphed into one of terror. His feet, frozen in place only moments before, began shuffling backwards as his arms came up in a futile effort to ward off the now inevitable. Seeing his defiant gesture, the two guards who had detached themselves from the squadron moved their hands closer to their rods.

Than threw caution to the wind and broke into a run. Not Elias; anyone but Elias. The thoughts screaming through his brain overrode his survival instincts and pushed his legs to greater speeds. He planned as he ran. They could slip down the side alley on the opposite side of the path and lose the guards in the maze of shacks. After that, they could hide in the resistance's underground headquarters or even out in the wilderness. People survived out there; they could make it. They were both fast and built for endurance. Unfortunately, so were the guards, and they would reach Elias first.

This was a nightmare the likes of which had not touched Than since he was a small boy, comforted by the lyrical voice of his sister, Gilla. He watched in impotent horror as the guards each grabbed one of Elias's upper arms and pulled them forward, ready to shackle. Unable to act and desperate to intervene somehow, Than shouted. "Stop! Take your hands off him. Take me instead."

Pausing briefly and turning to their commander, confirming the rumour that guards were not especially chosen for their mental acuity but merely brute strength, they watched Risoth's head swivel towards Than and zero in on the young man. A gleam lit the head guard's eye, and he opened his mouth to speak.

At that precise moment, Elias struck. By using his own body weight and hooking his arms tightly around the limbs of the guards holding him, he managed to drag all three of them off balance. They fell into the side of a dormitory and slid to the ground in a tangle of limbs. His fists flew immediately, prepared as he was for the impact. Years of intense heavy labour and his need to protect his family fuelled his rage and tightened his aim. It would have worked if he'd been fighting humans.

Unfortunately, the guards took only moments to recover, and instead of returning like for like, the largest simply reached for his rod and touched it to the nearest section of exposed flesh while the other moved out of the way. Elias pulled taut, every muscle in his body strained in rigidity, before convulsing in waves, unconsciously curling into the foetal position. The guard pulled back and hit again in a different location, and then again, and again. Within an incredibly short period of time, Elias was a moaning, quivering mass on the floor between them. The smaller of the two once again reached for the shackles.

Than approached the melee and was about to strike the nearest guard when Elias stopped him.

"Run," he breathed. The single word that Than was positive sounded as a shout in Elias's mind came out as a mere whisper through teeth clenched in agony. Than paused. Indecision tore his insides until the choice was removed by the next words he heard.

At the same time Risoth calmly commanded, "Him," in Than's direction, Elias pleaded in desperation, "My family."

Than only heeded the second voice. An image of his sister and young niece flashed across his mind, and the look in his friend's eyes cemented the impact. He would survive, for their sake. Than backtracked as quickly as possible as Elias used the last of his strength to push a foot forward and trip the head guard. It caused just enough of a distraction for Than to skid around the nearest corner and charge towards the next.

Breathing heavily, he didn't dare stop or turn to check on his pursuers. He frantically weaved through the warren that was the slave settlement in seemingly random directions until his lungs screamed in protest. He slowed but continued to push himself forward. Misery nearly crushed him as he enacted the plan he thought they would follow together, knowing he had left Elias behind. Whether it was what the other man had wanted or not, guilt and grief began to overwhelm Than and tears streaked his face. He silently vowed to be the man Elias would have been, had he escaped, and to protect the family and unborn babe they both loved so much. Than's extra rations would go to them from now on, just as Elias's had, and he would move to their shack and see them safe.

Of course, in order to do that, he would first have to survive himself. He ducked into a doorway to catch his breath and attempted to clear his head and think. He needed to make sure he'd lost the guards and was in no danger of recapture or reprisal. Only Risoth had taken a good look at him, he hoped, and Selections generally only lasted a few cycles before they had their quota. The human men he'd glimpsed between the squadron were nearly exclusively from the uduin sector, and he was positive there had been none from manufacturing. A workable plan forming, his habitual smile attempted a return, but he squashed it into a hard, determined line.

∞

As soon as Than darted down the nearest alley and escaped, the fight left Elias and he slumped back onto the ground. Gritty dirt and blood from where he'd bitten his tongue while convulsing in pain filled his mouth. He'd never received so many consecutive strikes from a rod before and could barely move. Resigned to enduring however many more rounds of punishment the guards decided to inflict, he curled in on himself and tried to remove his mind from his immediate circumstances. He concentrated on the first happy image he could think of: that of his wife on the day she'd told him she was pregnant the first time.

He'd just arrived home from a gruelling shift, and Gilla had been standing in the doorway of their small sleeping chamber, her hair still rumpled from slumber. Her face had radiated joy, the warmth of which he could still feel to this day. Expressive brown eyes had been lit with excitement, and the smile she'd bestowed on him had made him feel like the richest man in the universe. Only the smallest flicker of apprehension at bringing a child into their life of slavery had crossed her features before being overtaken by anticipation once more.

As she'd shared her news, her hand had drifted to her abdomen and gently cradled the new life there, protective and nurturing even then. He'd known she would make the best of mothers and had only hoped at the time that he would live up to her faith in him as a father. He held the memory at the fore of his consciousness as he waited for the next contact of rod to skin.

The preparation had been unnecessary; the expected pain never materialised. He slowly opened his eyes to see Risoth turn away from him in disgust and wave for two of the remaining guards to retrieve his unresponsive body. Within a slow blink of his unbelieving eyes, he was yanked up and dragged over to the other Selected captives. His body hummed with pain and refused to follow his directives, but he was still conscious. Physically, things could have been much worse.

Emotionally speaking, he was a jumbled mess. He'd been Selected. There was nothing he could have done, or could now do, to change his fate. His throbbing body was proof enough of that. However, he could barely comprehend the numerous, horrific implications of what had just happened to him. The impact on his family would be devastating. They'd be vulnerable without him, and the thought would have brought him to his knees had he not been supported on either side.

He reminded himself sternly that he trusted God to protect them, but he still wished he'd been able to see them just once more. Gilla was heavily pregnant, Mirami was still so young, and they were lost to him forever. He would never know if he had a son or another daughter, and his youngest child would never know the tangible love of a father. Instead, the little one would have only a mother's and sister's tales as proof of his feelings. And he … well, he would probably be dead, or as good as.

Elias was slowly becoming clear-headed enough to recognise the facts of his predicament. He would be taken off U'du—something he'd previously only dreamed of—in the most nightmarish of circumstances. What would come next was a mystery none had ever solved, or more specifically, none had ever returned to tell. He prayed to God that he would face whatever it might be with honour and faith, and be able to show the Esarelians what true courage humans were capable of. Thus decided, the rest of the Selection passed in a haze of shouted commands and cries of desperation and despair.

∞

Half a cycle after his escape, Than was wearing a borrowed blue manufacturing uniform that strained to contain the width of his chest and shoulders. He ran a hand nervously over his head, still surprised at the feel of the freshly, hastily shorn locks. Stopping often to check his surroundings and listen for tell-tale sounds, he carefully circled back around to the main thoroughfare and stopped in the shadows between two buildings.

He didn't have long to wait before the Selection squadron, captives in tow, paraded past on their way to the flight centre. Having noted their disinterest in a few men walking stiffly in the opposite direction, Than surmised that the quota for the Selection had been met. That boded well. His heart beat frantically in his chest for what he was about to do next. He ignored the physical reaction, used to dealing with such trifles during his frequent spying missions for the resistance. Half turning his face away, he moved forwards into view and waited, tensed to flee, for a shout of recognition from Risoth. None came.

Than let out a whooshing sigh of relief and, abandoning all subtlety, eagerly scanned the prisoners for signs of Elias. Towards the back of the group, supported on either side, Than spotted the drooping yet distinctive head and shoulders he knew so well. He edged towards the procession as the tail end passed his position and let a low bird call escape his lips. Nothing happened to begin with, so he tried again. Slowly, with obvious effort, Elias dragged his head upright, and hazel eyes, bleary with pain, found Than's. Than held the contact for as long as he could and then, unable to speak in the circumstances, nodded once. Elias nodded in return, his lips attempting to twitch into a smile, before he slumped forwards again.

Than melted back into the shadows of another alley, his message delivered and understood. There was nothing more he could do here, and he had somewhere else he needed to be, as quickly as possible. Unfortunately, for all concerned, his next task would be much more devastating to complete.

∞

Draped between two guards, with his feet dragging along the ground, Elias half stumbled along the main path towards the flight centre. The work sectors rose on his left, their menace no longer a concern to the group of Selected men he trailed behind. He found the revelation amusing for reasons he couldn't currently explain, even to himself.

Something caught his attention. A sound off to the right was out of place. It was significant, but his muddled brain couldn't figure out why. As he mulled it over, he heard it again. This time he knew exactly what it was and who had made it. Ignoring the agony the movement caused to his neck and shoulders, Elias raised his head and searched blearily with unfocused eyes to find Than.

Elias held onto the connection for as long as he was able. In Than's eyes, he read the anguish of helplessness along with a determination to make him proud. Elias hoped it was clear from his own gaze that Than had already accomplished that particular goal. When Than nodded, Elias knew that Gilla, Mirami, and the little one would be provided for.

He smiled, though he felt his lips barely lift, at the thought of the impulsive twenty-two-year-old taking on responsibility for an entire family. He wouldn't argue, though. It gave him a modicum of peace to know that Than would be there for them, and Gilla would need all the support she could get in the months and years ahead. Elias nodded solemnly with the last of his strength and let his head fall forwards again.

Where were they taking him and the others? What would happen to him when he finally left the only place he'd ever known? He didn't know, but the cargo doors to the transport tub gaped ominously in front of the group, luring them into its cavernous black depths. His fears receded. It didn't matter where the Esarelians took him or what fate they forced him to. His family would survive, watched over by God, Than, and the rest of the resistance until they could escape this place.

A pang of regret shot through his chest once more at never meeting his youngest child, and he rubbed the spot over his heart to ease the ensuing ache. Unwilling to contemplate his likely short and tortuous future off-world, or the consequences for his family, he focused instead on recollections of happier times.

He was thirteen when he first met Gilla. She'd been huddled against the wall of his dormitory when he'd set out for his shift one blistering afternoon. Only a muffled whimper had stopped him from passing right by without noticing her. There had been a moment of indecision while he'd calculated the probable outcome of being late before he'd sighed and moved cautiously closer to the small quivering form.

A cascade of wavy brown hair had hidden all but the barest hint of a blue arm with a training band circling the thin bicep. He'd crouched down in front of the girl and stretched out a hand, resolved to helping her in whatever way he could. Offering comfort the way he'd seen his mother do, he'd stroked the soft strands away from her grubby, tearstained face and made soothing noises until she looked up at him with wide eyes.

He'd smiled encouragingly. He remembered her seeming so lost, so fragile in that instant that he'd felt a strong need to protect her from whatever had made her so upset. His young mind hadn't known what that would entail, but he'd been determined to cheer her up somehow. He'd shifted until he sat beside her with his legs stretched out in front of them, nearly touching the building opposite. Even then, he'd been tall for his age.

"What's wrong?" he'd asked simply, not having a clue how to ease into conversation with a sniffling girl.

She'd bitten her lip and looked around, presumably making sure they were alone, before answering him just as forthrightly. "I'm s-scared. I don't want ... to go to training any more. I just w-want to go home..."

But you know you can't, he'd finished silently for her. That explained why she'd been hiding down the side alley next to his dormitory. Her parent's shack would be the first place the guards looked when she was reported missing. And she *would* be reported missing, if she hadn't been already.

"What shift are you on?"

"I'm su-supposed to b-be on th-the afternoon shift." Her voice had hitched several times but remained strong enough to be heard, which he'd taken as a good sign.

Deciding what to do next had been much easier than choosing to stop in the first place. Clambering to his feet, he'd held out a hand as he said, "Come on. I'll tell you about the time I ran away while I walk you to your sector."

Her eyes had opened even further at his admission, and he'd seen her debating whether to accept his offer in the furrow of her brow and the way she'd bitten her lip again. After only a slight pause, she'd slipped her tiny hand into his and let him pull her upright. She'd only reached his chest, and he'd again felt an inexplicable responsibility for her.

As they'd started walking, she'd quietly said, "I'm Gilla."

"Elias," he'd responded, mentally kicking himself for not thinking of introductions earlier. He'd gone on to tell her about the time, early in the first year of his training, when he'd been told to climb the netting above the uduin tanks and had been so scared by the height, he'd run out of the building and all the way home. He'd been punished but, thankfully, assigned to the pumping floor ever since.

By the time they'd reached the manufacturing sector, she'd told him how she'd made a mistake fusing one of the circuit boards in a docking mechanism the day before and had been reprimanded by a passing guard. The experience had frightened her so badly that she was terrified of returning to face him again.

Elias had reassured her the only way he knew how. He'd prayed for her, explained that God would always be with her, and promised to accompany her every day until she felt better. Leaving her at the checkpoint with a small smile on her face, he'd raced to his own sector and arrived just in time to avoid notice.

They'd walked to work together each afternoon from then until she'd turned twelve and been assigned to a different shift pattern. Keeping in touch after that had been harder but worth it. When he'd eventually worked up the courage to ask her about courting four years later, she'd been surprised, thinking of him as only a friend, and he'd had to work hard to make her see him as anything more. By God's grace alone, he'd prevailed.

Elias smiled at the memories, despite his residual pain. He would always love Gilla and his children, and nothing—not time, distance, or the Esarelians—could ever change that fact. By the time the transport tub was ready for him and the others to be loaded aboard like a herd of cattle, he was moving under his own power and ready to face whatever life was left to him. He would trust God in all things, as he always had.

∞

Than made his way cautiously to the manufacturing sector, still half suspecting the guards would pick up his trail and haul him away with the others that had been Selected. Thinking about them made him feel sick, so he mentally brushed the image away and focused ahead. Scanning the area for signs of trouble, he found nothing of immediate concern. In fact, it seemed the sector had been left entirely alone this time. The buildings in front of him looked as imposing yet calm and orderly as always.

He casually sauntered towards his primary destination with his shoulders hunched inward and his arms held loosely at his sides. The last thing he wanted was to appear as a threat to any hyper-aware guards possibly lurking in the vicinity. Even managing a nonchalant whistle, he approached the largest building at an oblique angle before slipping inside.

Once through the main doors, his nose wrinkled at the acrid burning smell of fused metal, so unfamiliar and different from the pungent aroma of the water in the uduin buildings. He again paused to assess. Having never been inside this sector before, he hoped the general layout was the same as in his. His only plan at this point was simple: try to find Gilla. Beyond that … well, no amount of planning could help him soften *that* blow.

There was a row of supply carts lined up along one section of the huge left-hand wall, and he decided to use one to blend in. Pushing it firmly before him, he made his way systematically through the lines, looking for his sister.

Two-thirds of the way through the large, open space, he spotted a familiar-looking woman. One of Gilla's friends, he tried to recall her name. M... Man, Mena... Amina! That was it. He urgently whispered her name and, when she turned, surreptitiously waved her towards the end of her row. She frowned at him, and for a moment he thought she would refuse his bidding, but on closer inspection of his face, her eyes widened in recognition, and she began to move.

"What have you done to—"

"Never mind that now. Where's Gilla?" he demanded quickly, interrupting what was no doubt going to be a long series of questions regarding his new looks, clothing, and presence in her sector.

Frowning again in disapproval, she jerked her head in the direction of the far corner. He thanked her with a quick peck on the cheek and a squeeze of her hand and moved away before she could speak further.

There were no guards in the immediate area that he could see, but to be sure, he took a circuitous route towards the line Amina had pointed out. Slowly, he made his way to the work station where his sister was currently stretching on tip toes to reach a panel far above her head. He swallowed, reached out a hand towards her shoulder, and dropped it, trying to formulate the words he needed to speak. Closing his eyes and swallowing again, he did what had to be done.

"I need a word with you."

"Oh!" She jumped and tottered backwards into his chest. Before she could spin and give him the pummelling he deserved, he steadied her, his hands gently but firmly gripping her upper arms. She glared up at him over her shoulder and whisper-shouted, "Are you trying to kill me?"

He let her go as he stepped back out of reach and put a finger to his lips to quiet her. Getting her first good look at him, shock slacked her jaw, and then her eyes narrowed in suspicion. To prevent Gilla from voicing her thoughts, he stepped forwards again, bent down, and put his mouth close to her ear. "Not here. Wait until I'm out of sight, and then make your way to the prep room. I'll explain everything there."

Returning to his cart, Than continued down the line and around to the exit, hoping she'd be able to follow without running into problems with the guards and praying to God that his news wouldn't break her in her current state.

A short while later, Gilla rounded the corner into the prep room and came to a standstill, scanning the room for any sign of him. He checked behind her to ensure they were alone and then stepped into view. Before she could do or say anything, he pulled her into his arms and enveloped her in a long bear hug. He needed it. The past few cycles had taken his usually steady nerves and frazzled them with one adrenaline-fuelled exchange after another.

Knowing time was against him, he led her to a bench and held her hand as she settled back onto it. When he had her full attention, he began.

"There's no easy way to say this, sis, so I'm just going to tell you straight. There was a Selection today, and Elias was taken. I'm so sorry." Than paused, but as yet, there was no reaction, so he continued. "I came here because I needed to tell you myself but also because, if we hurry, I might be able to sneak you close enough to the flight centre to say goodbye before they take off."

When she still didn't respond, he began to worry. "What are you thinking? Are you all right? Of course you're not. This is terrible, and I've probably said it all wrong." He stroked the back of her hand gently, hoping to elicit some small acknowledgement with touch where words had failed. Her fingers remained limp and unresponsive.

"I tried to help him, really I did. If I could change places with him, I would in a heartbeat. You won't be alone, though. I promise I'll be here for you and Mirami. I told Elias I would, gave him my word, well, my nod, but it's the same thing. Please believe me. I tried to help him, but there was nothing I could do."

Growing desperate, Than crowded into her face, forcing her to meet his eyes. Though his tone was urgent, he spoke slowly, enunciating each syllable clearly so she would understand. "We need to go if I'm going to get you there in time…"

His rambling apology and assurance of support trailed off as he realised something finally must have triggered the understanding that what he was telling her was reality and not some cruel jest. She slumped forwards and then fell onto her knees, a low keening sound coming from her that filled the room and reached down to the pit of his stomach, twisting it into knots.

Than watched her, helpless to know what could possibly comfort the sister who had sung him to sleep and kissed his bruises better as a small child. Before he could even bend to rub her back or gather her into another hug, the noise she was making changed dramatically. The quiet, heart-wrenching moans became a short, sharp gasp of pain.

She clutched her stomach and expelled three words on her next breath. "The baby's coming!"

It was Than's turn to stare in stunned incomprehension. It took several moments before he gathered his wits enough to say, "Are you sure?"

In answer, he watched as Gilla bent double again, clutching her distended abdomen and crying out. The fear etched on her face, combined with the knowledge that she was still over a month away from her due date, sucked the air from Than's lungs.

Galvanised into action, he tucked one arm around her shoulders and the other under her knees and hefted her into the air. Cradling her securely against his chest, he strode as fast as he was able out of the building and towards the med-wing of the Nursery. As he moved, he whispered soothingly into her hair. "I know I'm not Elias, and it's not the same, but I'm here for you, for as long as I live. I promise, Gilla, you're not alone. You've always looked after me; now it's my turn." He made the vow before her and God and prayed he would be enough.

Early the next morning, Than held his brand new nephew for the second time, leaning down and inhaling the slightly sweet scent of fresh baby sweat. The tiny boy looked up at him as if to ask who he was and what he was doing. He wasn't sure exactly what the tiny bundle's smile meant, but he didn't think he could go wrong interpreting the yawn. He gently laid the boy back in his cradle of blankets and squatted next to him. After a few moments, Than's index finger was released from the child's surprisingly determined grip as he succumbed to sleep.

Than padded silently over to where the unconscious form of his sister lay pale and sunken on the sleeping mat. Torn between wishing for her to flutter her lashes open and come back to him or for her to avoid the inevitable and regain her strength before she woke, he simply watched the slight rise and fall of her chest as his mind wandered back over the events since her initial collapse.

The baby had been early, but not dangerously so. After the initial frenzy of their arrival at the med-wing—where personal detail checks, scans of Gilla's vitals, and the move to a private delivery room blurred together in a stream of panic he was unable to control—all had proceeded in as calm and orderly a fashion as any event of this nature could. The midwife had taken pity on his general wide-eyed confusion and explained that that was often the way. Second children were usually much quicker to deliver, and she'd seen no reason his sister would break that pattern.

It had been a strenuous few cycles for Gilla, who had initially held up well, given the circumstances surrounding the onset of labour. She'd fixed her eyes on his as she followed the instructions alternately to push and breathe with each contraction. Tears streaming down her face, she'd silently pleaded for him to find some way of returning Elias to her, begged Than to tell her it had all been a mistake and that her husband was, even then, racing to be by her side as she gave birth to their child. Instead, Than had only been able to grip her hand in his, as if pouring his strength into her body through the connection.

At the first cries of her baby, she'd fallen back against the support frame in exhaustion. He'd watched, fascinated, as the assistant cleaned and wrapped the precious, wriggling body and inserted his universal translator chip before placing him gently in Gilla's waiting arms. She'd taken one look at his scrunched face, inhaled sharply, and slumped sideways, unconscious.

Just in time, Than had reached forwards to cushion her fall and protect the child from toppling from his mother's arms and onto the floor. He'd awkwardly transferred the baby into his own embrace, while the midwife had managed to wrangle Gilla back into a safe position and set the scanner next to her head.

One look down was all he'd needed in order to understand what had caused his sister to faint. Large hazel eyes, the exact same shade as his father's, had blinked innocently up at him.

That had been a few cycles ago, and Gilla still hadn't regained consciousness. The on-call medic, after gleaning all the pertinent details, had assured him her state was the result of repeated shocks and that it would be better for her to wake up naturally than to bring her round with stimulants. Than wasn't so sure, though, and could barely keep himself from the frantic pacing of earlier. He'd made one promise—to look after her and her children. A fine job he was doing so far.

Kneeling next to the sleeping mat and carefully lifting her hand in his, he tentatively started to pray. "Lord, I know I don't come to you often enough, or listen to your direction when I do, but Gilla is everything to me. Please be with her as she grieves for Elias. Send her back to us, so I can help her raise her children in a way that will make him, and you, proud. Please guide me in what to do. I'm nothing on my own. Please, please Lord, give me a chance to make things right. Amen."

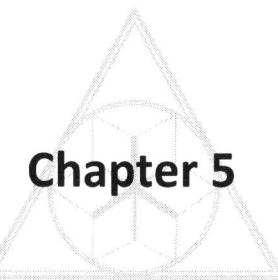

Chapter 5

Day: 21 Month: 06 Year: 6428
Location: Planet U'Du, main slave settlement

"...Davian, Joss, Lukarr ... Elias." Dannon, who had been reading a list of the men taken during the Selection three days earlier, stumbled over the last name. The news had hit them all hard, as well as dealing a devastating blow to their cause. It had taken this long to confirm the forty-eight names on that list, seventeen of whom besides Elias were members of the resistance, and put in place what support they could for any families left behind. The majority had been uduin workers and would have shared their additional rations with their loved ones. The loss would be felt in more ways than one.

Order had inevitably been restored, however, and they were back in the musty underground room with its perpetually stale air, additional ventilation holes notwithstanding. It was where their most valuable supplies and information were stored and where their most sensitive discussions were held.

Only six, no ... five now, knew its location, the entrance hatch hidden beneath the sleeping mat in a shack indistinguishable from any other without knowing the precise series of notches to look for on the outside wall. The woman who harboured their hidden headquarters, painstakingly chiselled from the rock beneath her home, would take their secret to the grave, as had many before her.

After a moment of silence for the men stolen from them, Dannon dropped the databloc to the rickety table and looked around the group before his eyes reached Than. "How is she?" he asked quietly.

Than dragged a hand down his ragged face, feeling scruff on his cheeks that he hadn't even noticed during the last few days of sleep-deprived worry. Even his perpetual movement had ground to a halt, surrendering to fatigue. He shrugged a helpless gesture at the situation and simply said, "Still unconscious."

Aronin leaned over, grasped his shoulder, and asked, "Is there anything else we can do?"

Than assured them with a shake of his head that there wasn't. Members of the resistance weren't the only ones who could be persuaded to cover or swap a shift in the case of an emergency. They were, however, the only ones that regularly put such measures in place for any that needed it. They had long ago learned that, to Esarelians, one human pretty much resembled another. As long as the correct number of workers were counted into the sector at the start of a shift, and all stations were occupied so that work could progress on schedule, the guards didn't care who performed each task. Rosters were only checked against names when a workspace was found empty, a fact that Than and his compatriots had often exploited to their advantage.

He never imagined he'd need it for something like this, though, and he was grateful it had allowed him to stay with Gilla. Damaya had taken Mirami to stay with her family until Gilla was back on her feet, and he'd been getting plenty of help from the medics with the as-yet-unnamed baby. He'd moved his blankets, spare jumpsuit, stool, eating bowl, and canteen into Gilla's shack during the two cycles he'd been forcefully persuaded to leave her side the day before. It hadn't taken long. Aside from that, and this meeting, he'd not left her since she'd been admitted to the med-wing.

"In that case, just know we're here for you both and praying daily for Gilla," Aronin finished.

Before the atmosphere could turn maudlin, Than pulled himself together and attempted to re-direct the meeting. "So, what do we do now?"

"Yes." Willan spoke for the first time. "What do we do? They can't keep getting away with this. We need to strike, soon, before there are none of us left to do it. If we'd done something sooner, Elias might still be here." His intense gaze was just this side of a full glare, showing his hurt and frustration.

Than surprised even himself when he was the first to respond. "Don't go there, Willan. Elias wouldn't want us fighting amongst ourselves, and nothing would please the Esarelians more. We'd be doing their jobs for them. We've got to focus on the future, on gaining our freedom."

Dannon agreed, wondering aloud, "Could we find out where Elias and the others have been taken at the same time? Maybe do something to get them back?"

Aronin shook his head sadly. "You know that's not possible; we've tried before. No, there's no point chasing their trail, much as I wish otherwise. There's nothing we can do for them now but pray. We *can* do something for the rest of our people, though. It's clear we need to act as soon as possible, so we'll have to recruit and train as we go. If you're still with me..." He scanned the men before him. "Then here's what I propose we do—"

"I can't take the lead." Than interrupted in a rush. "I still believe in what we're doing and want to be part of the strike, but I can't be at the front or put myself in any more danger than necessary. Gilla can't lose me too. I'm sorry."

"I already figured that would be the case." Aronin paused, as if choosing his next words carefully. "Are you sure you're ready for this? I hate having to promote you so soon after Elias ... and into what would've been his role. That can't be easy for you."

"I'm fine, really. I just have to dial back on risk-taking now that I have more responsibility. Wow, never thought I'd be saying that so soon." His smile was easy but still failed to reach his eyes.

Aronin's was genuine. "Well, I adjusted my plan accordingly. It's not entirely risk-free, but your role is the safest I can give you. Here, see what you all think." He activated their stolen databloc, and a detailed 3D holovis of the entire settlement, including the work sectors and surrounding area, hovered between them, casting their faces in a flickering white-blue light and turning the areas behind them into black nothingness.

He pointed as he talked. "This will be a multi-pronged, simultaneous attack. The first and largest group, led my me, will strike here." He indicated the main checkpoint to the guards' private sector on the projection with a thick calloused finger before enlarging the display to give a more detailed view of the interior buildings. "Then we'll move here and here inside, fusing these doors shut and holding this entrance. Hopefully, that will subdue the majority of the guards at their base of operations and prevent them from interfering with the rest of our forces. If we can do that, there'll only be four squadrons left across the entire settlement for the rest of you to have to deal with."

Leaning back, he pulled out a crate that had been tucked underneath the table and carefully placed it next to the databloc. "We'll need weapons.

A small selection of blast rods have been provided by my contact, pre-calibrated to stun. After all, we're not murderers. That's the only physical help he can give us without being detected, though.

"At the same time, Than and Willan will take a smaller group to this staging point"—Aronin swept the holovis view sideways to show a marker on the eastern edge of the settlement—"and take out the guards on patrol before securing the flight centre. There should only be two three-man squads you'll have to deal with, one along the perimeter of the settlement and one inside the buildings. I can't see you having any problems with them, especially with the element of surprise and the weapons we have.

"Willan will need to move as quickly as possible to the control station and jam all signals off-world with whatever gadget he's been working on... I assume it'll be ready in time." Willan nodded in response to Aronin's questioning look.

"Than, the rest of your group will secure the supply depot and any tubs they find. If we're really planning to get off this planet and away from the Esarelians, we'll need to be able to feed large numbers for an indefinite period of time. If we can time this right, there'll be additional tubs there too. My contact on the cruiser is going to send details in the next few days of a large shipment planned for some time next month. The more spacecraft we can get our hands on, the better. It shouldn't be too dangerous, there's minimal guard coverage out that way, but it is vital to our success. Is that okay, Than?"

Than appreciated the older man's consideration of his new situation and let his eyes show it. Compared with Aronin's task, Than's role seemed relatively tame, and he felt relieved he could still be part of the operation while keeping his promise to make Gilla a priority.

Aronin moved the holovis display again, creating streaks of white between them until it came to rest on a detailed miniature of the north-western side of the settlement. "Finally, Dan will lead the attack on the Uduin sector. If we want to cripple the Esarelians badly enough that they'll be too busy scrambling around to be able to come after us, we need to hit them hard. That sector's the best chance we have for that."

Than whistled under his breath, finally beginning to appreciate the scope of Aronin's plan and astounded by its sheer audacity. Like everyone, he knew how important uduin was to the Esarelians. The yellow base of the plant-like life forms was necessary for all their bio-technology, particularly their bio-suits. A lucrative profit was also made by selling blocks of the flowering lavender tips as a nutrient-rich food across the galaxies around their Empire. Each organism was priceless.

Destroying, even disrupting, the main supply would be a huge blow, costing billions of credits and setting their bio-tech research back by decades. There hadn't been a strike on this scale since ... well, since before Than was old enough to know of such things. The last attack had been on the space port as an attempt to cut off trade and weaken the Empire. It had ended badly when the explosives had accidentally triggered early, blasting out into space instead of knocking out the sub-space gateway.

This, though... If it worked, this would cripple the Esarelians and provide an escape for all of their people in one fell swoop.

Than tuned back in to hear the rest of what Aronin was saying. "Dan, yours will be the smallest group, between six and eight men only, as you'll need to rely on stealth. You'll stage from here." Again, Aronin pointed at the display, this time at a spot between the pipelines at the edge of the sector. "Send men to these points along the shore to lay charges next to the main pipes. Use your knowledge of the building layout and shift patterns to get all our men out of the blast area before you cause the maximum internal damage you can with the remaining charges. Hopefully it'll be enough to take the uduin harvest out for a long time. Oh, and see if you can get on the same shift as Than so he can cover any final recon you need to do.

"The only other thing we need to do is secure some power cells to use for the explosions. Willan, I know you're working on the jamming device, and you've already arranged for the remote detonators to be smuggled out of the manufacturing sector. Have you had any luck yet with the cells?"

All eyes turned to Willan in the dim light as he shook his head. "I've got no access to that area, and the man who was going to get them was just Selected. I'm sorry, but if I try, I'll most likely fail and jeopardise the entire plan. I'm just not sneaky enough, and they've watched me more than the others ever since I suggested those modifications in the grav-sims on the new cruiser. I couldn't help it, what they were planning was ridiculous and... Sorry. You don't want to hear about that," he said, realising they weren't interested in the technical details he himself found so fascinating. "Anyway, I thought I might be able to cobble something together, but without cells to fuel the explosions, the result will be more of a pop than a bang."

Aronin thoughtfully stroked his beard, his fingers unconsciously following the long scar down his cheek that he'd partially disguised beneath it. Eventually, he turned to Than. "Gilla works in that section, doesn't she?"

Before Than could voice a protest, Aronin held up his hands and rushed on. "Don't worry. I wouldn't dream of asking her to do it. Besides, she's on maternity leave for a month, so it'd be suspicious if she turned up to root around in the supply station. *But,* she must know someone we could trust to ask. We can't leave this to chance, and approaching the wrong person now could ruin everything. Do you think she'd give us a name to contact?"

"If she was awake, yeah, I'm sure she would, but who knows when that will be?" Than drooped against the uneven wall behind him at the reminder of her condition.

Reaching over again, Aronin clasped his hand. Dannon took the other in a strong, sure grip. Joining in a circle, they bowed their heads as Aronin led them in prayer. Silently, and more confidently than the first time in Gilla's room, Than added his own.

Chapter 6

Day: 22   Month: 06   Year: 6428
Location: Planet U'Du, main slave settlement

Gilla was floating. She was warm and comfortable and safe. Snippets of a life outside the blanketing fog danced just out of reach, but failing to grasp any, she was content to ignore them. That was but for one word that snagged her attention and pulled her uncompromisingly towards a thin crack of blinding light—baby. She tried to attach meaning to it but, again, failed to comprehend the full significance. There was only one thing to do. She pushed up.

Her eyelids fluttered infinitesimally, brightening and enlarging the crack. It was almost too much to bear, and she longed to return to the familiar darkness. Nevertheless, the word forced her to try again. Her eyelids eased further open and closed, then again, further, before finally opening halfway. Forcing almost forgotten senses to obey her commands, she moved her neck and tried to take in her immediate surroundings.

Above her sat a rough, mid-grey ceiling. The walls were the same colour, uniform with only one open doorway at the bottom of her sleeping mat. Thick blankets draped her body, which didn't look quite the right shape for some reason. Emanating from a single globe stuck high in the centre of the wall to her left, a soft glow provided the only light. She had no idea what time of day it was. The smell was clean enough, but there was a slight something in the air that tickled a memory, something sour and milky … and then it was gone again. Indistinguishable sounds floated from somewhere beyond the small room. A motion in the doorway broke her concentration, interrupting her mental catalogue.

"You're awake! Thank God."

The voice was familiar to her. She just needed a moment to place it. Before that happened, a shadow passed over her face, and large, brown eyes peered into her own.

The eyes expected some sort of response; that much was clear. Gilla's throat felt dry and swollen with disuse. Swallowing experimentally a couple of times, she attempted to moisten it.

"Here, let me help you." The eyes were replaced by a canteen, which was tipped slowly and gently towards her mouth so she could sip from the opening. Surprisingly refreshing, the water washed away more of the gravel coating her insides, enough to try speech next. She would start with the word that pulled her from the void.

"Baby," she croaked through still-parched lips.

Moments later, there was a rustling sound and a heavy, warm lump of cloth was placed in the crook of her right arm. She looked at it blankly while her mind fitted a jigsaw of memory together. Something fell into place, and it all came rushing back to her: Than appearing at work; the sudden early labour pains; the baby … his eyes. Elias's eyes. Elias!

Shock and denial battled for dominance within her beleaguered brain until, only moments later, the truth won out, unlocking her body and emotions from their mental prison. She cried out, and tears she wouldn't have thought she possessed enough liquid in her body to produce trickled from the corners of her eyes and down into her hair. The brown eyes became Than as he settled on the mat next to her and held her with one arm while he cooed soothing nonsense. Her own arm instinctively gathered her son in to her chest and held him there, his warmth proving a balm to her broken heart.

Moments or cycles later, she gathered her courage and reluctantly pulled back to wipe her face with the back of a hand. For the first time since waking, she truly looked at her not-so-little brother. What she saw shocked her nearly as much as the previous day's events. Gone was the tumble of locks hiding his eyes and curling over his ears. Instead, a short stubble of hair covered his scalp. Fully visible now, his eyes were completely serious for the first time in her memory and shadowed underneath by dark purple-black smudges. The small smile he managed was missing any sign of the trademark cockiness. In fact, it looked sad and tremulous.

He waved away her concern before she could voice it and turned his attention to her son. "I just fed him; he'll need changing soon."

She followed his lead, knowing that practicalities would keep her mind from other, darker thoughts. On closer inspection, while avoiding looking at his eyes, she noticed the colour and plumpness in her baby's cheeks. Surely the wrinkles of birth would take longer to leave his skin? Something wasn't right here. "How long have I been asleep?"

Looking away, Than replied, "More than three days. I've been so worried."

"Three days! What... How...? I have to go."

"It's all right, Gilla." He tugged her back from where she'd been attempting to rise from the mat and gripped her hand in his. "Everything's all right. Mirami is with Dee, and I've been taking care of the little one here. All you need to do is concentrate on getting your strength back. It'll take some time before you're ready to get up. Try anything before then and you'll most likely just fall over."

"He's right." The masculine voice came from the doorway and surprised them both. "Sorry. I'm the medic on duty, Benn. I was with another patient just down the hall and couldn't get away when I heard you yell. By the way, I thought we discussed that already." The last was directed at Than with a firm look that spoke volumes and reminded her of those he'd frequently received from their father when they were children.

Before she could comment, the short, sandy haired man entered and held a scanner above her brow. "He was right though; you shouldn't risk getting up yet. Your muscles aren't used to moving, and you'll still be tired, the last few days notwithstanding. Let us look after you just a little longer, and then you'll be able to run around as much as you want." He studied the scanner intently before relaxing. "Looks good for now, but you'll probably want to sleep again soon. Drink as much as you can, but only in small sips, and I'll have some uduin waiting for you later on today." With another glance at Than, this time accompanied by a reassuring smile, he was gone.

Than untangled his limbs and carefully took the baby from her. When she started to protest, he reassured her that they wouldn't be far and that he could look after the little one while she rested. Gilla would have argued further but found her eyelids drooping. Without further complaint, she snuggled back under the blanket and let the darkness claim her once more.

The next time she woke, Than was squatting on a stool beside the mat with the baby propped against his shoulder. Feeling much better, she reached for her child, needing his weight and warmth to anchor her. Than studied her, unmoving, for a long time. She knew he was trying to ascertain whether holding the baby would push her over the edge of sanity, or maybe consciousness, again. That knowledge flipped a different switch in her, and she sat up, lashing out at him.

"Give me my baby!" The echoes of her shouted demand rolled around the otherwise silent room until reason returned and she flopped back against the mat. "I'm sorry, Than. I can hold him. I'm feeling better now, I promise." She gave him a weak smile as further apology.

It took another long wait, but eventually Than handed the baby over, expertly transferring both him and his burping cloth to her waiting arms. Practice over the last few days while she was unconscious must have given her brother new confidence. She felt a combination of guilt and gratefulness for his aid.

Humming softly, Gilla looked over her son. A square face, plump with baby fat, and a determined jut to his little chin; tufts of dark brown hair, silky as down, poking out at angles from his head; strong, active limbs, waving their own hello; intelligent eyes of green-brown with dark blue edging and a thick fringe of lashes—all were clear signs that he was, indeed, his father's son. The thought both floored and buoyed her.

She closed her eyes as her heart cried out. In that moment, she vowed to be strong, for him and for Mirami. They would feel the loss of their father, but they would never suffer for it. She would protect and provide for them and would do everything in her power to ensure their happiness. She would dedicate them to God, raising them to trust Him in all things, and He would help her cope with their shared loss. He would give her the strength she needed. A sense of peace settled over her pain and sorrow like a thick blanket around a small child, not stripping them from her but tucking them in and away where they could do no harm. Gilla opened her eyes once more.

Looking back down at her child, she mumbled, "You need a name. If I don't give you one soon, Uncle Than's 'little one' will stick."

"I think it already has," he quipped.

She sighed theatrically and then narrowed her eyes on him and teased back. "I wouldn't draw my attention, if I were you. I've yet to receive a satisfactory explanation for your new…" She trailed off and waved a hand in his general direction. "While you're at it, you can tell me what else has happened while I've been sleeping."

"Are you sure you're up to hearing all the details? I mean, you've been through a lot and should be resting. I promised the medic I wouldn't cause any more problems." Her unwavering gaze silenced his protests, and he reluctantly explained the circumstances surrounding his altered appearance. He also tried to update her on all of the goings on since then. Unfortunately, as he'd barely left her side since he carried her into the med-wing, it soon became apparent to Gilla that there was little information to extract from him.

"There are just two last things," he finally muttered, twisting his fingers in a loose strand of the blanket over her legs. A deep frown creased his forehead, and his eyes fixed on a point somewhere around his knees. The only sounds in the room were the soft snores of the little boy still tucked safely into her neck.

"What is it, Than?" she prompted, with a gentle hand on his knee. Although he gripped it tightly, he still didn't speak for a long time. Eventually, he squared his shoulders, took a deep breath, and gave her a direct, determined look.

"I'm sorry I couldn't get him out of there or get you over to see him before... Well, I am. More than you'll ever know. I'd do *anything* for you and... I promise that I'll be here for you now. Whatever you need..." His stilted words and the broken sound of his voice matched the welling tears that he blinked back and refused to let fall. It was the most vulnerable she'd ever seen him.

Her own tears threatened, but Gilla took her cue from him and fought them off. With blurred vision but a dry face, she leaned forwards and cupped his cheek in her free hand. "There is nothing to forgive between us, little brother. *Nothing.* We'll be here for each other, as we always have. All right?"

"All right." The whisper was enough.

"Good, because I miss your annoying ability to make me laugh and want to tie you down at the same time. And I'll need that, Than."

A small twitch of his lips eased her chest. It might take time, but her carefree, energetic little brother would return to her. She sighed internally with relief and remembered his earlier words. "What was the second thing?"

"Ahh. That's another delicate matter. Um, the resistance needs someone in manufacturing—"

"I can't do anything to help, Than. Not now. I have to focus on my children, and I can't get caught—"

He snagged her arm before she did some damage with its flailing. "Whoa! Slow down. I wasn't asking you to do anything, sis. I wouldn't do that to you, especially not now. Besides, you're on a month of maternity, remember. It'd look more than a little suspicious if you tried to walk in there anytime soon." She settled at that, so he continued. "All I want from you is the name of someone you think we can trust to help us get a few things out of your building in that sector. Our man there was taken, and as you know, we can't afford to approach just anyone." He paused, thinking. "What about your friend, Dee? Would she be able to do it?"

"Damaya!" Gilla made a noise that was half splutter, half chortle. "That woman couldn't smuggle a dune-tick out of the building. She's so loud-mouthed and troublesome that they check her every time she sets foot through the entrance to the sector, in either direction. She'd never get whatever you need through without notice."

"Well, who else is there? I don't know many people in that building, and we need to move fast."

She studied him while she flipped through names in her head, wondering just how serious the mission was. After some deliberation, Gilla reluctantly settled on one person—Amina. Her hesitance didn't stem from an unwillingness to trust her friend but from an understanding of the sacrifice she would be asking of her.

When she told Than who she recommended, he agreed with her assessment. "Are you sure she's the best option? I mean, after what happened to her husband *and* son..."

"I know. It left her extremely bitter and fatalistic, but she worked with the resistance occasionally before the Selection that took them. Maybe this is what she needs to get some of her spark back. It's worth a try. If nothing else, at least you can be assured she won't turn you in..." Gilla shrugged. "The other reason she's perfect is that the guards will never suspect her; she's carried a beaten air for years now."

"Okay. I'll get Dan to talk to her. She might take it better coming from him. Thanks, sis."

A glint twinkled in Gilla's eyes as she changed the topic. "Now, go and get in the nearest cleansing cubicle, then get some sleep and eat a serious amount of uduin rations. You look like you've gone ten rounds with a pain rod. Oh, and make sure he speaks to Ami in private. If Dee finds out, she'll want to help, and well, you know how that'll go."

"Okay, okay. I get it—shower, eat, and no Damaya near the resistance." He gave a mock salute before he paused, and a soft smile transformed his face. "It's good to have you bossing me around again, sis. Dee's been great, but she lets me get away with way too much."

Gilla put a hand over her heart in mock horror and defended herself. "I don't *boss*; I *care*!" Her smile beat his into the ground in terms of wattage. "Dee being a pushover is no surprise, though. Did I ever tell you about the time she once took Gerom for a ride on a skimmer?"

By the time Gilla's friends arrived to see her, Than had the baby changed and down for a nap, and they were laughing together over some of Damaya's more memorable exploits. "... and all he could think to do in the situation was reduce her rations by half for a month. He never did find them all." Gilla chuckled, her stomach aching with the forced merriment. It was worth any pretence, though, to hear the genuine guffaws of her brother return once more.

"Are we interrupting anything?" Damaya's question set them off again, and she looked at them as if they were strange, exotic creatures she thought might bite her. As if deciding she wasn't fazed in the slightest after all, she bounced into the room to bestow hugs all round. Behind her, Menali entered more sedately.

Although younger than the others, at only twenty-one, Menali had become a good friend to Gilla since taking on Mirami's class three years earlier. Shorter than most and naturally shy, the teacher's quiet demeanour and gentle disposition often left her beauty overlooked. Long, loose hair hid a fine-boned face with porcelain skin and large eyes framed by the longest lashes Gilla had ever seen. Her friend would be stunning if she ever gained the confidence to stop hiding from the world. She stood just inside the doorway with her head lowered, twisting her hands together nervously.

Than stared openly at Menali, and Gilla thought she heard him whisper, "It's you..." As she opened her mouth to ask what he meant and quiz him on why he was staring at one of her friends, Than shook his head and his face shuttered, locking away whatever emotion had caused him to freeze in place. Gilla resolved to ask him about it later, when he would be less guarded in his response.

He stood and offered his stool. With a wink at Gilla, he said, "Excuse me, ladies. I need to take care of something."

As he started to move, she said, "Make sure you go home and rest now that you know I'm going to be all right. I can do without you for a while, especially if Trouble over here stays." She indicated Damaya with a jerk of her head and then softened the nickname with a smile in her best friend's direction.

Catching Than's wrist, she added, "Oh, and one more thing…" Pulling him nearer, she made an exaggerated sniffing sound and cast him a swift smirk. "There's a distinct whiff of baby vomit around you, so a quick trip to the cleansing cubicles on your way out might be a good idea."

Uncharacteristically, he ducked his head, red splotches creeping up his neck as he muttered, "I've already been through three times since I got up today. That stuff just won't come off."

As Menali approached the stool, a strange look that Gilla couldn't immediately interpret crossed Than's face and was gone. She would have thought she'd imagined it if not for his earlier reaction and the additional flicker of his eyes in her friend's direction on his way out of the room. Before she could determine the reason, her focus on it flittered away under the onslaught of Damaya's second, longer embrace.

"Dee, Menali, I'm so glad you're here." It was all she could, or needed to, say. Grief she had kept hidden in the face of Than's distress overwhelmed her defences, and she broke down in anguish. Her friends sandwiched her between them on the sleeping mat, the three women clinging together until the flow of her tears ebbed and retreated. It took a long time. When at last she felt stuffy in their combined body heat rather than comforted, she pulled back, and they disengaged themselves.

She felt the need to qualify her tears, despite their unquestioning support. "I just miss him so much, and I can't cry in front of Than. He blames himself. Stupid, really, as if he had any control over a Selection. It's just that we've never been personally affected before. We were so lucky. I can't imagine how Amina coped, losing her son as well as her husband. I'll never complain about any negative comment she says ever again. Only the grace of God has brought me back from oblivion. Well, God, Mirami, and this little one." She huffed at her own use of Than's nickname. "I've been praying every second that God will be with Elias and keep him safe. I know I'll never … see him again, but…"

"But God is telling you that he's still alive somewhere, and that comfort keeps you going for the sake of your children," Menali finished. A gentle smile warmed the space between them.

Gilla smiled in return. There was no reason to explain after all. Her friends knew her well enough to know how she felt and how she reacted, who she turned to in times of great need and emotional upheaval. She was still lucky. Damaya fidgeting with her jumpsuit distracted Gilla from her musings, and she asked, "What in the universe are you doing? Surely your clothing didn't get *that* skewed during our hug?"

"Wasn't the hug. This was digging in my side." She produced a large, flat square of lavender-coloured uduin and proceeded to split it into three. "I thought you might want something to eat while we chat."

Before Gilla could comment, Menali beat her to it, berating Damaya for breaking the rules, especially when they were together, and reminding her that Gilla received a small extra ration while in the med-wing anyway so the gesture was unnecessary. Menali's shocked indignation that Damaya might have landed her in trouble or, worse, used her as cover for her devious plots was almost as effective in restoring Gilla's good mood as the other woman's rambunctious ways.

Disapproving or not, Menali didn't turn down her portion, and all three tucked in as they filled in the gaps of Than's update for her. Apparently, those gaps were large enough to fly a transport tub through. People were grieving, and the settlement was turbulent with emotion—as always after a Selection. Attitudes were affected in different ways, and responses were varied. Some became more subdued, defeated, and bitter after the loss of loved ones, as Amina had. Others became more determined to act, to end the cycle of pain and humiliation suffered at their overlords' hands. Yet others went into shock and walked about in a daze that could last for months. A small minority, hated by all, became convinced that the only way to avoid such loss in future was to ingratiate themselves with their masters, turning traitor on their own people in hopes of sparing their families. It was hard to tell who to trust in the current climate, and her friends had been spending their free time trying to offer simple comfort where they could.

The Esarelians had lowered the work age from twelve to ten and the training age from eight to seven. The decision had forced Damaya's son, Gerom, into a full-time worker's position instead of merely being a trainee in the processing sector. Thankfully, as far as Damaya was concerned, the dormitories were currently unable to take the sudden influx of new children, and the age to move from parents' shacks had been left at twelve for the time being.

Apparently, Gerom was coping well with the change in status, even liking his new green uniform jumpsuit. Damaya had spoken privately with Aronin, who had promised her on pain of severe, yet unnecessary, retribution that he would watch out for the lad and arrange ways for his burdens to be lightened or shouldered by others until he became strong enough to handle them alone. It had reassured her enough to stop constantly checking on his progress, and she declared she would only sneak over to that sector on occasion from then on. She was incorrigible, but none could question her love for her son.

The other implication of that change in policy stabbed Gilla to her core. Mirami had also been positioned. She was so young to be thrust into the world of constant labour, even as just a trainee, without her mother there to offer comfort or council. The one positive in the situation was that Mirami had been assigned to the Nursery with Menali, who assured Gilla that her daughter was being well taken care of. It was a relief. The work there wasn't as strenuous as elsewhere, and her daughter had always loved being around younger children. She quizzed Menali for as much information about Mirami's welfare as the other woman knew and was finally satisfied that her precious girl was coping well in her new position.

Gilla sat back on the sleeping mat and allowed all she'd been told to percolate through her brain until the churning sensation behind her eyes settled and she felt the need to move in order to gain much-needed perspective. Swinging her legs towards the floor for the first time since her arrival, she attempted to get up on her own. It didn't work. Her legs buckled, and she swayed precariously as the room spun in circles around her. Listing to the left, she half collapsed, half eased back onto the mat with the aid of hands suddenly supporting her.

"What do you think you're doing? You've only been fully conscious for less than a few cycles, and you're trying to … what? Lie down and … hold the little one if you need to feel useful." Damaya whirled to pick up the sleeping babe while Menali helped settle Gilla back into a comfortable position. Their concern touched her, and while the inactivity chaffed, she could hardly argue her case for strolling around the building yet.

To distract her, Menali asked, "Have you decided what to call the baby? After all, we can't keep calling him 'little one' forever."

"I totally agree, although Than and Dee seem quite content with the moniker." Gilla thought for a moment while she watched the soft rise and fall of her son's tiny chest. She and Elias had discussed possible names several times over the course of her pregnancy but had not come to a consensus, thinking they had plenty of time before the child's arrival. Seeing him now, none of them really suited or felt right. In fact, there was only one name that sprang to mind as he sleepily opened his eyes and locked gazes with her. "Elias. His name's Elias, after his father."

Menali nodded and wiped at moist eyes. Damaya leaned over to hug them both and welcome little Elias to their extended family. Gilla just smiled at her son and thanked God for the piece of her husband He'd allowed her to keep.

∞

Than leaned his back against the wall outside Gilla's room, his long legs stretched out before him, half listening to the hushed whispers within. He'd rushed over to Dannon's dormitory to give him the name they needed, along with Gilla's mandate to be gentle with Amina. Then he'd turned straight back to the med-wing, hoping not to miss another shot at impressing the woman who invaded his thoughts more and more as the days wore on. His mind drifted back to the first time he'd seen the beauty he now knew was Mirami's teacher and one of Gilla's close friends. Pushing away memories of the events immediately after that meeting, he wondered how he could have missed her before that day. How had he not met her through their shared connection?

Breaking into his musings, Menali stepped out of the doorway in front of him and, without seeming to notice him, turned to make her way down the hall in the other direction. He stopped her with a hand on her arm before thinking the move through. She started and whirled on him, her eyes wide and momentarily frightened before the realisation of who had touched her sank in and she relaxed, marginally.

Her eyes had haunted him. He'd dreamed about those eyes. Stupid dreams, where he'd tried to describe their exact hue and the way they made him feel. He knew a hundred words for the different shades of grey on the planet, purple too, but there was nothing with which to compare the brown of her eyes except the other varied brown eyes of his people. There were old phrases and words passed down from the ancestors, like mahogany or chocolate. Chocolate... He had no idea what the word meant, but he liked the sound of it. Dark chocolate globes that hooked him and pulled him into oblivion he could easily crave.

"I love your dark chocolate eyes." The words were out before he could stop them.

"My what?" Her beautiful face scrunched in incomprehension.

Great, he sounded like an idiot. He quickly backpedalled. "Uh, nothing. I have to go." Before he said something else that made him sound like a fool. He needed to end the encounter on a better note, though. Plastering on a roguish grin that never failed with the ladies, he said, "See you soon, Nali."

"Nali?" She sighed and looked away, breaking the spell. "My name's *Men*ali, not that it matters."

His smile dropped. "It does matter, to me." He let that sink in before lightening his tone once more. "But Nali suits you, and I like having something to call you that's just mine. So, I'll be seeing you soon, *Nali*, especially as you work in the building and Gilla will be here for a while." He winked and strode purposefully away before she could react or comment. He would let her stew on that for a while and then see about asking her out, preferably without saying anything dumb or letting her know how much she affected him.

∞

Menali watched Gilla's brother stride confidently down the corridor as if he could conquer the world. She wished sometimes she could be that brave. She frowned. He was brave but also cocky and arrogant. She'd seen him around the settlement occasionally in the past. Honestly, she'd never given much thought to the charming man who flirted with every pretty face he came across. She preferred to stay in the background.

The day he'd spoken to her for the first time, she'd been in a rush. At first she hadn't noticed him appear alongside her, too intent on getting the children's clothes back to work before she was missed. She'd taken them home a few days earlier to mend, but Petran had needed a spare set after playing in the dirt and getting sticky, grey goo all over his brown trousers and shirt. The boy would never stay clean. She'd been smiling at the thought of his skinned, bloody knees the previous time she'd let him out of her sight.

When she'd realised someone was talking to her, Menali had reacted without thought and hidden behind the bundle she carried. He would no doubt go away soon enough and leave her alone. Instead, he'd spoken again, the rumble of his voice near her ear making her jump.

She hadn't known what to say in reply, didn't really even know what he'd said to her. Out of her depth in social situations involving males above the age of eight, she'd looked down and tried to think of a response.

He'd saved her. He'd started to say something about "thinking she might" but then trailed off and looked away, as if already moving onto other things. She remembered thinking that he must have taken her for someone else and then not known how to back out of the awkward situation. Embarrassed, she'd mentally berated him for his thoughtlessness and roguish ways before taking the opportunity to slide quietly away and continue her trek back to the Nursery.

When she'd realised later what had happened and the true reason for his sudden retreat, guilt had swamped her for her snide thoughts. It was better that he'd left, though. She was totally wrong for a man of action like him.

Her opinion since then hadn't changed, except to include the off-putting certainty that he flirted with every female medic to check on his sister. Menali had heard a couple of them talking about his looks and arguing about which of them they thought he'd preferred. His arrogance and assurance that charm would get him anything he wanted was astounding. She could never be with a man like that. No, she would just carry on as normal and wait for him to move on to a more outgoing, vivacious woman that would be his match. It wouldn't take long.

In the meantime, she'd have to be careful to avoid him when she visited Gilla. His presence made her nervous. When she'd arrived earlier to find him in the room, she hadn't known how to react. She'd dithered and hated herself for her reaction to him. Thankfully, he left after offering her his chair. She hadn't even had to look at him or his devastating smile.

Here he was again, though, making her tongue-tied. Again. Menali had no idea why. *Dark chocolate eyes*, she thought to herself as she walked towards the school-wing of the building. *What in the universe was he talking about? The man's mad.* She was definitely better off with the little ones, whom she could help grow out of their precocious ways.

Chapter 7

Day: 04   Month: 07   Year: 6428
Location: Planet U'Du, main slave settlement

As she paced her room in the med-wing, Gilla bounced little Elias gently and attempted to lull him back to sleep. He'd started crying halfway through his afternoon nap a quarter of a cycle ago, his screams a siren blaring through the entire lower floor of the wing. Within the room, the noise had been almost unbearable and rattled her eardrums until he eventually wore himself out. Softly moving around the confines of their small shared space, her mind had time to ruminate on their situation.

She shouldn't be here, not any longer. Gilla knew it but couldn't bring herself to sign out of the med-wing and go back to the little shack she and Elias had turned into a home together. Even the thought of that space without him in it brought tears to her eyes and denial surging to the forefront of her mind. He hadn't been Selected. He was just at the uduin sector on an abnormally long shift and would be waiting in the doorway to their sleeping room with the smile she adored when she returned with their new son.

As long as she didn't leave the med-wing, the illusion could remain a pristine work of art in her imagination. She could continue to delude herself into thinking that everything was fine and that her married life hadn't come crashing down around her in the space of a single afternoon. In reality, she was being a coward. However, knowing this and acting on the knowledge to break the unhealthy spiral she was descending into were two distinct things. Making the frightening leap from one to the next was seemingly impossible, so she remained in her comfortable little bubble in the med-wing and waited for something to change. She couldn't help chuckling at the strange about-face in her thinking. When she'd initially woken, she'd wanted nothing more than to rush home, but a mere four days later, all she wanted was to remain where she was.

The excuse that little Elias needed monitoring after such a premature birth was beginning to wear thin. She could see the truth of that on the faces of the medics who came to check on them each morning and evening. He was miraculously healthy for one born so small and continued to gain weight on a daily basis. Still, none had commented directly on her overlong stay yet, and she wouldn't bring it up until they did.

Laying her precious bundle in the box-like wooden cradle next to her sleeping mat, she rocked it from side to side until she was assured he wouldn't wake again. Taking care of her son's needs was a balm to her troubled thoughts and, so far, had left her little time to contemplate the darker aspects of her new world. He was, indeed, progressing well for one born over a month early, and she praised God for his continued good health.

Gilla was deciding who to visit after Elias's afternoon nap when the door swung wide. Revealed in the opening were Damaya and Than, with Benn, the medic who had first attended her, barely visible behind them. Her friend would have swished into the room, chattering loudly in her usual exuberant manner, had not Gilla rushed to block her path. Ushering them back out into the hallway and quietly closing the door behind her, she warned them all to keep their voices down lest they wake Elias again. She would rather avoid the little tot starting to bawl at the interruption and disturbing the elderly man in the room next door for a second time within the cycle.

The grins filling their faces dimmed but soon returned full force as they hunkered down for what she could only presume was going to be a lengthy conversation. Wherever these two went together, mischief was sure to follow. They were lode stones for whatever crazy schemes floated through the universe. Assuming Benn, whose arms were folded and legs were planted shoulder-width apart in a firm stance, was there as supervisory escort, Gilla settled next to the door for an extraordinary tale of their latest exploits. She anticipated a diversion worthy of their combined capacity for trouble. She was wrong.

"We've come to bust you out of here," Than started.

Damaya finished, "By force if necessary!"

Pushing away from the wall she'd been leaning against, Gilla stared in near horror at their determined expressions. She could tell they were serious by the glint in Damaya's eyes and Than's unnatural stillness. He looked like a hunter eyeing prey, ready to leap into action and capture her should she choose to bolt in any direction.

They even had Benn in on their ambush. Before she could close the mouth that had dropped open at their statements and formulate a reply, he added, "It's time you went home, Gilla. You've been here too long already, and frankly, we need the beds." He raised his hands in an open, helpless gesture.

"I can't go yet… Elias is still under observation."

It was a flimsy excuse, and they all knew it. It was also an expected reaction and apparently why Than and Damaya had brought Benn along. She caught them exchanging fleeting looks before turning to him in unison.

Sympathetic though his expression was, he still said, "He's fine, Gilla. Better than expected, even. We can monitor him at home from now on so you can get back into a normal routine."

She glared at him, the unspoken label of traitor clear in her expression. They were forcing her to admit the truth aloud, and she resented them for it, especially as they had ambushed her so thoroughly in order to accomplish their goal.

Looking down to avoid the pressure of their gazes, she whispered, "I'm not ready yet."

From the corner of her eye, Gilla watched Damaya pull herself upright and walk slowly until she was directly in front of her. Taking both of Gilla's hands, she held them gently and squeezed once. The whole manoeuvre was performed as if she was afraid that Gilla would spook like a scared child and run at any moment. She wouldn't have been far from the truth. Gilla's heart had begun knocking against her ribs, and her mouth had dried at their proposal.

Damaya waited until she had Gilla's complete attention before squeezing her hands once more and looking directly in her eyes. "You *are* ready, and you need to do this. Trust us, please."

From behind, Gilla felt Than slip his arm around her shoulder and add, "I'll stay with you for as long as you need me; forever, if necessary."

"It's time to go home. Mirami needs you there, and Elias will too. You can do this; you're the bravest person I know." Damaya's mention of her children brought Gilla's eyes back to her and a spark of defiant indignation to her core.

"We'll be right there with you the whole time." Than finished the back and forth of persuasion-coercion before she could respond, leaving her nowhere to turn but to the medic.

He offered no hope of safe harbour when he said, "You'll still need to come back for regular check-ups over the next ten days. Don't worry, you'll soon find your feet again." The encouraging smile he gave her was almost too much, and she fought not to growl in frustration.

"Fine, you win. But I'm coming here every day. There are people here that I've grown close to and who rely on me to visit and cheer them up."

Benn rubbed his hands together, looking positively gleeful at her acquiescence. "That won't be a problem. I'm sure some of our patients will greatly benefit from your continued support and prayers. Now you'll need to liaise with someone in the infant-wing over the little one's schedule for feeding, changing, and naps. I can—"

Gilla held up a hand as she interrupted. "Don't worry. I've done this before. Elias," she stressed his name, mildly irritated with everyone's continued use of Than's nickname for her son, "will be in sync with the patterns of the baby factory by the time my maternity's over."

Benn had the decency to blush. Whether it was due to her implied reprimand or her description of the infant-wing, however, was unclear. Either way, it instantly made Gilla feel guilty for her less-than-charitable remark. The medic softened his voice when he said, "Come on, Gilla, it's not that bad. The routine's necessary with the number of infants they have, and they do care…"

"I know," Gilla replied wearily, "it's just that a month's so little time." She felt Damaya's grip tighten in understanding on the hand she still held.

Smiling again, this time in sympathy, Benn said nothing further. He merely turned and rushed away to sort out the discharge notice, presumably before she could change her mind.

Than rubbed her shoulder to indicate his approval of her decision and then squeezed so tightly she was forced to push him off. With an all-too-familiar grin, he said, "Now let's get you packed up and out of here so I can get some adult conversation in the evenings. Mirami tries, but it's not the same with a seven-year-old."

She put a hand out to halt his forward momentum. "First, do *not* disparage my daughter's conversational skills. You had nothing of substance to say until you were at least ten. Second, don't even *think* of going into that room while Elias is asleep unless you fuse your mouth shut." She modulated her voice from protective mother to soothingly open and continued. "I'm not stalling, honestly, but I only just got him down for his nap."

Looking for a moment as if he was unsure whether to be offended at her accusations or remain pleased with the progress they had made, Than narrowed his eyes at her in indecision. Not one to hang about, he bounced a few times on the balls of his feet and set off down the corridor in the direction of the common room. "All right, then, I'm going to get a drink while we wait. Want anything?"

Just in case he decided to do something childish to it, she shook her head, calling after him that she would get one herself later. Damaya said something similar and probably with the same reason in mind. Turning to each other, they shared a soft smile and exchanged a look of understanding.

Coming in for a proper hug, Damaya whispered, "I'm sorry we ganged up on you."

"It's all right. I guess I needed it." Taking a moment to process the outcome of their conversation, Gilla felt her body relax in acceptance—or defeat, depending on how she viewed it—and then immediately tense again in dread. She was going home. As she thought about it further, though, Gilla felt the rightness of the decision settle in her gut and soothe the tension there. She was going home. This time when she let the idea wash over her, the prospect didn't feel like drowning so much as cleansing, like a new beginning. Holding onto the insight, she centred her mind on her children and began the journey towards healing.

With the few things she'd accumulated during her stay in the med-wing tucked inside a blanket and slung over Than's shoulder, Gilla walked out of her room there for the last time. It had taken no time at all for Benn to arrange her discharge, and before she could say anything, Damaya was tugging her out of the main entrance to the building as she waved goodbye over her shoulder.

In the open, the sun blazed down on them, and Gilla pulled Elias's blanket further up over his face to protect it from the intense glare. The distance between the Nursery and her shack wasn't far, but she didn't want the heat or harmful rays to cause him distress. Walking through the centre of the settlement, she smiled, nodded, or waved greetings to those they encountered. Her throat had closed, preventing her from calling out to them, but there wasn't much that could be said anyway.

Stopping occasionally for friends and acquaintances to admire her son delayed the inevitable and made Gilla antsy. One woman, chucking Elias under his chin and cooing for him, commented on how much he resembled his father, with his unusual eye colouring and dark, almost black hair. As soon as the words left her mouth, the realisation of what she'd said and the implications of such a statement passed across her features along with a sneaking blush. Unable or unsure of how to backtrack, she self-consciously dropped her arm, mumbled an awkward apology, and scurried away down one of the many passageways between shacks.

The day would have lost its sheen of new-found possibilities had it not been for Damaya's rejoinder as she got them moving again. "Well, thank the universe he does! Better that than take after his uncle's ugly mug."

"Hey! This face is a thing of perfection. I have to beat the ladies away with a stick." Than's retort came fast and cockily, as expected. He jogged forwards a few steps before spinning to face them and preening as he walked backwards—and into a wall. The oomph forced from his startled body was lost amid their laughter.

Happily knocking him aside as she passed, Damaya said, "More like beat them blind before they'll even be able to take you seriously."

The light-hearted banter gave Gilla much-needed time to talk her limbs into co-operation and her nerves back into line before she had to face her home without her husband for the first time.

By the time they arrived, she was ready. They stopped outside, Than to her left and Damaya on her right. After glancing at each of them and receiving encouraging looks and nudges, Gilla took a deep breath and stepped forwards. Although it had remained in use by Mirami and Than over the last several days, in Gilla's eyes, the shack sagged with an air of abandonment, as if it knew its master was gone forever. It was probably her imagination, but she knew how it felt. Creaking on bark hinges as it moved slightly under her initial soft touch, the door felt warm and worn smooth with age and a thousand hands seeking entrance. Familiarity wormed deep inside. This was her home, and it always would be. The touches of Elias would be a comfort to her in the years ahead as she raised their children here.

Reminding herself that she'd vowed to be strong for them, and seeking the peace that had accompanied the decision when she made it, Gilla pushed the door the rest of the way open and stepped across the threshold. Inside, the shack was just as she'd left it that fateful morning that seemed a lifetime ago.

The scratched and scarred table sat to one side of the main room with the pair of rough stools Elias had made stationed at either end. He'd never been very good at building furniture, and the one nearest to the door forever leaned crookedly to the side, no matter how many times he'd tried to fix it. A solitary cupboard on the far wall held their rations of uduin for the week, presumably collected from the distribution point by Than before he came to fetch her from the Nursery. His things sat on a stool underneath. Canteens hung from scrap metal pegs hammered into the rock wall, and their globe was fixed to the centre of the ceiling, casting the entire space in a gentle light.

Hesitantly, she stepped across to the door of the sleeping chamber, hearing the others enter behind her. Having no additional light, the smaller back room was dim at first. As her eyes adjusted to the gloom, however, they cast over the sleeping mat covering two-thirds of the floor. Blankets were stacked neatly at the end, and spare blue jumpsuits could be seen peeking over the edge of the makeshift crate in the corner. A smaller version in yellow with brown training bands had been tossed near it but not quite near enough. Smiling at her daughter's haphazard ways, Gilla bent to fold the discarded clothing, smoothing out the wrinkles as she did. It seemed one of the others had removed Elias's red uniforms, and for that she was grateful. It would have been too much.

She moved back into the main room to find that Damaya and Than had stayed back, presumably to give her space to acclimatise. They still stood just inside the doorway, eyeing her as if she would break down or strike out at any moment. At the gesture, emotion welled, and for just a moment, the greys and purples of the shack's interior blended together into a dull blur, the only relief provided by their red and blue jumpsuits. She blinked the room back into focus and forced a shaky smile.

To reassure them that she was, in fact, dealing reasonably well with the move home, she took little Elias's things from Than's loose grip and began to put them away. As she worked, she felt rather than saw them relax. It loosened the knot in her own chest, and for the first time, she knew she would eventually recover fully from her loss.

That didn't mean she was entirely comfortable being at home yet. She told them so as she brought the canteen to the table and returned to the cupboard for some uduin. "Just don't leave me here alone yet, all right?"

"Whatever you need, sis. I told you I'd be here for you, and I meant it. Now how about you get this growing lad some food?" He winked and rubbed his stomach to emphasise his need to be fed.

Gilla laughed as Damaya slapped him across his solid chest with the back of her hand. The what-did-I-do look that he shot her cracked Gilla up even more, and she almost forgot her recent pain. With their help, she would undoubtedly be all right.

After Than and Damaya had gone, and before Mirami returned from training, Gilla spent some quality time with her son. She'd fed and changed him and now sat in a shaft of warm afternoon sunlight streaming through the open front door of the shack. Motes of dust flitted among the angled beams of light, creating complex patterns that lulled Gilla towards a restful trance. She felt the intimacy of the moment. Almost complete silence surrounded her and little Elias, cocooning them against the trials of the world outside and making it feel like they were the only two people left on the planet.

Looking into the sleepy, drooping eyes of her son was strange. They were so much like Elias's that she felt she was looking at an old soul rather than a new-born. Gilla put her little finger within reach of his blindly grasping hand, delighting in that moment of physical connection when he seized it. Lightly touching the soft down of his flushed cheek, she wiped a trace of drool from the corner of his rosebud mouth.

Soon he would sleep in earnest, and she would be alone with her memories, but for the moment she enjoyed spending time with her newest child, learning the nuances of his expressions and personality. Gilla loved this stage of raising children and remembered similar afternoons with Mirami when she was still a babe. *You grow so fast*, she thought as she hugged him close. *Before I know it, you'll be starting your training and leaving home as well. God, help me face all this alone.*

Readjusting herself on the stool, she felt a sense of peace wash over her like the rays of sunlight, bathing her skin in warmth that reached to her very core. She turned her face into the heat and began to hum an Old Earth lullaby passed down from her grandmother to her mother. It seemed to settle her son as much as it had soothed Gilla, and his fidgeting lessened as his breathing evened out.

Gilla looked down at him once more. If Elias truly was his father's son in more than eyes and name alone, he would grow to be a strong man of God with a calling to help his fellow slaves. She studied his fragile form. His fingers were so tiny, the nails barely the size of a wand tip, and his arms and legs were covered with a layer of baby fat that would thin far too soon. His chest moved up and down within the blanket wrappings, in time with the shallow cadence of his soft breathing, and his mouth scrunched from side to side as if mulling over matters of vast import.

She couldn't imagine what destiny awaited such an innocent, other than the harsh reality of life as a slave. Nevertheless, she would prepare him for whatever he might face, with lessons in trusting God and developing his faith along with every drop of a mother's love. She would teach him to care for others and give him as many verbal images of his father as she and Mirami were able to recall. Knowing that God would provide whatever else was needed, Gilla continued humming and rocked little Elias to sleep in her warm embrace.

Eventually, his eyelids fluttered closed for the last time and his long lashes came to rest on the smooth, round apples of his face. Careful not to wake him, Gilla rose, still humming the lullaby, and padded silently to the back room, where she laid him down in the crate that would form his bed for the next few months. Taking one last look at his sleeping silhouette, she turned to face the ghost of his father in the main room with renewed hope for the future.

Chapter 8

Day: 11 Month: 07 Year: 6428
Location: Planet U'Du, main slave settlement

It was mid-afternoon, the quietest time in the day on this side of the settlement. Elsewhere, shift changes would hide the other teams getting into position and draw the guards' attention from their own quarters.

Aronin crept silently along the outer wall of the guards' private living sector and signalled his team to take cover and hold their current positions. Scattered along the eastern edge of the slave quarters, the men were crouching in the small gaps between shacks and dormitories, hidden from view among the shadows. All was silent, bar the distant hum of activity in the work sectors to the north, and there was no one within sight. Should a random patrol pass their way, outlying scouts at the corners of those buildings closest to the most likely routes were ready to render them unconscious with their *borrowed* rods. Any such casualties would be secreted away in several of the nondescript shacks behind them, hopefully to be found by their compatriots long after his people had left the planet.

The team would do one final check of equipment and the surrounding area before continuing. Aronin slipped a pack off his shoulder and reached inside to extract the makeshift mirror-scope Willan had designed for just this occasion. Constructed of polished metal off-cuts and tree bark tubing, the device would allow him to detect any Esarelian movement inside the perimeter before he had to give the final command to go. Aronin raised it slowly up until it peeked over the top edge of the wall. With his second-in-command, Pinna, steadying it, he put his eye to the viewing hole.

As expected, the area between the wall and the first buildings was cast in shadows and quiet. There wasn't a living soul in sight. There were, however, occasional trees and shrubs providing cooling shade for the off-duty guards in the heat of the day and a more picturesque outlook from their windows than barren grey rocks. Aronin spotted plenty of places where his men could hide should the need arise. He breathed a sigh of relief; his contact had been correct. Sweeping the area again, Aronin watched for any sign of movement at windows and between structures. While he trusted his contact and would be struggling without the information he'd provided, Aronin believed it always paid to do his own reconnaissance. He wouldn't put the lives of his men in any more danger than necessary.

He gave a second signal, and five of his men materialised from the shadows. The first three scrambled as quietly as possible up to the top of the wall he was currently huddled against, using the linked hands and shoulders of their two comrades to aid them. After an immeasurable time lying motionless atop the thick wall, scouring the interior and committing a route to memory, they dropped down the other side and disappeared from Aronin's sight.

He prayed briefly for their safety. This being the most dangerous assignment of the entire operation, he'd requested volunteers and had had to choose from many more than the small number needed. They would skirt the inside of the perimeter wall and approach from the rear as part of a pincer movement to take and control the main entrance to the sector. His aim was simple: to surprise and overwhelm the guards at the checkpoint without alerting the eight off-duty squadrons within the boundary walls.

Giving the three men time to manoeuvre into position, Aronin raised a hand and pointed his finger to move the rest of his force forward on silent feet to the final staging point. At the appointed time, he and two others detached from the main group and crossed quickly to crouch under the windows beside the doorway.

After catching the eyes of both men, he pulled out the blast rod tucked in his belt and brought it up, ready. At a nod, they simultaneously rose. One of them turned into the doorway with him, the other into the window in a choreographed and well-practiced move. Sighting their targets, all three fired in rapid succession. It was over before it even started. Three stunned Esarelians sprawled on the floor at awkward angles, none of them moving more than an occasional twitch. So far, so good. They hadn't even needed the back up from inside the compound.

Aronin quickly holstered his weapon in order to disarm and bind the nearest guard, the others following his lead. They dragged the Esarelians into an antechamber and motioned the rest of their men to join them.

Positioning themselves strategically in case of a counter-attack, those assigned to hold the checkpoint wore a mixture of grim determination and excited anticipation on their faces. They were just settling into place when the flanking party joined them.

"It's really quiet inside the sector, sir," reported the most senior of the three in a calm, clear voice that betrayed no anxiety or fear. "We didn't see or hear anyone."

"That's good for us," Aronin responded, encouraged by the apparent viability of the rest of their plan. Everything hinged on Aronin's team being able to subdue the guards in the sector in front of him. He moved to the rear of the checkpoint and scanned the immediate area. All was, indeed, extremely quiet. Eyes narrowed in concentration, he gave his orders and watched as team after team melted into the shadows in the direction of their assigned buildings.

On the count of three, Aronin's team stormed through the main doors of the primary guard barracks. They expected to have to rush down the corridor, firing stunning shots into any Esarelians caught in the open and then into each private chamber to subdue what would be considerable resistance. What met them instead wasn't anything they could possibly have envisaged. The pristine corridor, rather than teeming with off-duty guards, was empty. The only sound came from their own shuffling, suddenly uncertain footsteps.

"Check the rooms. Pinna, find out if this happened at any of the other buildings," Aronin commanded in a voice more above a whisper than he would have previously thought wise. It also didn't crack with shock as he suspected it might. He made his way towards the first open doorway on the right to check out the guard accommodations for himself.

The room could only be described as luxurious in comparison with his own cramped dormitory. A raised sleeping mat contained additional cushioning and blankets in rich shades of red and yellow. No scavenged wood and twine made the furniture but smooth, solid, waxed pieces that fitted together as if made by a master craftsman. These included a corner desk and a chair with a complete back rest, an ornately carved chest and stand for clothing and personal effects, and shelves where several holovis images showed a number of Esarelians, presumably family members. On the opposite wall, a huge holovid portrayed a view of a jungle from atop a hill, branches swaying with the weight of some creature or other that was moving in a meandering line across the range. The grey walls were barely noticeable. Shaking his head at the disparity in conditions between slaves and guards, he returned to his more urgent problems and left the room.

As his men worked their way along either side of the corridor, clearing room after room, a barb of dread raked down his spine. This wasn't right. If they weren't here, where were the off-duty squadrons of guards? Maybe they'd been called to an impromptu inspection or training exercise his spies had been unaware of. Aronin could only hope so, because the alternative was unthinkable.

Against the Esarelians' superior strength and speed, the only advantage the resistance had was surprise. If they'd lost that, the consequences were sure to be disastrous. Something still didn't add up, though. They should have been met with a building full of surprised yet angry males or, assuming a leak somewhere in their ranks, a building full of blast rods pointed in their direction by prepared yet still angry males. Instead, they were met with ... nothing! It made no sense.

His feelings of unease intensified. He ignored those of his men who were curiously examining the private sanctum of their captors, flicking only a brief reassuring glance at the few shifting uncertainly in the unexpected pause in action. He needed to think. Where were the guards? What forces had the other teams unexpectedly encountered? Before he could formulate a coherent conclusion to the guards' mass disappearance, his attention was arrested by Pinna calling him from the still open main doorway. Aronin hustled over. "What is it?"

"It's the same everywhere. No sign of any Esarelians in the sector... Can you hear that, sir?" The young man stood statue like and cocked his head in the direction of the other sectors.

Following his subordinate's lead, Aronin listened intently, trying to tune out his own harsh breathing and the adrenaline-fuelled pounding of his heart. The rustle and occasional clatter of the men in the building behind him faded into the background. He instead focused all his attention on the distant sounds drifting across the settlement. He could hear the faint echoes of crackles and hisses.

All at once, his surroundings snapped back into focus as he placed the noise and realised what he was listening to—and what had happened. There was now no doubt that their plans must have been discovered. It was a trap.

"Get the teams back to the main entrance on the double. We need to help the others. God help them till we get there; they've walked into the full twelve squadrons."

∞

Than eased the unconscious body of the last Esarelian silently to the ground and secured his hands behind his back and then to his ankles. The guards had been exactly where they were supposed to be, and Than's small strike force had managed to subdue all but one instantly with the element of surprise.

Unfortunately, that one had been visiting the waste units at the time and, on his return, had managed to stun one of the team before they could take him down in crossfire. Than checked on the man and looked around for somewhere safe to prop his inert body until he returned to his senses in half a cycle. If he hadn't needed every man at his disposal to complete his mission, Than would have left someone with the unfortunate victim. That not being an option, he chose a rocky outcrop at the edge of the settlement to provide cover.

Returning his attention to the task at hand, Than joined Willan at the final staging point and examined the wide open space between them and the flight centre. Beyond it, two buildings, each the size of any three in the main settlement, stood a safe distance away from a large landing area. A tower of sorts rose from the larger structure on the right, antennas reaching from the roof towards the stars. Than was relieved to see a row of tubs powered down at the far side of the inbound traffic zone. They must have been sent from the cruiser to pick up parts for the new build, just as Aronin's contact had predicted.

There was no cover between Than's team and the buildings. He'd known this part of the plan would be the most exposed and dangerous, but his men had been divided into small teams for that very reason. According to the intelligence they'd been given, there should only be one more squad between them and their objective inside. The flight centre wasn't considered at risk under normal circumstances, being situated away from the settlement behind the guards' living sector, and was provided with a minimal contingent of one squad. No deliveries were expected until later in the day, and the Esarelians would be at their most relaxed.

It looked clear. Shaking out his limbs and bouncing on his toes a couple of times in readiness, Than checked on Willan and gave the signal for his group to move. They raced across the barren rock, careful of the extra spring the spongy ground added to their steps when running.

Just before they reached the other side, Willan stumbled, and Than reached out an arm to steady the older man. They couldn't do this without him. Willan was the only one able to set up, and recalibrate if necessary, the device needed to jam any signals between the planet and the space cruiser somewhere beyond the vast cloudless sky above them.

Willan was panting heavily by the time they hunkered down behind a stack of empty crates. Pulling a canteen from his waist clip, he gulped down a few huge swigs of water with trembling hands. *He really isn't cut out for actually participating in missions*, Than thought with wry amusement. Still, despite Willan's near-tumble, they'd made it to the edge of the flight centre undetected and were marginally ahead of schedule.

Waving the all clear, Than watched the next team run in a low crouch across the open expanse. They veered towards the line of tubs beside the landing zone, moving quickly and scanning for additional guards. That team would secure the craft and begin pre-flight checks while Than ensured Willan was set up in the control room and then joined a third group to procure the supplies needed during their escape.

The plan was solid. Even so, the responsibility Than had been given weighed heavily on his shoulders and made him more nervous than he would otherwise have been. Taking a deep breath as he watched the last group start out towards the main hangar, he vowed once again that he wouldn't let the others down.

Than allowed Willan a brief rest and used the time to scout ahead to find the three guards they expected to encounter before reaching their destination. Moving like a ghost, he slid inside the building on the right. Before him stretched a gigantic warehouse packed with rows upon rows of stacked crates full of uduin destined for distribution throughout the stars. To the right, in the far recesses of the building and currently out of sight, a staircase was built into the corner, winding up to the room that formed the control station for all off-world transport and communication. To the left, an oversized doorway, covering more than half of the internal wall, led to additional storage areas packed with supplies. Beyond that, a smaller door opened onto a thin path between the warehouse and the hangar next to it. Than knew that a similar door accessed the likewise enormous space where skimmers were stored when not in use and tubs were parked to load and unload cargo.

He wove his way towards the base of the control tower. Pleased that his intel had proved accurate, he noted that the positions of the guards were as expected. One stood at the bottom of the staircase, and the two on the main floor were moving in a regular pattern through the hangar, warehouse, and storage areas. Than waited for the nearest to pass his position before carefully making his way back to the door where the others waited.

"It's all clear," he whispered to the group. "We proceed as planned."

Receiving nods of acknowledgement, he stood watch as the others slipped through the partially open door. Finally, he and Willan gathered the remaining equipment and followed.

As soon as the door closed behind him, Than felt a difference. There was nothing specific alerting him to danger. However, a prickling of the hairs on the back of his neck wouldn't be ignored. He also noticed a thick, heavy sense of anticipation that wasn't present on his first foray into the building. Trusting his instincts, he whistled a low warning to take cover.

He settled Willan into the dark recess in the corner behind the door and gave the signal to stay put. The others melted into the stacks around them. When there was no more movement, silent as always, Than skirted around a tower of crates and tried to place the disquieting feelings pounding the insides of his skull.

He spotted the ambush moments before he would have sprung the Esarelians' trap and, backtracking a few paces, eased around a row of shelving to gauge their numbers. They were many. His brain stalled. How could this have happened? Had they been discovered ... or betrayed? The additional squadron wasn't there when he came through earlier—he was certain of that, if nothing else. Realising that they must have been in the hangar, he silently berated himself for not checking the entire complex thoroughly. With difficulty, he pushed that thought aside and focused on the steps he must now take.

He needed to get back to his men and get them out of the building before the guards had a chance to engage. If he didn't, they would be slaughtered. Something had gone horribly wrong, and Than thanked God that he'd discovered it before they'd gone any further. As long as they kept their heads, his team could still make it out in one piece. Than's heart plummeted at the certainty that this scene would be repeating across the sectors. His group might live, but he wasn't sure about the other teams' chances, and their best hope for freedom had definitely just been killed.

Before he reached the area where his team waited, Than heard behind him the tell-tale click of a weapon being charged to fire. Reacting instinctively, he launched himself towards the cover of a stack of supply crates. He rolled and scrambled into a crouch, feeling lucky to have avoided the shot. As he edged towards the corner of the crate to try to spot his attacker, his shoulder began to smart, mocking his supposed good fortune. When he shifted his head to see the back of it better, his heart shrivelled at what he saw.

Across the bulge of his deltoid muscle ran a deep channel the width of several fingers. It crossed the back of his upper shoulder and had cut cleanly through cloth, skin, and flesh alike. The open wound had been cauterised as it was inflicted, so at least it wasn't bleeding, and he couldn't feel much yet. He tested it gingerly and was relieved to find the blast of energy hadn't penetrated to the bone, a much worse injury to have to deal with. A tendril of smoke brought the smell of seared flesh to his nose that made him gag as his brain caught up with what had happened. He'd been hit.

The rational part of him clawed its way to the surface and demanded he move, before the Esarelian that had fired at him had a chance to do so again. There was nothing he could do but keep going and hope he lived long enough to tend to the damage later. Above all else, he must not be caught; he knew far too much about the resistance to fall into the hands of the guards. He undid the front of his jumpsuit and carefully tucked his now useless arm inside, wincing as it pulled at the impaired muscles. Taking another quick look around the corner of the stack, he drew on the last of his stubborn determination and moved quietly along the row in the other direction.

He ducked aside just in time to avoid the next blast and, abandoning all attempts at stealth, tore around a corner towards the door they had used to enter the building. As he moved, the stinging in his shoulder became a slow burn that flowed outwards from the site of the impact, until it filled his mind with the scorching pain. Explosions all around him forced his speed and dexterity to the limit of his ability, weakened as he was by the injury. Nevertheless, he ducked and dodged, managing to avoid any more direct hits. This was bad—very, very bad.

"Red! Red! Red!" Than shouted the distress code word as soon as he came into view, unnecessarily, given the sounds of attack behind him. His men knew what to do, and two lay down covering fire while the rest dashed through the door, scattering instantly. Seeing Tash go down under a barrage of blasts, Than slowed, ready to offer what little help he could with one arm out of action. There was no need. Lifeless eyes stared straight ahead, and a gaping hole smoked in the centre of Tash's chest. Unable to do anything more for his friend, Than shot off a quick prayer and a hastily aimed blast over his injured shoulder before continuing forwards.

As he reached the doorway, another member of the team fell. Less known to Than before this mission than some of the other men, Mattis had proved his worth during the last days of training. He groaned and clutched his thigh. Than glanced around, assessing his options. They were limited. With nothing else for it, he pulled the other man back to his feet with his good arm, ignoring the screaming agony shooting out from his own shoulder and the grunts of pain that could have come from either of them. He shoved Mattis through the door with the admonishment to move. They could stop later to treat their wounds, but until then, Mattis would have to bear it, just as he would.

Than hauled the equipment bag over his good shoulder, closing his eyes and clamping his mouth shut against the overwhelming pain the movement caused. Blackness crept in around his periphery, but the adrenaline in his veins forced it back. He pulled Willan from his hiding spot with the same hand and lunged through the door. Spinning around, Than took a moment to jam it closed behind them before he pushed the others into a sprint. They ran out into the wilderness, away from the settlement and beyond range of the guards' weapons. The constant pounding motion made him want to vomit once the initial shock had started to wear off, and he could barely see through the swirling haze before his eyes. He kept going though, knowing that to stop would be to ask for death at the hands of the Esarelians behind them—and not necessarily a quick one.

Planning to circle back later and re-join any survivors from Aronin and Dannon's teams, Than first needed to ensure Willan's safety. Determined to succeed in this one thing, if nothing else that night, he pushed Willan and Mattis in front of him and fought the pull towards unconsciousness in order to cover their retreat. The frigid night swallowed them as they moved farther and farther away from the chaos in the flight centre, and Than again had time to wonder what had happened and who had betrayed them.

∞

Dannon thought their entry to the sector had been too easy. Wearing borrowed red jumpsuits where necessary, his team had approached the checkpoint in small groups of two or three at a time. Having expected to lose some to the random identification inspections, he was surprised when they met at the first staging point that they had all made it through.

It was a busy time of day. Teams of slaves were moving crates of freshly harvested uduin to the edge of the processing sector on hover-transports. Guards stood watch over them, ensuring that their precious cargo reached the correct destination. Other slaves were heading in large groups to each of the many buildings surrounding the edge of the lake and stretching into the distance. Most didn't jostle or banter, they simply trudged towards their destinations with the weary acceptance of the defeated and oppressed. Some were still waiting to enter the sector at the main checkpoint and were becoming steadily more fractious at the possibility of being late to their posts. The sight of his people subdued never failed to make Dannon's blood boil and his skin prickle at the injustice of their situation. It renewed his determination to free them all from Esarelian rule.

Blending in with the throngs of slaves rushing to and from their shifts, his men quietly and unobtrusively slipped away to the lakeside. They concealed themselves between two of the large pipes, each as wide around as a man could reach, running from the water into every building. Teams of two, facing in opposite directions, scanned the narrow strip between the lake and the closest buildings, on the lookout for guard patrols while the rest readied themselves.

Dannon was already digging up the equipment when the last of the team arrived. Smuggled in over the last week and hidden in place, it had been assembled earlier that day by other trusted members of the resistance before being reburied.

While he distributed the explosive devices, he gave the men their final instructions, reminding them to ensure no workers remained in their assigned blast areas and became accidental casualties. The exterior explosions would go off first, allowing panic, reasonable and expected in the circumstances, to explain the mass exodus of workers from inside the buildings and cover their own escape. It was simple and should be relatively straightforward to execute, but not this easy. He hadn't counted on all of his team getting this far, and he had a niggling feeling in the back of his mind that wouldn't leave him alone. Deciding to shrug it off, he instead counted it a blessing, a sign from God that they were to succeed.

"If you see guards, act as if you're meant to be there and follow the lead of the uduin worker in your group. If they grow suspicious and there's no alternative, stun them with the blast rods as quickly as possible. Make sure you bind them tightly and stash them where they won't be found until after the mission, and check the area thoroughly for more squads."

"We know what to do. Don't worry, Dan. Everything's going perfectly." Callen winked and grinned at the group. The youngest in Dannon's team, he had no fear and saw the mission as an exciting opportunity to pay back the Esarelians for years of abuse.

Dannon huffed. "Too perfectly," he muttered to himself. Aloud, he said, "Good luck, everyone. Stay sharp." He directed the latter specifically at Callen and a couple of the other younger men.

As casually as possible, his group made their way into the first building with a couple of long paces between them. If the heat outside sucked strength from limbs, the heat inside was a suffocating wall that drenched each of them with moisture as they pushed through it. The heating vents looming high overhead kept the atmosphere thick and soupy. What air there was had a more concentrated sour taste in the enclosed space than that outside.

High-intensity wide-spectrum globes shone constantly from above, encouraging growth in the uduin but forcing the human slaves to squint as they laboured. Dannon raised a hand to shield his eyes while they adjusted to the harsh glare. His surroundings came slowly into focus, and he took in the all-too-familiar scene.

One of the pipes they'd used for cover jutted through the wall to his left, piercing the thin sheet of rock like a giant finger. He could hear liquid sloshing and gurgling inside the massive tube as it was sucked from the large body of water beside the building. The shiny black conduit split into tens of smaller ones that snaked along the numerous rows of oversized metallic vats, terminating at pumping stations at the end of each that were manned by teams of three.

Above them, Dannon caught a glimpse of uduin tips as the vast organisms half stood, half floated in the gentle current of purple liquid. There were so many in the large open space that they created an undulating cloud-like field with barely any gaps between. He'd seen it once when he'd had to climb one of the vats to make some repairs. Each creature resembled a cross between Old Earth cauliflower and sedum plants but was more sponge-like in consistency. Originally entirely light yellow in colour, the water on this planet had turned the veins and flowers a deep lavender shade that stood out against the bases and stems.

As he ducked between the nearest vats, Dannon signalled Callen and Tinnor to take cover while he checked the immediate vicinity. Everything seemed normal. The workers to his left steadily pumped the handle between them, studiously ignoring his presence as effectively as they ignored the sweat that ran down their brows and necks. He wished he had the pickers' vantage to see more of the space, but he knew that was impossible.

Sagging over the vast carpet of tips as if in surrender to the heat and humidity, an immense network of ropes formed a lattice through which those slender slaves clambered. Made from plant fibres native to the Esarelian home world to ensure strength and durability, each strand was more expensive than two slaves. Periodically, a yellow-brown braid snaked down from the quivering mass towards the side of each uduin that enabled the dangling pickers to snip the tender buds as they grew. Remaining on the flimsy cords was made more difficult by wide sacks slung around their necks and bulging with uduin. Dannon would stand out like a tamolut among dune-ticks if he attempted to climb up there, assuming the ropes would even hold his weight, which he seriously doubted.

The entire building pulsed with a tension that was ever present and easily discerned by those familiar with the sector. He searched again for signs of guards and, still seeing none, proceeded with his mission. They needed to warn the men in the building of the impending attack without tipping their hand to any who would betray them. Advising those he knew that a break to visit the waste units within the next cycle might be a good idea would suffice. Word would spread, but the lack of specific details would make reporting him extremely difficult.

By the time he reached the end of the first row, the men were buzzing with an undercurrent of hope they just couldn't hide. He decided the warning would pass quickly now, especially with the rest of his team to help it along. It was time for him to focus on placing the explosive device under one of the central vats. Somewhere halfway down the main line would be preferable, with the charge placed close to the pumping station to take out as many of the pipes as possible.

As he moved towards his goal, a slender man lowered himself down one of the ropes until he was dangling at head height a few paces along Dannon's chosen path. Purple stains splotched his jumpsuit where the thick gel that ran through the uduin's veins had bled onto him. His legs wrapped securely around the thick cords, and one hand gripped his half-filled sack as he gestured Dannon closer. The mop of tightly curled black hair seemed vaguely familiar, but Dannon was sure he didn't know the picker personally. That was often the way with those above; they were only

Courage

usually glimpsed during the change of shifts when his head wasn't bent to his own burdens. The clear eyes that met his gleamed with cautious anticipation, and Dannon moved closer to see what he wanted.

"Is it true? Should we be prepared to leave soon?"

The rumour must have already passed to the pickers in the lofty reaches of the building. Dannon smiled softly at the courage the man showed in descending to check its validity. Most would not risk being caught off task, having been cowed by their masters long ago and unwilling to chance the possibility of punishment. Dannon made a mental note to attempt to recruit the man to their cause, before remembering that if that day's strike worked as planned, there would be no need.

He gave the man a quick nod and the flash of a wide smile. Matching it, the man scurried back up the rope and immediately began snipping at the tips of the nearest uduin as if he had never left his post. Only the straightened, more confident set of his shoulders and a small smile that was barely visible from below gave away his new-found knowledge. Dannon was sure he would soon pass the word to his fellow pickers.

Continuing to edge along the row of vats, Dannon again scanned the area for signs of guards. There should be at least one squad patrolling inside. Right on cue, Lamesh, one of the commanders, appeared from around the far end of the line. Dannon felt relieved at the normality of the routine way the Esarelian walked and watched the workers, especially after worrying that their lack of presence portended ill. About to duck out of sight in order to plant the charges, he caught something less routine from the corner of his eye. Another guard had stopped at the other end of the long line of vats. Compounding Dannon's sense of disquiet, he noticed a third guard step out from behind the pumping station.

Heart racing in his chest, Dannon silently signalled Callen and Tinnor before dropping and crawling under the vats to the next line. The situation there was no better. More guards filled either end. The same was true of the next, and he could see their feet filing into any area that led to an exit. He should have heeded his instincts when they begged him to distrust the quiet and ease of their incursion. He'd known something was wrong but carried on regardless, not wanting to let Aronin down and relying on God to protect them in this vital mission. Unfortunately, his team would likely all pay for his mistake. They were surrounded.

Scrambling back to his original position, Dannon watched as Lamesh drew a blast rod from his side, the other guards following his lead and beginning to walk steadily down the aisle. Blast rods, not the usual contact rods, Dannon registered. They had definitely come prepared. He searched for a defensible spot to hold them off while he thought of a way out for as many of his people as possible.

Between two of the large vats, he wedged as many of the closest innocent bystanders as he could in the small gap and formed a protective shield with his body. He watched with pride as Callen did the same on the other side of the aisle. Blasts rang out before he had finished pulling his own weapon.

The noise was deafening. Weapons fire, screams, and shouted orders combined to create a cacophony that drilled his ears painfully. Bodies dropped all along the aisle, the stench of cauterised flesh a sure indication that the weapons they faced were not set to stun. Chaos erupted fully. Workers ran in all directions, desperate to escape the net of lethal rods steadily closing on them. Dannon saw a member of his team farther down the row fall lifeless to the floor and redoubled his efforts to punch a hole in the guards' ranks through which his people, resistance fighters or not, could run to safety outside the building.

The explosive device knocked against his side as he leaned around the edge of the vat to fire. An idea sparked. It was risky—but so was doing nothing at this point. He opened his mouth to call across to Callen and froze in horror at the scene playing out before him.

As if in slow motion, Callen leaned in front of one of the workers he was protecting to return the blasts aimed at the man. At the same time, a thin streak of blinding white entered his torso from the back and pushed him forward a pace with the force of the impact. That put him directly in the path of the first guard, who didn't hesitate. Callen's body jerked, his eyes wide with shock and pain, his mouth gaping open. Nothing happened for a moment, and Dannon wondered if Callen's injury was less severe than he'd assumed. The young man's body slumping to the ground proved otherwise.

Callen, grimacing and using the last of his strength, managed to turn onto his side. Raising his hand a fraction, he called weakly to Dannon, fear and agony written across his still boyish features.

Dannon tried to respond, to reach him, but the continual fire from the next intersection had him pinned down and unable to get to his young friend. "It's okay, Callen. It's okay." It was all he could offer, and it nearly choked him to get it out. He watched as alert light brown eyes slowly glazed and locked in place, as the short, jagged breaths came twice more and then not at all. Callen was gone.

Dannon closed his eyes in desperation. Sucking in a lungful of air, he set his sights on the guard who had just killed Callen without any hesitation and fired a shot in return, wishing he could do more than stun the monster. Determination flooded his veins. If this was to be where and how he died, he would make it count and save as many as he could with his sacrifice. He yanked the explosives from his pocket, ripping his jumpsuit in the process, and reprogrammed the device as quickly as he could with fingers that were suddenly too large, as sparks rained all around him from the impact of several blasts.

Counting down from five in his head, he sent off a succession of shots towards the squad of guards hunkered down behind a nearby pumping station. Then he spun and hurled the device towards the other end of the line like a hurried shot-put. Before the device even reached its destination, Dannon was crouched in the recess between tanks and pushing the workers he'd been covering even farther down, yelling for them to cover their ears.

The explosion slammed into Dannon, knocking the air from his lungs and his feet from under him. Dust and debris filled the area in huge billowing clouds that swept out in a consuming greed for the little clear air left in the building. Not waiting to examine the impact on the Esarelians, Dannon grabbed the nearest man and shoved him towards the ragged gap in the building wall that was slowly coming into view through the clearing smoke. "Run!" He growled.

Laying down covering fire, Dannon worked as quickly as he could, pushing men towards the newly made exit. Others joined him, and they soon had a stream of men and women trickling through the gap in the Esarelian net. Feeling the pressure to get as many out as possible before the Esarelians regrouped, and knowing they wouldn't have long, he ordered the rest of the fighters to follow the workers across the rubble and help them on the other side. Tinnor was the last to scramble across the wreckage before it was Dannon's turn.

He nearly made it. He would have if not for the cries of a dying man distracting him from his mad dash. In the time it took for him to realise there was no hope for the poor soul, who had been caught in the chest, a blast took out his own right hip and sent him spinning to the ground as agony raced through his torso. The last coherent thought he had before the blackness took him was to pray that the others made it to safety.

∞

The scene that greeted Aronin like a nightmare brought him to a momentary stand still. Following the sounds of weapons fire, his team had raced towards the uduin sector to offer their friends what support they could. Lungs heaving with the effort of sprinting across half the settlement, it took a while for his brain to switch focus to another organ and process what his eyes were seeing. He hauled himself atop a storage tank and confirmed his initial impressions. It was worse than he had been imagining on the way over from the guards' sector.

Before him, he saw guards swarming around each of the buildings. They were everywhere. It seemed as if the entire contingent of guards on the planet had been concentrated in this sector, bent on his men's utter destruction. Aronin watched in horror as they blocked every entrance and fired blast rods indiscriminately into the fleeing backs of distraught workers.

At several central locations, huddled groups of slaves had been forced to their knees in the grey dirt, hands spread on their heads, while heavily armed guards lunged at them with activated contact rods and laughed at their distress. He noticed some of the resistance fighters amongst the prisoners, drawing the guards' retribution on themselves where possible. They, at least, would likely live through the night. He would have to see what he could do about the rest.

Smoke rose from one of the buildings, drifting into the night as a bedraggled banner of defiance. From the same direction, shouts and the distinctive sizzle of discharging weapons echoed through the air.

A grim resolve settled on Aronin's shoulders as he vowed not to leave his men to this fate. He jumped down from the tank and turned to find Pinna, ashen and slack-jawed, beside him. Aronin shook him by the shoulder until wide, horror-filled eyes met his. Having got his second's full attention, Aronin rattled out commands and watched Pinna snap back to himself as he carried them out.

Their team spread out through the sector. Some gathered those fleeing the area and organised a safe retreat. Others began freeing any they could reach who had been captured but not yet incapacitated or killed. Yet more provided covering fire for the few who had found safe places to hide in the chaos and aided the men still fighting in small pockets of diminishing resistance. The rest took and held the checkpoint to help those of their fellow slaves who had reached the edge of the sector to disappear either into the settlement or surrounding scrubland. They moved as units, stunning any guards they came across and seeming to sway the course of events. Aronin drew strength from the new sight before him, believing at last that God would help them overcome. Thus reassured, he joined the fray.

As he started to move forwards, an explosion rocked the ground beneath his feet and knocked him backward. Through the thick, acrid smoke, tumbling rocks cascaded and scattered across the pathway, along with the moans of a couple of Esarelians caught in the eruption. An uneven, gaping hole appeared in the side of the nearest building and men began to pour through, slowly, uncertain and cautious at first, but then faster as they became more confident of escape.

"Cover them!" Aronin yelled, as he brought his own weapon to bear. Pinna and the others in his unit followed their commander's lead and fired blasts into the black chasm above the heads of the fleeing humans.

Aronin saw one of Dannon's group, Tinnor, leap through the gap as the stream of men dried up. Hope sprang for his friend, who would be covering the escape, and then died as the next face that appeared through the wall was that of an Esarelian. Raising the weapon he'd temporarily lowered as he waited for Dannon to appear, Aronin aimed at the creature and fired over and over, heedless of anything but the need to give the last of his men time to retreat. The attack was over, their plans in ruins. It now came down to ensuring survival for as many as possible, even at the cost of his own life.

When his weapon misfired, he threw it down and searched for another, anticipating the searing pain of being caught by a return blast in the ensuing stillness. Looking around with a finally clear mind, he realised the immediate vicinity was clear of slaves. Pinna confirmed his assessment when he reported that the last of the surviving men had made it through the checkpoint, and they were the only ones left.

Nodding his understanding, Aronin clamped a hand on Pinna's shoulder and said the only thing left to say. "Now, we run!"

They did. Through the checkpoint, along the path leading to the west of the settlement, and on until the only sound was that of their own laboured breathing, and the only light came from the twin moons above and the distant soft glow of the settlement globes. The sole piece of good news in the gruelling trek was that the heat of exertion prevented the night's freezing cold from creeping into their bones.

Darkness changed the landscape. What was a monochrome grey palette during the daylight cycles became blurs of charcoal and nearly black on full black. Picking their way between clusters of boulders became more difficult as the night progressed, forcing them to slow their pace from time to time. Eventually, when they were all gasping for breath, Aronin called a halt.

The pause for rest gave his thoughts a chance to return to those left behind. They had no final count of the dead or captured as yet, but one name he knew with certainty: Dannon. Hunching down into a crouch and then allowing himself to fall backwards onto the ground, Aronin saw his best friend behind his eyelids as clearly as if Dannon stood before him in reality. A solid, dependable man, quick to ease tension and calm discord in a group so often highly charged with testosterone, he would be greatly missed.

Aronin's grief brought to mind the reason behind it. They had been betrayed! But by whom? Aronin could find no clue in his memory or assessments of his men as to which of them it could have been. There was certainly no valid reason he could see why any who joined the resistance would have turned on their own kind in this way. All that planning, all the secret training in the wasteland, all those lives; it was all for nothing. God had truly abandoned them. What would they do now?

"Sir, we have incoming," Pinna called quietly.

"Direction?"

The young man pointed out into the darkness. "From the wasteland, travelling parallel to the settlement. It looks like a directional globe."

Aronin scanned the distance in the direction Pinna indicated and could just make out a faint point of light moving towards them. His tension eased slightly. An Esarelian squadron would be more likely to approach from the direction of the settlement and have more light. It might be one of the other teams. "Take what cover you can among the rocks, and let them get closer before we decide how, or if, we'll engage."

They waited. The single light bobbed and occasionally weaved and blinked, presumably skirting large boulders. Slowly but steadily, it drew near enough to make out. Any residual tension completely left Aronin's body when he recognised the outlines of the two men in the lead. One reasonably tall and athletic, the other short and wiry, it could only be Than and Willan. Others materialised behind them and Aronin counted eleven in all, one of them limping between two of his comrades. Most of Than's group had made it. Aronin moved into the open and waited for them to get close enough to speak to.

Than spoke first. "Aro, thank God we found you." He came forwards to greet his leader. "It was a trap; they were waiting inside the buildings. We lost Tash, and the rest of us barely made it out. We haven't seen anyone from the group I sent to the hangar, but we caught up with the second team lying low in the wastes. Mattis was hit in the leg, and we've had to carry him most of the way here. We stopped to bandage it, but he needs attention as soon as we can get him to a medic."

"That can be arranged." Aronin waved a couple of his men forward to take care of Mattis. As they supported the drooping man and half carried him to an area where other injured men rested, Aronin turned back to Than.

In the dim light, he looked incredibly pale and had started to tremble. Aronin didn't think it was entirely from the cold. "What about you? How serious is that arm?"

"It's just a nick; I'll be fine. I can't even feel it any more."

"It doesn't look like just a nick. You look like you're about to fall down."

Aronin called someone over to see to the wound, and reluctantly, the younger man sat on a large boulder to let the medic take a look. When the material of Than's jumpsuit was pulled back, it exposed a gaping furrow across his shoulder that was nothing but blackened char on the surface. After some gentle probing, the medic looked up from behind his patient and met Aronin's gaze with a small grimace. Than's pain must have been excruciating until his current numbness set in, and Aronin wondered how he'd managed to keep going. He hoped they would be able to get to a med-wand before it was too late to reverse the damage. As a distraction, Aronin asked Than questions about his team's escape until the medic had finished salving and binding the shoulder.

"We were circling around to see if we could find other survivors," Than said, "but Mattis faded quickly, and it's taken us longer than expected. What happened to you?"

"There was no one in the guards' sector when we got there. They must have doubled or tripled all the usual patrols and then concentrated the rest of their numbers in the uduin sector. It was a massacre. We did all we could, but by the time we arrived... We lost so many."

Aronin watched Than scan the rest of the group, presumably looking for familiar faces among those scattered through the surrounding rocks. A worried look on his face, he turned back to Aronin. Feeling again the crushing weight of defeat and loss, he couldn't bear to say anything and simply shook his head, knowing Than would understand.

"No!" The young man whispered. "Not Dan too? First Elias and now..." The expression on his face reflected Aronin's inner turmoil. How would they cope, having lost those closest to them?

Aronin drew on the last of his reserves to say what those gathered around him needed to hear from the man they followed unfailingly. "We go on, for them. Because that's what they would want us to do—get our people out of slavery and somewhere safe, where they can be free. God will not forsake us. He's been with our race since the beginning of time and will show us what to do next. For now, we go back to the settlement. Get into small groups, and we'll sneak back in a staggered pattern from random directions to avoid the Esarelian patrols. Wounded and medics go first." He gave a pointed look to the medic behind Than with the order, "Stay sharp, they'll be expecting us."

They would survive. They would go on. Aronin knew this beyond doubt. While their failure was a huge blow, it was not entirely one-sided, he reminded himself. The uduin sector was in shambles, and it would take many cycles of hard labour before the Esarelians received any more of their precious resource. That would cause them numerous problems. They also knew now that humans were a force to be reckoned with and not a race of weak, submissive beings. Maybe they would think twice before pushing their slaves too far again.

Another thought occurred and was swiftly brushed aside. Unless they planned on punishing random individuals and further reducing their now even more vital work force, there wasn't much the Esarelians would do about the events of the night. Most had escaped and would drift back into the settlement before dawn, becoming indistinguishable from any other slave there. The Esarelians were not known for their ability to distinguish between individual humans, seeing them all as vague brown haired, brown eyed bodies to use at their own discretion. Those that hadn't escaped were now either dead or would refuse to divulge any information. He knew he could trust them. Except ... he didn't know that, not any more.

Oh, God, he pleaded, *why have you abandoned us? What do we do now? I told the others you were still here, but are you? I can't see how you could be with us and let something like this happen. Do you not care?* Exhausted, as much from his swirling thoughts as from the circuitous route he had taken around the settlement, Aronin rose once more and trudged on through the darkest night of his life.

Chapter 9

Day: 14   Month: 07   Year: 6428
Location: Planet U'Du, main slave settlement

Gilla sat on a stool next to Than's sleeping mat in his room in the med-wing. It was a role reversal that was not lost on her. Neither was the fact that she could have lost him so soon after her husband. She leaned over and stroked the side of his face, bristling with three-day-old stubble that scratched against her palm. Her hand trailed ever so gently across the thick bandaging around his damaged shoulder before skimming along his arm and slipping under his hand to squeeze it in hers. He was too still, lying under a thin brown blanket without even a wrinkle to indicate his perpetual energetic movement. She missed it.

For what seemed the hundredth time, she found herself waiting for Than to regain consciousness after a round of treatment. She sat by his side, as she had each day from the moment she'd heard he was admitted. Other than for a few cycles to sleep each night, she'd refused to leave him alone until either she knew he would regain full use of his arm or he was discharged. Even Elias's crib had been moved into Than's room to allow her to stay near him and still care for her son. It was the least she could do for the baby brother who had been through everything with her since the Selection and was the only adult family she had left.

The wound in his shoulder had been through several regeneration sessions since the morning after the resistance attacked his sector. Although the medic had been able to use a med-wand to repair the majority of the muscle, Than had been brought into the Nursery too late for the Esarelian tech to heal him completely. Only a med-pod with expensive regenerative fluids would be able to achieve that, and access to such a costly resource was impossible for slaves. A few sections of the burned outer layers of flesh and skin had simply had to be cut away.

The rest of his recovery would have to take the old-fashioned route of salve, dressings, pain meds—if the stubborn fool would take them—and time. She wouldn't even mention the stretching and strengthening exercises recommended for after his skin was whole again lest he attempt them too soon.

According to Aronin, Than had been nearly unconscious when he finally arrived at the wing and had been knocked the rest of the way under by the medic who worked on him. After the first, extended session, she'd wished he would come round quickly so she could knock him out herself for worrying her so badly. Instead, she'd waited anxiously for him to wake up, just as he had for her less than a month earlier. Watching his face for any signs of movement, she'd prayed for his complete and speedy healing.

When Than had eventually returned to her, the scolding she'd promised herself she would deliver had drained from Gilla's mind, replaced by a profound sense of relief that he was all right. Nothing else truly mattered. He was still alive and had still been his irreverent self, asking if this would get him out of cloth changing duties with the little one. Half sobbing, half laughing at his question, she'd squeezed his good hand and shaken her head in reply. She wouldn't be left alone with her two young children, and they wouldn't lose another male role model and family member.

Since then she'd been talking to him while she sat at his side, telling him each time she heard of a new development in the aftermath of the failed strike. The most significant piece of news circulating the settlement was the death of Head Guard Risoth, who'd apparently been caught in one of the explosions in the uduin sector. Which of his seconds would take his place, and the implications of such a change, was currently the subject of much quiet debate among the general populous of the slaves.

The pair also discussed likely punishments and retaliation. What form those would take was one thing they'd been equally concerned about. That the Esarelians weren't going to arrest him, or even be looking for him specifically, was something Than had emphasised often since he'd heard the good news the day before.

Aronin had been to visit him while she stepped out to feed little Elias. By the time she'd returned, they were talking quietly with their heads bent close together. The image had made her stomach lurch with dread that they were already planning their next move against the Esarelians. Her muscles had only released when Aronin had turned and beckoned her over to join their discussion.

His contact had informed them that none of the faces of the resistance fighters at the flight centre had been seen, at least not well enough to be picked out of the entire populous of the settlement. Flashes of skin and brown hair had been recalled here and there, but on the whole, only the colours of uniforms were reported, which were worthless for identification purposes. Besides which, the military, who'd taken over in the wake of Risoth's death, were focusing all of their resources on investigating the main uprising as it was being called.

From the number of injured admitted to the med-wing and the talk throughout the settlement, it was clear that the guards had been firing indiscriminately into the crowds in the uduin sector. That had made it impossible for them to tell who'd been part of the attack and who'd been merely an innocent bystander. As the list of casualties was so long, the Esarelians couldn't detain them all and had therefore been forced to let everyone remain in the med-wing to receive what care and treatment could be provided for so many. Than's friends had been able to slip him and some of the others in with the crowds during the inevitable chaos that ensued, but they were only now sure that the risk of discovery had passed. Their names would be recorded, and the list shown to collaborators, but it seemed, so far, that additional scrutiny in the months to come was the extent of the expected repercussions for any wounded.

She'd been so pleased to hear the news that, without thought, she'd thrown herself on Than in a massive bear hug that had accidentally caught his injured shoulder and caused him no small amount of pain. Feeling terrible, she'd fussed over him for the rest of the afternoon until he practically ordered her from his room. Still, it couldn't dim her joy at his lucky escape. The knots in her stomach had finally uncurled, and she could breathe somewhat easily again.

As for any general retaliation, rumours of new double shifts had spread through the settlement over the last few days. Work details had been ordered to clear away the rubble and rebuild the damaged buildings in the uduin sector. They were apparently expected to complete the repairs on top of their usual shifts and with no additional resources or access to technology. It was a gruelling task that many thought almost impossible.

Aronin had heard several angry denouncements of the resistance in the days since the failed strike. A few vigilante groups had also sprung up, led by known collaborators but including regular civilians. They were calling for an end to the movement and promising retaliation for what they considered inflammatory actions against the Esarelians. The backlash from fellow slaves was limited but vocal, and it obviously weighed on Aronin, showing in the marked lines around his mouth and eyes. Gilla wasn't sure what she thought about it all, but she was glad she was exempt from work for the month after Elias's birth and that Than would also be on light duties until his arm healed.

Aronin had informed her during the quiet hours of the previous night that a few of the prisoners taken at the time were civilians with no knowledge of the attack or anyone connected with it. He'd been almost wild as he spoke to her in the quiet corridor outside Than's tiny room while they waited for yet another round of regeneration treatment to end. The comfort of Aronin's reassurance that Than would be all right and should be safe from reprisals was lessened by the mixture of defeat and concern in his eyes for those prisoners. She knew he felt a great weight of responsibility for all of his people, whether part of the resistance or not.

Having no other way of offering support, and feeling an acute sympathy for the large, broken man, she had sat next to his slumped form on the floor of the corridor outside Than's room. They had been cocooned in a bubble of privacy, seemingly the only two awake in the quiet, still middle of the night. With their backs pressed against the wall and her hand occasionally patting his as she held it in a small reassuring gesture, she had listened to his regrets and self-recrimination. He gave her none of the details of their strike, for which she was grateful, but apparently took comfort from her presence as he pieced himself back together through the darkest cycles of night.

Why he'd chosen her to unburden himself to, she had no idea and didn't want to ask. Other than happening on him at his lowest point and being willing to listen, he had no reason to trust her with so much of his inner turmoil. They had been good friends before that night but were, quite reasonably, not as close as he was to Elias, Dannon, or even Than lately. However, in that lonely, quiet place, they forged a bond of shared loss and mutual anxiety for their closest loved ones. For the first time since her husband had introduced them many years ago, she felt they truly understood each other and had formed a deep and lasting kinship that would stand the test of time.

As the sun rose in the morning, so did his spirits and a new strategy for the foreseeable future. The resistance would lay low, remaining hidden while they cautiously regrouped. They would support their fellow slaves through what punishments came and gather intelligence only. There would be no missions, no open resistance, and no more attempts at freedom. They would not give up, but their focus would be to survive and create a more tolerable existence for the rest of their people until their lot changed enough for freedom to be viable once again. He stood behind her now, waiting for Than to wake so he could share his thoughts.

Gilla looked up at Aronin from where she sat. She was about to suggest he take over her spot while she went to retrieve Elias from Damaya, when she felt Than's fingers twitch beneath her own. His eyelids fluttered as she watched him struggle to regain his senses. Stroking his arm to orient him, she waited for his eyes to open fully before flashing him a huge grin. "That was the last one, little brother. The rest is up to you and God."

"Less of the little," he croaked. "I've been bigger than you since I was twelve."

She handed him a canteen of water to sip and ignored the familiar jibe. He might not be fidgeting yet, but he was back, and she would endure any amount of his teasing to have him remain so.

"How does it feel?" Aronin leaned around her shoulder to check on his friend.

"Numb for now. I guess I'll find out soon enough, though. The medic said it would take about a month to heal completely, but I don't think it'll be that long. I've always healed fast. Right, Gilla? Remember that time I tried following Dad to work and broke my leg jumping off the sector wall?"

She mumbled a noncommittal response, remembering the anxiety that incident had caused her mother and how intolerable he'd been while waiting for treatment at the med-wing.

Aronin admonished him for wanting to rush his recovery, telling him to take it easy, not push himself too fast, and that there was nothing to get back to until the after-effects of the attack had blown over. While supposition was rife, the final Esarelian reaction had yet to be either announced or enacted. The entire settlement waited with baited breath as they crept and scuttled about their duties.

Not wanting to continue along such maudlin lines, Gilla turned their attention to more personal matters. She listed the friends and acquaintances who had stopped in to pass on their best wishes while Than had been unconscious earlier and then described Elias's latest antics and some of the stories Mirami had told Gilla of her training. Aronin added some tales of his own, and the two men spent the next half cycle trying to out-do each other in terms of the ridiculous escapades of their youth.

By the time Aronin had to leave and return to work, Than's colour was good and he had hoisted himself into more of a sitting position. Gilla smiled when she noticed the fingers of his good arm tapping against the blanket over his leg. Saying goodbye to their friend, she determined to make sure Than stayed safe and sound for as long as she was around.

As soon as Aronin closed the door, she pounced. "Than, you need to step down. The resistance is finished for now, and you need time to concentrate on your shoulder, and—"

"All right, all right. Slow down, sis. I already told Aro I'm done for the foreseeable future, and he's fine with it. He even said it was a good call and that he would have recommended it himself if I hadn't. You don't need to worry so much, you know." He looked directly into her eyes for a moment before his face softened. "Come here." He tentatively tugged her into a one-armed hug, and she relaxed against him, relieved that he saw sense for once in his stubborn life.

Pulling back, she smiled and said, "Thank you."

There was a light tap on the door, and they looked over simultaneously to see Menali poke her head around the edge on her way in. Her large eyes scanned the room, alighted on Than, and widened even further. Her cheeks flushed, and she stumbled to a halt, evidently torn between apologising and running. The darting of her eyes in the direction she had just come from gave the impression she would choose the latter, but she gripped her hands together and raised her chin slightly.

"Oh. I'm sorry. Dee sent me to this room to see you, Gilla, and Aronin said you were inside. I just assumed... They never told me it was Than's room. I can come back later." She looked directly at Than for the first time when she added, "I hope you're feeling better, Than. What happened was terrible."

Turning to go, Menali had barely taken a step before Than called out to her. "Wait! It's good to see you."

Gilla glanced at her brother and remembered the looks he'd thrown Menali the last time they had been together. It was suddenly so obvious that Gilla wondered how she'd missed it before. He liked her friend. And this was no casual flirtation, as was his norm. The longing in his eyes was plain to see for someone who knew him well; he had finally met someone he was genuinely and seriously interested in.

She couldn't be happier for him. Menali was a wonderful friend and would make any man a wonderful partner. What remained to be seen, however, was whether he would make a wonderful partner for her. Gilla had no illusions where Than was concerned. He had flitted from woman to woman for years, charming them all with his smile and friendly nature but getting close to none. He would need to be ready to settle down if he intended to approach Menali, or Gilla would shut him down herself.

Knowing her friend was extremely shy and interpreting her jittery behaviour around Than as possible attraction, Gilla decided to give her brother a chance. "Yes, come on in, please. You can do me a favour."

Menali sighed quietly and shut the door before approaching the other side of the sleeping mat, where Than struggled, without success, to hide his feelings in front of Gilla. Menali asked innocently, "How can I help?"

"Can you stay with Than while I go and feed Elias? He might not admit it, but he's still in a lot of pain, and someone should be with him in case he needs help." As she spoke, Gilla rose and straightened her jumpsuit, giving Menali little chance to refuse her request. It was true that she didn't like leaving her brother alone, and she really should get Elias, but Gilla knew she was interfering and experienced a momentary stab of guilt. Sweeping it aside, she internally justified her meddling. "I won't take long, I promise."

Menali sat down on the stool Gilla had just vacated and looked at her hands for a moment, as if gathering her resolve. Tilting her head towards Gilla, she flashed one of her brilliant smiles and said, "Go on, I'm sure I can handle him while you feed Elias."

"I'm sure you can, too," Gilla agreed. Turning to face him, she pointed a finger at Than. "And you ... behave yourself." She gave him a surreptitious wink while Menali wasn't looking and hoped he appreciated the opportunity she'd just given him. Walking out, she clicked the door shut and wondered what she'd left behind her.

∞

Silence. They were left in awkward silence that Menali had no idea how to fill. She wondered why Damaya had sent her up here instead of letting her wait for Gilla downstairs. She also wished she'd quizzed Aronin more carefully as to the room's occupants instead of just asking if Gilla was inside. Either way, it was too late now, and she would just have to make the best of the uncomfortable situation.

She asked him, "Can I do anything to make you more comfortable?"

"I was about to ask you the exact same question," he snorted. His voice held a note of resignation when he continued, "It's all right, Nali. I know you only wanted to see Gilla, and now you feel stuck. I'll be fine if you want to go, really."

Wincing internally at how close to the mark his words struck, she determined to start again with him and act as any true friend would. Ignoring his comment, she focused on his face and noticed the strain around his eyes and mouth. It made her see him in a different light and garnered her genuine concern. "How *is* your arm? Are you in any pain?"

He answered warily, probing her conscience further. "A little. The medics have done all they can, but I went too long without treatment, so there was only so much they could do. I'll have an impressive scar when it eventually heals." He attempted a casual shrug with one shoulder that didn't quite work but made her respect his bravery in the face of a long, possibly painful, natural recovery. Since the advent of med-wands and other regeneration technology, relying on traditional medical methods had become a rarity that most wouldn't wish on anyone. She found herself reluctantly drawn to his plight.

"I'm sorry to hear that, Than." Searching for a way to lighten the conversation, she added, "At least you'll have regular access to all the female medics while you're convalescing. That's got to be a bonus for a guy like you."

His eyes immediately flashed. "I have no interest in any of the medics here, or any other woman. I'm only interested in you."

The forthright statement stunned her. He couldn't be serious; she wouldn't believe it. Any warm feelings towards him that had been building in her fled. Her decision to treat him as a friend went right out of her head, replaced by a self-preserving instinct to bolt. He was lying in the med-wing suffering acutely from an injury he'd sustained during an uprising against their oppressors. He was lucky to be alive. Even if they had been well suited, she would never put herself in a position to go through that with someone she loved. Constantly fearing for their safety was not how she would spend her life with someone.

Besides which, Than was a flirt. He would move onto someone else soon enough, despite what he claimed. It was probably the pain medication talking anyway. She was shy and serious, while he was full of life and charismatic. It wasn't that she thought she was beneath him or not worthy of his attention. On the contrary, she had a healthy self-esteem in her own way. She just knew they were completely different and wouldn't suit in the long run. No. He couldn't be seriously interested in her, and she wasn't interested in anything temporary, with anyone.

She did the only thing she could. Mumbling an incoherent excuse, she jumped up and lurched to the door. She ran from the room, a frustrated groan from behind her echoing around her head alongside a renewed mantra to avoid him at all costs.

∞

Gilla had fed Elias and was rocking him against her shoulder, humming a tune her mother had taught her when Than was still a baby. As she patted his back, she tried to list all the things she had to be grateful for—another trick of her parents during times of trial. While she was thinking of something for number eight, the door to her shack burst open, and Menali flew inside. Unlike earlier, there was nothing timid about her entrance.

"How could you leave me alone with him like that?" Her chest heaved a great breath, and she placed her hands on her hips as she waited for a defence.

Jumping initially to the wrong conclusion, Gilla asked, "What's wrong? Is he all right?"

Menali waved one small hand in the air as if swatting away an irritating insect. "He's fine, physically. It's not that; it's him. He's just so … insufferable. He never responds the way I expect him to. And I made a complete fool of myself by overreacting."

"Ahh. Come sit down and tell me all about it."

Menali flopped onto the nearest stool, looking more flustered than Gilla had ever seen her. *Oh, little brother*, she thought, *what have you done now?* When Menali related her conversation with Than, Gilla blinked in surprise. It took her a few moments to process the implications of what she'd heard. As realisation dawned, however, a grin tugged at the corner of her mouth. She corralled it, not wanting to upset Menali any more than she was already.

Than really did like her, and he was serious enough to tell her so. This was a huge step for him, unprecedented even, but one that she knew was currently lost on her embarrassed friend. She made a mental note to explain a few important things to Than when she went back to visit him. In the meantime, her calming influence would be useful as she reassured Menali that all would be well. Her own worries faded into the background as she focused on repairing the damage her crude attempt at matchmaking had caused.

Chapter 10

Date: 311.428.147
Location: Esarelian Primary Space Cruiser, throne room

Nishaf half listened as Lorith gave his report detailing the recent events on U'du. He inwardly fumed with impotent rage at the audacity of the insidious creatures. Their pathetic attempts at a rebellion should be squashed decisively, wiping out every last one of them as one would do with any other infestation, not discussed at length during a private meeting of the inner tier of the Ra'hon. It was insufferable. But suffer through it he must, or he would damage his standing with the old male.

"How many casualties?" Ashal asked.

Lorith grimaced before replying, "Two dead, and one more in a med-pod with critical injuries. He will live, but it is using up half his allowance of regeneration therapy. Fifty-three humans so far. Reports are still coming in of their casualties."

"How could this have happened?" Ashal's fist banged down onto the arm of his throne, sending vibrations through the metallic black floor of the room. He closed his eyes and breathed deeply to regain his composure.

Before Lorith could continue, Nishaf asked in his most bland tone, "Where did they get blast rods from? They should not have access to weapons of any kind, especially not those used from a distance. We do not allow anything but contact rods on the planet for this exact reason."

Nishaf saw Lorith's eyes twitch to him for a fraction of a second, but he could not remove the smirk that pulled at the corner of his mouth at seeing Ashal's favourite pulled down a notch in front of others. If he played this right, Nishaf could raise himself even higher while further reducing the other male in Ashal's esteem.

"They had help, Ra'hon," said Lorith. Nishaf noted how the Na'hor ignored his own questions and kept his eyes on their superior. *Let him*, he thought, *it will not matter...*

"From whom? I want them found and eliminated, or sent to the mines on Pyteg as an example. This cannot be allowed to happen again."

"We are attempting to find their Esarelian contact, but all leads have proven to be dead ends. Apparently, the informant Risoth used to foil their plans had a relatively small role in the attack, and the only leader they knew of was killed at the scene. Risoth unwisely decided to handle the situation himself, presumably in an attempt to gain favour, instead of reporting it to his military Hor. His employment of blast rods set to kill and injure rather than stun was another poor and unsanctioned decision.

"We have since taken control of the few prisoners and are interrogating them. However, the ringleaders have evaded capture, and no names are forthcoming, no matter how thorough our questioning of those seized. It seems they are either innocent of any wrongdoing and were simply caught in Risoth's bungled attempt at a trap, or they are reasonably well trained and would rather die than betray their co-conspirators. The compartmentalisation of their plan was strategically clever, leaving us little means of further investigation." He paused. "What would you have us do with the prisoners, Ra'hon?"

Ashal looked around the table, effectively opening discussion.

Sunath suggested moving them to the mining operation on Pyteg. *He would*, thought Nishaf. The old fool cared nothing for making a statement of strength, for showing these humans their place, only for production and profit. As if he needed any more profit. Nishaf's mouth watered in anticipation of what he would do with the wealth currently controlled by Sunath. One day, soon.

Clearing his throat, he offered his own opinion. "We should execute them in the public square of the colony as a warning to others who would attempt such foolish actions against us. They must be made to see there is no way out for them."

Lorith turned to Ashal for his final decision without saying anything more. Why was he not speaking? Surely the *great military commander* would argue for leniency and caution, as usual. He only ever seemed willing to kill in the heat of battle. Nishaf narrowed his eyes and studied the other male objectively for a moment. While Ashal was the largest living among their race, as Nishaf grudgingly admitted was the Ra'hon's birthright, Lorith was nearly as tall and muscular, his regular training giving a toned, lethal edge to his fitness. His cobalt eyes were clear, intelligent, and focused on the throne at the head of the table. The uniform jumpsuit he wore, while of good quality material, was simple in design and unadorned except for the insignia over his left pectoral. Nishaf loathed the male for his precious honour and dedication.

Eventually, Ashal made his choice. He ordered the executions, though they would take place immediately and privately. Lorith quietly sighed, probably relieved at seeing an end to his humiliation and not further incurring the wrath of his beloved Ra'hon.

"With respect," Nishaf quickly added, "I am not convinced that this will be enough to dissuade the rebels. The humans are growing too numerous and are rebellious by nature. This latest plot has shown how easily they could destroy our main source of uduin if we are not constantly vigilant. I believe more drastic measures are necessary to safeguard our resources and ensure timely completion of your new space cruiser, Ra'hon."

Nishaf had their attention but paused to emphasise his last remark. His hand rose towards the scar on his neck of its own accord, but he corralled the unconscious impulse, knowing it indicated his potential weakness, and instead stroked the neatly folded pleats of his kilt. He thought, witheringly, of Lorith's relatively plain military jumpsuit. Unlike *others* in the room, Nishaf liked the full ceremonial robes of office he wore over his bio-suit. The pristine white headdress with its thick band of purple reaching up over the crown of his head, which was the widest stripe allowed before that of the fully purple Ra'hon, showcased how far he had risen and that he was a force to be reckoned with.

His golden belt and matching shoulder chain, draped across his thickly muscled chest, were studded with jewels that offset his navy-blue eyes and made his translucent skin seem to glow. He was a magnificent example of pure male Esarelian, and Reemah should—would—be honoured to have garnered his interest. Shutting down that line of thought quickly before it showed in his even features, he brought his attention back to the current situation, searching for the next words needed to bend it to his advantage.

Rising elegantly, he paced the room towards a marginally pretty holovis of Esarel as it used to be, before the stripping of natural resources left it barren. Blue leaves of danta trees fluttered in the breeze, rippling over a nearby river where uduin hugged the shoreline in delicate pale-yellow blooms. Too pastoral and banal for his tastes, Nishaf would have the image replaced if, or rather, when, the time came. His capable mind lit on an idea that would more than suit his needs, and he turned back to the others with a conciliatory smile already in place.

Before he could open his mouth, Sunath re-joined the conversation. "We could move more of them off the planet. Spreading them out through the other slave colonies will prevent their ability to plan or do much damage, even if they do continue to rebel. They will also have less opportunity to reproduce as a pure species. Interbreeding might remove their stubbornness."

Ashal looked as if he were considering this option, so Nishaf spoke quickly to regain his momentum. "Hmm, that may work. It would be interesting to see the results of an interbreeding programme, in any event…" He let his words trail off as if in deep thought and then clicked his fingers to show an apparently sudden realisation. "But restructuring the workforce at this point would interfere with completion of the new cruiser. We would have to train those sent to the planet to replace the humans. There is also much heavy manual labour to be done on U'du. Would we use our own kind for that?"

"No," Sunath agreed. "It would be disastrous to send Esarelians there. We use all our criminals on Pyteg already. Esarelian workers for U'du would have to come from the underclasses, and I would rather deal with a human rebellion than one from within our own ranks."

Lorith finally contributed. "The humans are easier to contain with the resources I have available if they are all in one location. I will not use warriors for such demeaning work, and few choose to train for the lower status of guard positions."

"Remove all non-vital technology from the planet. I want tight control kept of the rest. Have them use manual tools only in the uduin sector from now on. They will be too tired to rebel if they have to do more of the labour themselves, and they will have no access to anything they could use in any case." Ashal gave the orders with determination, inviting no discussion of them. None was needed.

Nishaf worded his next proposition with care. "There is one further thing we could do that would serve a dual purpose. It would send a clear message that we are not to be tested, breaking their spirits along with their will to resist. It would also reduce the numbers of the humans without interfering with their work rate until long after the scheduled completion of the new space cruiser." Looking around the group, he saw he had their full attention and continued. "We kill the young human males."

The silence that met his statement was deafening, pressing in on his ears and making his cold blood feel warm as it hummed through his body. He waited for a reaction.

Lorith, looking shocked and virtually uncomprehending, recovered as fast as expected of one with military training and pushed out a response. "How would that even be accomplished? Surely, it would cause even more rioting?"

"Not necessarily," Ashal interjected in a calculating tone. "We could have the midwives kill all males at birth."

"With respect, Ra'hon," Nishaf responded hastily, "I do not think that they will comply with the order. The human midwives will probably make excuses and let them live. They will say they got there too late or were not called to the labour. We cannot rely on them, and our own people would be less squeamish about such actions in any case. A show of force would also send a decisive message at this point."

Ashal considered for a moment only. "Very well, send the guards in, but make sure they do it properly. And have Risoth's informant executed if that has not already been taken care of. I cannot tolerate disloyalty, even if it did lead to our discovery of the rebel plot."

Lorith again spoke. "The Head Guard, Risoth, was one of those killed in the explosions the renegades set off. It will take time to coordinate the guards left on the planet and choose a replacement. The chaos and potential rioting this action would cause will only impede that process. Maybe if—"

"Oh, yes. Of course." Nishaf gave Lorith a calculating look before cutting him off. He then turned to Ashal and smiled solicitously while countering the other male's apparent hesitance. "I support Lorith's request that you allow him the honour of going personally to supervise. The catastrophe on U'du was, as we all know, down to Risoth's ambition and can in no way reflect on Lorith as a commander. His loyalty to you and his exemplary record as Na'hor make him the ideal person to ensure your wishes are carried out efficiently and that no problems arise that may be missed by one less capable."

Ashal agreed with a slight softening of his features as he looked at Lorith, who simply nodded his acquiescence and swiftly exited to prepare.

It annoyed Nishaf that he was forced to praise his rival in order to achieve his aim, but there were larger issues at stake. This time he was unable to stop his finger from slowly rubbing the thin line that ran across the side of his neck. He would keep the scar until the last human had suffered beyond endurance and been exterminated. He smiled softly. With a little luck, the next few days might remove Lorith as well as more of the insufferable creatures on U'du.

Chapter 11

Day: 17   Month: 07   Year: 6428
Location: Planet U'du, main slave settlement

Having decided to spend her penultimate day of maternity leave visiting one of her friends in the med-wing, Gilla waited in a side room while one of the medics reviewed the elderly man. The empty room she'd found to feed her son in was just off the main corridor of the ground floor and suited her needs perfectly. Rocking little Elias gently as she paced, Gilla sang one of the old tunes quietly to him. It had always put Mirami to sleep after a meal but didn't seem to be having the same lulling effect on her active son. His little feet tried to kick through the blanket swaddling him, and his wide-awake eyes roamed the small space for anything interesting or new. If this carried on, he would have no nap before his next feeding and then be grumpy all evening. She sighed and turned to trek back towards the door.

Before she reached it, Mirami appeared in her new yellow uniform with the brown training band round her arms. Amina trailed behind her. Seeing her brother awake, Mirami raced across and rose up on her tiptoes to see his face. She cooed and tickled his chin with her little finger, which he promptly tried to bite. Tutting and softly tapping his small nose, she didn't seem at all fazed by his attempt to mangle her digit.

"Can I take Elias while you have a break with Auntie Ami?" She looked at Gilla and held out her arms patiently, expectant anticipation shining in her eyes. "I don't mind, really. It's one of my jobs while I'm training in this wing, and anyway, he's my little brother. I love spending time with him."

Gilla transferred the wriggling bundle to his sister. She was already a natural at holding him with the crook of her elbow supporting his head, and it lifted Gilla's heart to watch them together with her looking after him so carefully.

"Come on, little one. Let's leave Mama and Auntie Ami to have a chat while we go have a nice rest together in one of the back rooms..." She was still talking to him as she left the room and walked down the corridor, her cheerful voice growing fainter with distance.

Amina stepped into the room, looking anxious. She shook herself, as if throwing off dark thoughts and walked forwards to greet Gilla with a long hug. When they drew apart, she perched stiffly on the edge of the sleeping mat, gestured towards the doorway with her head, and asked, "How's she doing?"

"Good. She's only just started, so they're rotating her around the three wings to give her a taste of each before the intensive training starts. She's been able to get a few moments free once or twice a day to see us." Gilla smiled. "It's been great being able to watch her; she gets such a focused look on her face sometimes. And she's wonderful with Elias. I'm so proud of her... I can tell she's missing her father, though. She doesn't say anything—wanting to be strong for me and her brother, I guess..."

Gilla's smile turned wistful, and they sat together in silence for a moment. Amina picked at an imaginary spot on the leg of her blue jumpsuit before looking up at Gilla with troubled eyes. "And you? Why are you still spending your days here instead of at home?"

Avoiding the other woman's gaze by folding spare blankets and placing them neatly at the end of the sleeping mat, Gilla stalled for time before responding. When she still hadn't answered by the time the stack was three high, Amina rested a hand over Gilla's and squeezed. Understanding and compassion shone in her friend's eyes. It gave Gilla the courage to admit what she had been hiding.

"When we were first released home," she said quietly, "I came back to visit some of the people I'd met here. Now, though... I'm just not comfortable at home yet. There are too many reminders... Two more days, and then I'll be back at work anyway."

"I understand. When Fin and Ralton were taken, I couldn't bear to see the ghosts of their presence everywhere I looked. It's why I moved back into one of the dormitories. You're much braver than I was."

"I still have the children. I have to keep going for them. Two days. Then all three of us will go back to living normal lives at home again." As she said the words, Gilla felt the rightness of them settle into her bones. She felt lighter somehow, as if a suffocating blanket had been thrown off.

Amina patted Gilla's hand again. "It gets better."

Gilla leaned over and hugged her friend again before brightening her voice and saying, "It's a good job you came alone today. Dee tries, but…"

A smile finally worked its way onto Amina's face. "She thought it might be better coming from me, seeing as I've been through this and she hasn't. Don't tell her I told you it was her idea, though, or her head will swell even more, and she's bad enough as it is." The smile dropped, and she went back to picking the threads on her thigh. "She'll get herself in real trouble one of these days. She's done nothing but complain about the new tech rules. They are bad, though. I never thought they'd do something like this." A look of anguish flashed across her features and was gone.

"We'll survive the new rules, Ami, just like we've survived everything else they've done to us."

If anything, her attempt to comfort her friend seemed to make things worse. Amina jumped up from the bed and began to pace, her arms wrapped protectively around her middle. Gilla was worried. "What's wrong? Is it really that bad?"

Before Amina could respond, there was a commotion in the common area at the centre of the Nursery. The room they were in was only a few doors down the left-hand corridor of the med-wing, and they could hear loud voices drifting through the doorway from that direction. Heavily booted feet stomped across the floor in synchronised steps that could only indicate a squadron of guards. The scrape of chairs and startled protests and denials also confirmed their unprecedented presence in the building.

Amina's agitation reached a peak. Suddenly squaring her shoulders, she faced Gilla directly and said, "I'm sorry—for everything. I have to go. Goodbye, Gilla, and good luck." With that, she turned and made her way towards the door and the Esarelians.

It took Gilla a few confused moments to process what Amina had just said and then start to follow in order to find out what in the universe she'd meant. As she crossed the room, she could hear Amina, clearly and with only a small quiver in her voice, call out to the guards.

"I assume you're here for me," she said. "There's no need to cause problems searching for me. I'm right here, and I'll go with you willingly."

Gilla still didn't understand what was happening, but the guards obviously knew. She heard one of them mutter something before asking, "Are you Amina Lang?"

Gilla had just reached the door when a blast reverberated along the walls and through her body. The stench of burned flesh clogged her nostrils, and a buzz of static raised the fine hairs along her forearms.

Fearing what she would see, yet unable to turn back, she stole a glance around the corner.

She was just in time. Amina stumbled back into her arms, and they crashed together to the floor inside the room. Gilla scrambled to get out from beneath Amina's twitching body and, on hands and knees, peered into her pale face. Gilla didn't dare move her eyes lower. Her courage only went so far, and she feared what she would see if she examined her friend's torso. Instead, Gilla patted around until she found a hand feebly grasping for her own and latched onto the fingers tightly. Scooting forwards, she used her other hand to raise Amina's head gently and rest it on her lap.

Gilla couldn't wrap her mind around what had just happened. Why would the Esarelians blast Amina of all people? What could she have possibly done or said to warrant that? Were they blasting everyone they found? With too many questions tumbling around the inside of Gilla's head, she shut them down to sort out later. For now, she looked down at her friend and stroked the soft hair back from her forehead.

Light brown eyes, hazy with pain and filled with unshed tears, looked through her towards some distant image only Amina could see. They blinked a few times and refocused on Gilla's. Haltingly, after a few false starts and wheezing, bubbly breaths, Amina said, "But ... they promised..."

"Hush, now. Don't try to speak. It's all right, Ami. A medic will be here any time now, and then you'll be fine. Don't worry about anything. Shhh."

"No. Need to tell... They promised ... when, when they caught me... Promised I'd be with Fin and Ra-Ralton again. I'm so ... so sorry..." Her voice became so faint that, by the end, Gilla had to hunch over with her ear hovering just above Amina's mouth in order to hear her words. When Gilla was sure there wasn't anything else, she pulled back and looked down at her friend, trying to fit the pieces of what she had said together in a way that would make sense.

As Amina's breath stilled and her eyes glazed in death, the horror of the meaning behind her final whispered words washed over Gilla, leaving her frozen in stunned disbelief. It couldn't be true. Not Amina. The guttural groan worked its way, unbidden, up her throat and out of her mouth.

"Noooo! Ami, why would you trust them? How could you do that?" But she knew. She knew how desperate and broken Amina had been and that she would have done anything to have her family back. Grief threatened to crush Gilla as the full implications of Amina's deathbed confession hit home.

Something else nibbled at the back of her brain. Why would they kill Amina here? Why send so many? Something wasn't quite right with the whole situation. Forcibly pulling herself together and wiping her tearstained face, Gilla allowed the world outside their private bubble to crash in on her once more.

The guards were still in the building. She could hear high-pitched, feminine cries and the deeper rumble of male voices. Interspersed between them were the unmistakable sounds of weapons firing and the occasional crashing of furniture against floor or wall. Needing to see with her own eyes what was happening, she eased Amina's head to the floor and took a moment to cover her with one of the blankets she had so recently folded.

Crawling across to the door, Gilla edged around the frame until one eye could take in the view beyond. The immediate vicinity was completely empty. There were no signs of Esarelians anywhere in the corridor. With her heartbeat pounding in her ears, she crept forwards in a crouch until she reached the common room. After taking a moment to steady her nerves, she slowly peered beyond the opening.

Signs of a struggle littered the floor, but the only people she could see from her limited view of the room were a squad of stationary Esarelians. Gilla ducked back behind the wall. Why were they here? What were they doing? Despite the risks, there was only one way to find out. Cautiously, she looked again.

They stood in matching, ready stances on either side of the double-width main entrance doors, ensuring none entered, or left. Their rods were in hand, already charged and glowing at the ends, but that was the only clue as to their intentions with those inside the building. She needed to see more. Taking a breath, she scurried to the other side of the corridor to get a better view of the far side of the open area. Her jaw dropped when she looked across at the infant-wing.

It was almost beyond belief. Esarelian males were doing something to the babies. Hauling them out of small, private rooms and group areas alike, they were piling the tiny, silent bodies along the corridor as if displaying wares in a market. A few of the women in yellow Nursery uniforms were fighting back, trying to protect the children in their care. They were stunned with rods before they could offer any real resistance and left to lie slumped where they fell. Others were huddled in a group against the wall, crying and holding each other in their shared despair.

Gilla pulled her head back, out of sight. Her mind swirled with inconsequential details, unable or unwilling to deal with the horror before her. Those were military grade weapons, she absently mused, the kind able to switch between settings with the flick of a wrist. Only the warriors had access to those. She took another, closer look at the Esarelians. They weren't planet guards.

They wore sturdy, thick-soled boots that fastened past their ankles and up half their long calves. Their jumpsuits were a pristine white that clearly showed the limited time they spent on a planet surrounded by inescapable grey dust. Utility belts of the same brilliant colour held a few items Gilla couldn't identify in the short time the scene held her eyes in thrall. A faint glimmering sheen across the side of a pale, hairless scalp indicated where they had pulled their bio-suits fully over their heads to protect them from the non-existent threat of return fire. Grim expressions of resolve set their faces into masks of impending death and completed the frightening ensemble.

They moved in well-practiced synchronicity in units of three, just like the planet guards. Unlike their counterparts, they displayed a fluid grace and economy of movement that spoke of many decades in training. The deaths they delivered were quick and efficient yet sure and unyielding. There would be no escaping these men once caught. They were much more deadly than anything the humans had experienced before at the hands of the regular guards. Gilla's mind, full of information from her overtaxed senses, slowly came to the understanding that the Esarelians had sent elite military troops into the Nursery to kill innocent babes in their mothers' arms.

She couldn't understand why. What possible reason could they have? She thought, bitterly, that they didn't need one, and any that existed would never be explained to the likes of her anyway.

Just then, a woman in blue shot out of a room farther down from the Esarelians and attempted to run behind them towards the exit. The closest warrior turned and, almost casually, blasted her in the centre of her fleeing back. She fell forwards, the wailing bundle flying out of her arms and skidding across the floor to come to rest against the side of the corridor. The cries were cut off by a rod pressed to the side of the child's head by a different warrior.

The corridor began to whirl as Gilla tore her eyes away from the unbelievable sight. She spun and retched. Dropping back down to her knees, she couldn't stop until her stomach ached and her throat felt raw.

Finally, she managed to regain control of herself. Her thoughts jumped ahead, unreeling scenarios before her closed eyes. They were probably working their way through the building, starting in the infant-wing but not stopping there. Elias! Her eyes snapped open. She had to reach her son, had to get him to safety.

She didn't bother to move quietly. There was so much noise coming from beyond the common room that no one would hear a single woman moving in the opposite direction. As she ran, she thanked God that she'd been visiting the med-wing instead of the other babies across the building and that she still had a little time. Praying for His protection and guidance, she pushed herself even faster along the corridor.

Gilla almost collided with Mirami when she reached the doorway to the large, open room where her daughter had taken Elias less than a cycle earlier. With her brother wrapped in his blankets and firmly supported against her shoulder, she was heading towards the indistinct and puzzling sounds. She asked Gilla what was happening as soon as they steadied themselves.

"Never mind that now, we must hurry. Give Elias to me and stay close."

Mirami's face scrunched with confusion, but she made no protest as she complied with her mother's terse orders. With her hands free and her uniform bunched at her wrists and ankles, she looked young and vulnerable. The competent girl had vanished in the face of such uncertainty, and only the scared seven-year-old remained.

Gilla knew she needed a mother's reassurance. Shifting into a crouch directly in front of her daughter, she stroked her soft hair back from her forehead and cupped the side of her sweet face. She spoke in a soft but clear voice. "Warriors have come. They want to take Elias away from us, but we're not going to let them. We're going to hide him until it's safe to come out. I need you to be brave and help me. All right?"

It took a moment, but Mirami nodded.

"Good." She gave a bright smile and one more caress of her eldest child's precious head before rising. "Now, we need to get to the back exit as quickly and quietly as possible. Follow me."

With Elias clutched firmly against her chest and his baby smell working its way into her nostrils, Gilla felt her panic recede and was once more able to think clearly. Mirami shadowed her mother's every step as they skirted the wall towards the far end of the corridor. Gilla wasn't hopeful of their chances at escaping in that direction, but it was the best place to start. It would also give her a chance to see the placement of the troops at the rear of the building.

When they reached the last corner before the doors to the outside, Gilla slowed her pace and listened intently. Hearing nothing, she risked a quick peek. There was no one in the immediate area. Giving Elias back to Mirami, Gilla raised a finger to her lips. It took mere moments to hurry across to the outer wall and duck beneath the window ledge. After another quick scan around her, she slowly rose up enough to peer over the edge of the window and outside. Although thin, the dura-panes evidently cut off the noise made by three huge shadowy figures gathered around the doorway. There would be no escape here.

She scurried back to Mirami and retook possession of Elias. Looking down at his face, she wondered how he had managed to sleep through the events of the past half cycle. He really did take after his father. Thanking God that his ability to sleep through anything at least ensured he made no sound to alert others to their presence, she began to figure out their next course of action.

Mirami beat her to it. She tugged on Gilla's arm and indicated for her to bend down so she could whisper excitedly in her ear. "Mama, I know a door we could use. We went past it on our tour the first day of training. It's back the way we came and has a load of supplies in front of it. I asked where it went, and the guide said to the old incinerator block. I can show you the way."

"That's perfect, Mirami. You go first, but keep an eye out for warriors."

Mirami led them back through the wing, via a short side corridor and several adjoining rooms, thankfully still clear of warriors. She stopped by a door that was, indeed, well hidden behind crates of supplies. Once again, Gilla transferred her sleeping infant to her daughter and proceeded to move the top couple of crates as quietly as possible. By the time a small window had been revealed in the centre of the door, Gilla already suspected what she would find beyond. As if called by her thoughts, a guard shifted closer to the other side of the exit and she jumped out of sight.

Across from her, tears welled in Mirami's eyes, and she whispered, "I'm sorry, Mama."

Crawling across the floor, Gilla pulled both children into her arms and held them tightly. "It's not your fault, Mirami. You've been very brave. God will help us find another way out."

Despite her words, her own panic began to resurface as the hopelessness of their situation hit her once more. This wasn't going to work. The warriors must have finished in the infant wing by now and would be searching the rest of the building for any babies they missed. If Gilla didn't find an unguarded exit soon, she and her children would be caught. She couldn't let herself think about the consequences of that.

Pulling Mirami to her feet, Gilla set off once again, praying aloud as she moved. "God, please help us."

She looked up, as if to search the heavens for a response to her desperate plea. Instead, directly above them, she saw an air vent. The panel in the metal tube snaking across the ceiling was fairly small, but Mirami was still only a child and Gilla had always been slim. Praying she'd lost enough of the baby weight from carrying Elias, she hatched the beginnings of a faint plan.

A short time later, after having once again braved the main corridor to follow the route of the pipework, they stood beneath a similar ventilation panel in a little used room on the farthest side of the med-wing. The tubing here finally breached the outer wall of the building, providing a possible means of escape. Gilla removed the panel with a makeshift tool, clambering inside to unscrew the external grate, while Mirami cut a blanket into strips and tied them together to form a rope. They were ready.

"You go first. I'll lower you down to the ground on the other side and then pass Elias to you before climbing down myself. When we get outside, run. Don't wait for me or look back, just run. Get to Auntie Dee's shack and stay there until I come for you. If you hear or see anything that makes you worried or scared, hide until they leave and then keep going. Okay?" At the little girl's trembling nod, Gilla added, "You can do this, Mirami. I know you can. Everything's going to be fine."

Gilla gave her daughter one last swift hug and hoisted her into the air. She waited until Mirami had gripped the ledge of the vent, pulling herself partway inside, and then boosted her the rest of the way into the confined space. When Mirami had moved far enough along, Gilla laid Elias just inside the gaping hole and climbed up behind them.

She knew lowering Mirami to the ground with Elias in front of her was going to be difficult, but there was no other option. She was too big to fit him alongside her or turn back to get him afterwards. It would have to work like this. Sliding her arms along either side of her son, she gripped the blanket rope tied under Mirami's arms and braced to take her weight. The angle made her arms scream in protest at even the slight weight of her daughter, but she held on as Mirami shifted and slid over the outer lip of the vent. Hand over hand, she carefully lowered her to the ground outside the building.

As quickly as she could, Gilla shuffled forwards and passed Elias gently down. Then, holding onto the upper lip of the vent shaft and pulling her legs out until they were free, she dropped the short distance to the alley floor. The sponginess of the ground softened her impact, and she was instantly reaching for Elias again.

Nudging Mirami into a run before he was even settled, she watched the girl vanish silently among the shadows before turning in a final sweep of her surroundings to make sure they hadn't been spotted. She was too late. A large warrior appeared at the far end of the alley, his bright blue eyes locked on her own.

Chapter 12

Date: 311.428.149
Location: Esarelian Primary Space Cruiser, Ra'hos private suites

Reemah was bored. It had been only one month since her mandatory confinement to the space cruiser, and she was going stir crazy. There was nothing for her to do on-board that did not drive her to madness. Although trained and proficient in the art of political manoeuvring, it did not give her the sense of accomplishment that drew the rest of her race to what they viewed as a sport. As a result, she had spent the majority of her time in the rooms she now viewed as an extremely well-appointed prison.

They comprised a vast main chamber where she could sleep, entertain, or study, each area of which could have been private, had she bothered to submit a floor plan to the engineers for internal walls; a spacious prep room with a cleansing cubicle large enough for at least two; and a dressing room where her formal robes and ceremonial sheaths were stored in pristine condition behind a well-used pile of stark but comfortable white jumpsuits. On the uppermost level of the cruiser, the suite offered the best of Esarelian ingenuity and design. She even had floor-to-ceiling windows along one wall, which she had covered to prevent her being tempted to disobey her father's mandate by the view. Though luxurious, the walls were beginning to shrink considerably around her, and she felt a desperate need for real, wide open spaces and the freedom of speed.

In an over-stuffed chair, Selah, her friend and cradle-mate, sat reading and looking perfectly serene. Her beaded shift dress was tucked neatly beneath her and the matching necklace and arm bands of gold and precious jewels gleamed in the soft glow of the globe over her head. Sometimes Reemah envied her friend's ability to be at peace with the strictures of their elevated positions and wondered if her own family would be happier with Selah among their ranks. If it were not for the incontrovertible proof of her eyes, Reemah thought they might have been switched at birth. Selah's eyes, however, were the usual blue of her race, with a light hue that matched the sky on Esarel.

As if reading her thoughts, Selah raised her head and looked over at Reemah's tapping fingers. She shut down her databloc and set it on a side table of danta wood with inlaid tamolut ivory. "Do you want to take a trip to one of the pleasure bays? Or the garden suite?" she asked. "The pa'shulins are in bloom until the end of the month and are quite beautiful this year."

Reemah's wrinkled nose was enough of an answer, and her friend sighed in resignation.

Saving her from any more of Selah's perfectly respectable yet dreadfully dull suggestions, the entry chime sounded. Reemah scrambled upright on the raised sleeping dais and checked the viewer of her personal unit to see who it was. She stifled a cry of relief and commanded the portal to open. Standing jauntily on the other side was Velay, arguably her closest friend.

Selah's mouth firmed, but she gave no other indication of her views on the interruption to their quiet afternoon. Reemah knew she mildly disapproved of her friendship with a half. While Selah had nothing against Velay personally and would accept her inclusion in their group easily enough at Reemah's request, she held the ideals of the majority of their race. To Esarelians, blood was everything, and with an Oeal mother, Velay was often shunned by her supposed peers. Only her close friendship with Reemah saved her from worse treatment.

To her credit, Velay had never let it interfere with her personal agenda or outlook on life. Instead, she used her mixed heritage to her advantage. Wide green eyes, the only outward indicator left of her half status, were batted captivatingly at any who opposed her, while she employed her empathetic skills to get her own way. It was a subtle manipulation but extremely hard to counter, a fact of which Reemah had no personal knowledge thanks to a pact made as younglings. Velay's abilities were one of the reasons they had got into, and out of, so much trouble together. So much so, in fact, that Reemah's father had tried to ban their friendship several times.

Velay sauntered into the suite and, after removing a couple of abandoned datablocs from the soft cushion, threw herself down on one of the chairs with one leg swinging over the armrest. She wore a fitted vest and a jumpsuit with the top half tied around her sinuous waist, looking the polar opposite of Reemah's other companion. Her one concession to social mores for female Hos were rows of earrings along each lobe, the small jewels winking in the light and casting rainbows of colour on the brilliant white wall beside her.

"Am I interrupting anything?" she asked, cocking a brow at Selah.

Selah narrowed her eyes before turning away and staring fixedly at Reemah as she answered. "We were just relaxing and trying to decide where to go to stretch our legs. And before you say anything, I do not want any of your nonsense influencing that decision. Reemah has to show she can be civilized and decorous."

Reemah snorted at the word choice and then covered it, badly, with a cough.

"Would I do that to you, Selah?" Velay's innocent expression and hand over her heart did nothing to convince anyone in the room that she was the least bit serious. Selah still refused to make eye contact with her. Giving up, Velay turned her attention fully towards Reemah and winked. "I do have a suggestion for relieving the tedium—see, Selah, I can use big words too—imposed by your father's punishment..."

Selah rolled her eyes but Reemah simply waited for her friend to deliver the punch line, intrigued by the slightest possibility of a deviation from routine at this point.

Velay continued, "We could go flying."

Reemah slumped against the wall, narrowly avoiding a priceless tamolut ivory carving. Distracted by the possibility dangled before her, she shifted along the pristine expanse of panelling at her back, nearly knocking the piece from its place. With a roll of her eyes at the lecture she knew she would receive if it remained skewed and was noticed, she begrudgingly nudged the present from her mother back into alignment as she replied, "I told you, he took my access away. I can't bypass the block. I tried the other day for a couple of cycles but nothing worked."

"You did not?" Selah gasped. "You promised you would abide by the rules laid down—"

Reemah held up a hand to stop her friend's diatribe. "I wasn't actually going to take one out, just see if I could. Besides, it didn't work. He must've had Shonel do the block. That male is a genius with code and nothing could break his encryptions. So," she turned back to Velay and shrugged, "there's no way I can even board an arrow, let alone fly one. Boats are no good either. All personal pleasure craft power down at my approach."

The grin that spread across her friend's face promised adventure. "We can take a tub."

Reemah stared blankly for a moment before the gears in her head started turning and she began to nod. An answering grin lit her own face as she realised the potential. The lowliest of all spacecraft, in Reemah's opinion, transport tubs were slow, clumsy beasts but, in the current circumstances, her only option if she wanted to escape the cruiser. The hangars they were kept in were not on a secured deck like those for the more expensive or classified craft. They also held several passengers at least, unlike single flyer arrows, so she was more likely to be able to get aboard one and have someone else fly it out. Why had she not thought of them herself? Too used to luxuries like arrows and boats, she guessed.

It was Selah's turn to snort. She immediately covered her mouth with one hand at the indelicate noise she had made. "You cannot be serious. They are dirty and disgusting, smelly too. What would you even do in a tub?"

Velay already had an answer, which she addressed to Reemah, rather than Selah. "We could go out to the asteroid belt and set up a new course for when you're free. It'll take some time to do, so we shouldn't get too bored for a while."

"Oh, I like it. It'll give us an advantage in the races when I'm allowed back out, and no one will bother us all the way out there. Yes, it's perfect." Reemah felt a tingle of anticipation run across her nerve endings. Endless possibilities of course configurations using the various-sized asteroids along the edges of the belt scrolled through her mind. She would have to be careful not to go too deep, but the potential danger just added to the excitement she felt. Besides, tubs were tough enough to withstand a few impacts. She said firmly, "Let's do it!"

"Well, I will leave you two miscreants to your adventure. I am certainly not getting on a tub." Selah gracefully rose from her position and started to make her way across the plush carpeting of the room.

Reemah and Velay cut off her escape. Stalking towards her as she backed away from them, they exchanged looks, ensuring they were thinking the same thing. When Selah stumbled backwards into an upright chair by Reemah's cluttered desk, they came to a halt. Towering over her, Reemah spoke for them both. "Of course you're not. You're going to cover for us."

"Oh, no you do not. I want nothing to do with this. Just because you can technically get on a tub, *if* you can, that is, does not mean you are supposed to. I just wanted a nice quiet day reading or strolling through the gardens, not lying to the Ra'hon about his daughter's whereabouts. Oh, how do you get me into these predicaments?" She refused to look up at them, twisting the rings on the long fingers of her left hand with those of her right.

Velay put on her sweetest smile and most innocent expression. "Please, Selah. You won't have to lie, not exactly."

A quarter of a cycle later, Reemah and Velay left a dazed-looking Selah in Reemah's comfortably air-conditioned suite and made their way quickly through stuffy, little-used secondary corridors towards the lower hangar. They had to duck through a random portal once to avoid Nishaf walking in the opposite direction, but otherwise, it was an uneventful journey. Reemah vaguely wondered why her father's scientific advisor would be heading towards the private area reserved for royalty instead of the throne room but pushed the thought aside when they neared the huge portal behind which several tubs waited.

"Do you think Selah will be up to covering for us? I hate getting her into these things." Reemah knew she would have some major making up to do when she got back. It would probably have to include something cultured and appropriate like the gardens or a pleasure bay full of stuffy old holovis. She shuddered.

"Don't worry about her, she'll be fine. Technically, the last time she saw us, I was heading out the door and you were going into your prep room for a long massage followed by a nap. Besides, the hack into the internal sensors is virtually untraceable and will show you in your suite for the next fifteen cycles at least. As long as your PU stays powered down until we get far enough away from the cruiser, no one should even question her, and we'll be free. Now I already bribed the controller for this hangar to let us take off, so all we have to do is look confident while we pick a tub and get out of here."

"Solid." Reemah threw back her shoulders and stepped briskly forwards when Velay opened the portal.

They chose a mid-sized tub with the traction tech needed for moving asteroids into a challenging course. Designed with the pilot's cabin in the forward section and a large cargo bay behind, passenger seats lined the sides aft of the doors separating the two. Towards the rear of the craft sat the control station for the traction net, traditionally used to link additional cargo containers in a line behind the tub on long distance deliveries. The main loading doors into the craft covered almost the entire back end, with a smaller crew hatch at the side. Painted a dreary beige colour with designating marks under the forward window, it looked ungainly compared with the sleek, midnight black arrows Reemah usually flew.

It was just as slow as she had imagined it would be and was far less manoeuvrable or responsive than either of them was used to. They laughingly dubbed it Buln after the giant sand slugs on Lurinel. Taking the controls while Reemah strapped in behind, Velay flew until she deemed they were far enough away for Reemah to take over.

The relief at having her PU back online washed through her like a balm. She did not like the feeling of being so cut off from everything, even if that was what enabled her to get out for a while. Her excitement at the thought of freedom was palpable in contrast. She set a course for the asteroid belt and settled back to watch the stars through the dura-pane forward window. The view before her was one she was more than familiar with. Pinpricks of light from far-off stars winked at her, offering a multitude of secrets and possibilities to explore. Nearer objects, from tiny asteroids and a speeding comet to the lumbering giant planets slowly turning in their orbits, alternately fascinated and excited her. Space would always be her favourite place to decompress from the confines of her father's Empire.

What felt like only a few moments later, the tub slowed to a crawl, and a vast expanse, crowded with rocks and ice blocks of varying sizes, filled her field of vision through the screen before her. While some were stationary, others rotated or crashed into each other, sending yet more ricocheting through the masses. It was an extremely dangerous place to consider flying; very few who ventured farther in than the outer edges made it back alive. The twisted metal remains of a craft floating between two rock giants were testament to that fact.

Reemah studied the configuration of the closest section intently, mentally calculating possible pathways they could expand, enhance, or create.

Velay whistled at the display from over Reemah's shoulder. "Wow! Would you look at that? This course is going to be pure adrenaline!" She rubbed her hands together in glee before swinging into the rear to the traction controls. "Ready when you are, Ra'hos."

They spent the next few cycles moving asteroids into position and blasting those that refused to stay in place. Reemah had a complicated route mapped out in her head that was beginning to take shape. She was having the most fun she had had in a month and was so focused on what she was doing that she did not hear Velay approach until she spoke.

"We need a break. Those stiff controls are making my back ache, and I'm dying to hear all the court gossip."

Reemah wrinkled her nose in disgust at the word gossip but knew she was Velay's only real source of information. Honestly, if it were not for Selah, Reemah would have none to tell. She did not care in the least about the latest political scandals or the sordid personal affairs of her peers. She had better things to do. Seeing the hopeful glint in Velay's eyes, though, she huffed in resignation and sat back to think.

"Well... Selah thinks that Noree will drop out of the council to train as a warrior. Oh, and I heard Ourin has made a fortune on the Pyteg operation with Sunath..." From the corner of her eye, she noticed Velay shaking her head and suppressing laughter. She frowned. "What? You know I'm no good at this stuff."

"You're going to have to *get* good someday, you know. The freedom you have now won't last forever. Pretty soon you'll have to settle down and find a mate and a way to make your mark."

"Ugh! Don't remind me." She folded her arms as if warding off that eventuality.

Velay leaned forwards and grinned. "What about Nishaf? He's not that much older than you, and it's obvious to anyone with eyes that he wants you. He can never take *his* off you when you're around him."

"And that's precisely why I can't stand him. He's so creepy, turning up wherever I happen to go, especially since father confined me to the cruiser. I don't trust a word that leaves his mouth, and I want to poke his eyes out for the way he stares at me. He thinks I don't notice; it's disturbing. I was almost afraid he might be looking for me when we hid from him earlier. Selah would've let us know if he went to my suite, though."

Velay held her hands up in surrender. "Very well. Very well. Not Nishaf then." An evil smirk turned up the corner of her mouth. "What about Maran? He's available again by all accounts."

A steady glare was Reemah's only response. She never wanted to even hear that name again, as Velay well knew.

Nonchalantly, Velay said, "Lorith's nowhere near as creepy as Nishaf."

Reemah found herself unaccountably starting to blush and forcibly reversed the physical reaction. "No, he's not," was all she said.

Her *friend* continued, prodding at an apparent weak spot. "He's achieved a great deal for one of his age."

"I suppose so."

"He's not seeing anyone..."

"Mm hmm."

"And he's good looking, too," Velay prompted further.

"Fine." Reemah threw her hands up, not for the first time wondering briefly if Velay had broken their pact and read Reemah's emotions. "He's extremely good looking *and* extremely cold. I know strong feelings aren't exactly common in our kind, but I at least want someone who can be affectionate with me. I'm not sure Lorith is capable." An image of his disapproving blue eyes flashed across her mind. "Besides, I'm not in the least bit interested in getting involved with anyone for at least another fifty years.

"Now, this is a depressing conversation, and we're supposed to be having a few cycles of fun." She shoved Velay back to her station and shook a mocking finger at her. "So, young lady, get back to work."

"Solid." Velay winked and turned back to her small viewer and the mass of ice and gravel still caught in the traction net.

Chapter 13

Day: 17   Month: 07   Year: 6428
Location: Planet U'Du, main slave settlement

Cool and detached, with all his emotions turned off, Lorith supervised what Nishaf had dubbed the culling from the front of the Nursery. The large building was impressive by colony standards. It rose several stories high and had been allocated thin dura-pane windows, a rare luxury on slave planets. Set adjacent to the original slave barracks, and across from the uduin sector, it formed a T shape with the cross-section facing the front. The three wings housed units dedicated to basic education, infant care, and medical emergencies, which met in a central atrium comprising a huge common room with notice points and a guard station.

Lorith blinked his inner eyelids against a flurry of dust and allowed the heat of the strong sunlight to warm his blood and ease his resentment. He was the Na'hor of the Esarelian Empire. He should not have allowed himself to be manoeuvred into coming down to the surface of U'du to perform such a repugnant task. This could cause him serious problems, as if he did not have enough to concern him. He should not be here.

He would not be if it was not for Nishaf, Lorith reminded himself. The odious, manipulative creature was up to something, as usual. The question was what? What could he possibly hope to gain by ensuring Lorith's presence during the culling? It was no secret they were rivals, opposites in many ways, with often discordant views. Lorith also had certain suspicions regarding the other male, which he was, as yet, unable to prove. The moment he was finished here and got back to the space cruiser, he would check on the males he had tasked with tracking Ashal's chief scientific advisor. He had a feeling it would not be a moment too soon.

Hearing a scraping noise from a side alley to his left, Lorith cocked his head in that direction and listened intently. He heard it again and then more incongruous rustling. This time he sighed. Could those planet-bound guards do nothing right? Their deployment should be covering the back entrances at the rear of the building. If they were messing around back there or out of position, he would have their hides. He strolled towards the corner, ready to demand obedience to his orders, but froze in his tracks when he got a good look.

A human female stood two-thirds of the way down the dark, narrow passage underneath an open vent, holding a small bundle protectively in her arms. There was only one thing that could be. His inner eyelids blinked in surprise. All possible exits to the building should have been accounted for and covered; the guards assured him they had used the schematics to double check. The incompetents obviously missed one. He frowned. He would have to deal with this himself.

In his momentary hesitation, the female darted behind the next building and out of sight. He huffed. She was fast, for a human. Shaking off the inconsequential thought, he reminded himself that he could not afford to let anyone escape the culling, not if he wanted to keep his position. Nishaf had seen to that much at least—goading him in front of Ashal in the apparent, yet futile, hope of seeing him make a mistake that Nishaf could use against him.

Lorith quickly returned to his command post and ordered two of his warriors to give chase. He watched them disappear around the bend, scanner and weapons ready. The female would not get far. Sighing once more, he turned his attention back to the gruesome task at hand and the interim Head Guard, who was hovering in an obsequious manner by his command post for the third time that day.

"What is it, Lamesh?" Lorith snapped, aggravated by the male's continued attempts to ingratiate himself. His insistence on wearing the full regalia of office was annoying enough on its own. Lorith had always preferred comfort and practicality rather than symbols of power, and he distrusted those who clung to such emblems.

Lamesh bowed his head, as was proper before addressing one of Lorith's station, and then stepped forwards to present a holovis of the settlement, sectioned into a grid pattern. "Na'hor, I have brought the plans for stage two of the culling. When you are finished inside the Nursery, my guards will hold the entrance. They will assist in gathering and detaining the humans here while your warriors sweep the rest of the settlement. I have assigned numbers to the search areas and will send a male with each of your squads to act as a guide through the unfamiliar terrain of the outer settlement."

The recital of Lorith's own plan as if it were new and highly valuable information had him grinding his teeth in frustration. All he had requested was a more detailed holovis of the settlement than he had used in the initial planning stages, with the sections coded to each of his squads for dissemination among his warriors. The guards' supporting role at the Nursery had been an addition to his strategy, designed solely to keep them out of his way in the outer settlement.

Lorith ground out a reply that would be sure to let the male know his place. "You may deliver the holovis to my second, Horath. He will see it is uploaded to the warriors' PUs. As for your guides, they will not be necessary. My warriors are highly trained operatives, more than capable of navigating a disorderly collection of slave dwellings. Your guards will hold the central location and accompany the humans we find to the Nursery building, as planned."

The glint of impotent fury that flashed in Lamesh's eyes was immediate and telling, but to his credit, the male quickly masked his feelings and smiled in acquiescence. Lorith did not give it a second thought, as the subordinate bowed again and took his leave. He did not like the interim Head Guard, finding him too ambitious by far. In fact, he would not have put it past Lamesh to have, himself, planted the explosives that killed Risoth. The rebel attack would have been a good cover for such a Foh'mahn.

Nevertheless, Lorith's orders were clear. As Risoth had proved to be ineffective in curbing the rebellious tendencies on the planet, Ashal wanted a stricter regime in place. The notion had probably come from Nishaf, but there was nothing Lorith could do about the increasing influence his nemesis held. Regardless, from what he had seen of Lamesh, the male would fit his new role of harsh overseer well. Contingent on the satisfactory result of the current operation, Lorith was to promote Lamesh officially to the position of Head Guard before returning to the cruiser. If things continued as they were, that would prove to be the case, and Lamesh would have the next step in his advancement before the end of the day.

∞

Gilla ran. She could hear the warriors behind her, their steps heavy and in complete sync. The first one must have called for back-up. They would be strong and fast, but she prayed she would be able to lose them in the seething mass of the settlement shacks. There, she would be able to blend in and hide easily, while they would struggle to navigate the serpentine alleys. Their scanners would pick up every living person in the area and be virtually useless in tracking one lone female. From the sounds behind her, she could tell that they were also unused to the spring of the ground and were overcompensating in their gait. For the first time since they walked into the Nursery, she gave thanks they were warriors trained on cruisers instead of lowly guards who would have been as used to the terrain as she. Keeping her thoughts positive, she continued to run.

Ducking down another tentacle of the great octopus of slave lodgings some time later, she sidestepped inside the second doorway she came to and flattened her back against the wall next to the window. She needed a moment to regain her equilibrium and think clearly. Taking deep breaths in through her nose and out through her mouth, she checked on Elias.

He was no longer asleep. Instead, he looked up with inquisitive eyes and gurgled a smile at her. She stroked the tiny hand that he had worked loose in all the chaos and was waving towards a hank of her hair that had come undone. He gripped her finger and immediately began to tug it towards his gummy mouth. "Later, little one," she whispered to him soothingly. "Right now, Mama has to keep us safe, so you have to be a good boy and stay quiet. Can you do that, Elias?"

Another smile and twitch of his round cheeks was all the response he gave. She took it as assent and risked a look outside. It was all clear. If she was going to move, and she knew she must, now was as good a time as any. Looking back at Elias, she tucked his blanket more firmly around him and threw a quick prayer heavenward for protection and courage, before once more darting into the narrow alley.

She sped down the passage and around a corner, only to find two warriors at the far end of the row of shacks to her left. Dodging across the limited open space, she squeezed through a narrow crack between two rundown homes and down another path. She spotted two more warriors around a dog-leg of shacks and then more at the end of the next alley. She had taken too long. They must have finished at the Nursery and be starting a systematic sweep of the entire settlement. The warren was full of twists and turns, paths and alleys merging and shooting off in an organic sprawl, which tumbled out into the wilds. However, with enough men, even this maze could be conquered, and it seemed the Esarelians had committed more than enough warriors to the task.

Fear consumed her, tearing her heart from her chest with its force, but she looked at her son and forged on. Breathing heavily through the terror, she kept putting one foot in front of the other for his sake. She ran until her legs wobbled and collapsed beneath her, unable to take another step. Her lungs were burning, each breath gasped through a parched dry mouth and throat. She needed a moment to regain control of her body. Not yet, though. It was too soon to stop. She needed to put just a little more distance between herself and any pursuing warriors. She pushed up and onwards, dogged determination to save her son the driving force behind each painful stretch of thigh muscles.

Lord, she thought, *I could do with your help here*. There were warriors all over the settlement, and though she could avoid them for a while, it wasn't a long-term plan. How could she save her son from their cruel rods?

Her thoughts skittering in random directions, she crashed into inspiration and changed direction without a conscious decision. Heading generally towards the manufacturing sector, she mentally followed the steps she would have to take in order to ensure Elias lived. Only that mattered.

She realised she would need help for even a slim chance at success. Changing course again, she headed for home, praying that Mirami had made it back to their shack safely and that the warriors were not right behind her.

By the time she reached her shack, Gilla was hiding from patrols more often than not, and making short bursts of progress each time they passed. When she darted through the front doorway and straight into the back room, she was relieved to see Mirami huddled on the sleeping mat. Her tearstained face popped up from where it had been resting on her bent knees and transformed from terror to relief in an instant. She struggled to rise and wrap her arms around Gilla's waist, trembling the entire time. "What are we going to do, Mama? What's happening?" Her voice quavered and broke into sobs that wrenched at Gilla's already shredded gut.

She held her little girl with one arm, gently shushing her. Gilla needed this as much as Mirami did, the shock of the day's events still numbing her. She heard a whisper again and pulled back to hear more clearly what her daughter was trying to say.

"I'm scared, Mama. What if they catch us?"

Gilla ducked level with her face and tried to look as confident and determined as possible. "They won't. God will make sure of it. Have you prayed about your fear?"

"Yes. In my head, I've been asking Him to save us the whole time." Her little forehead creased, and she added, "Maybe I should have stopped for a while to listen to His reply?"

Pride filled Gilla, banishing her own demons in the face of her daughter's simple faith. "That's a wonderful idea, Kiddo. I've prayed too, and I know God's going to help us escape from the warriors if we follow His lead. So there's no need to be scared of them. Trust me. Their arrogance is going to work for us. From what I've seen, they only brought short-range scanners that will cover each shack as they search it but not much farther. They believe their numbers will block off any escape outside." She paused and forced a wide smile. "They don't know the settlement like we do, though. We were born here, have roamed these alleys, passages, and paths our entire lives. We know which gaps to use as short-cuts and which lead to dead ends. We can get through their net. And then, we're going to hide your brother somewhere none of them will ever be able to find him."

∞

Than had been out of his mind with worry for Gilla and her children since he first discovered what was happening in the settlement earlier that afternoon. Knowing she still spent the better part of each day visiting a new friend in the med-wing rather than facing the ghost of Elias at home, his first concern had been their safety. He was certain she wouldn't have left the building before he came for her at the end of his shift. She hadn't since she was released.

He'd abandoned his work station, ignoring the demands of the guards to stay where he was, and slipped out of the uduin sector to dash towards the Nursery and his sister. When he'd arrived, an impenetrable wall of Esarelians had blocked the way inside, and he could do nothing more than stand and listen to the terror-filled cries from within. His heart had shattered with each scream as he imagined horrific scenes, progressively worsening, with Gilla's broken face on each mother. It was too much to bear after losing Elias so recently. Unable to take the pain, which sliced through his chest much more fiercely than anything he had felt during his own recent injury, he had slumped into a nearby alley to await the inevitable conclusion.

The warriors—he was lucid enough to recognise the differences between them and local guards—finally allowed movement into the building when all sounds from within, except a mournful wailing, had ceased. Than felt like he'd been waiting for days, although, in reality, it had been a mere half cycle. He had failed. On unsteady legs, he pushed up and shuffled forwards with the rest of the growing crowd, watching the Esarelians march out of the Nursery and consult briefly with their commander.

The Esarelian in charge had stood outside during the entire massacre, in full view of the human slaves being prevented from aiding their families, with a face void of all emotion. His clothing didn't mark him out as anyone special, only his bearing, and the speed with which his orders were followed. The warriors split into squads on his mark and loped into the surrounding area, following various tracks and pathways.

Than could easily guess at their purpose, though he was sure he didn't want to. Instead, he focused on getting into the Nursery and to Gilla. Pushing through to the front of the crowd, Than dreaded what he might find inside. His imagination hadn't abated its onslaught of gruesome scenarios since his arrival, and he felt sick at the thought of having let his sister down. The one promise he'd made Elias was to look after her, and he'd not been able to. It ate at his insides even as his entire body jangled with nervous tension.

It was only as he entered the building that the true horror of what the Esarelians had done broke over him, chills and nausea fighting for dominance and creating a whirling, churning sensation in the pit of his stomach. He blocked the images of the corridor to the infant-wing from his mind, afraid that to acknowledge them would be to descend into madness and grief.

Even more terrified of what he would find, he ran to Gilla's friend's room, preparing to offer support and comfort to the sister he adored. He skidded along the last span of corridor and swung himself into the room by the garn wood doorframe. Splinters of plum-coloured wood bit into his palm, but he ignored them, the sight before him taking all his attention. Blinking in hopeful disbelief, he surveyed an empty chamber.

His frantic search for Gilla took Than through the entire building more than once. With emotions swinging in a constant pendulum between hope and despair, he scoured every corner of every room, even ransacking the supply cupboards and opening the incinerators.

He caught sight of Nali at the side of the main common room on his second time through. A hank of her hair had pulled loose from her work braid, forming a tangled nest of ebony behind her ear, while her uniform, usually so neat and clean, bore streaks of dirt and grime as testament to the trauma she'd endured. The glazed, horrified expression on her face pulled at him, making him long to stop for a while and comfort her. At the same time, however, he couldn't give up on his family until he knew what had become of them.

Torn between the competing urges, he convinced himself that he would meet both needs by asking for her help. He changed direction and headed towards her. When he reached her side, he gently took her trembling hand in his but realised quickly that she barely noticed his presence, let alone the comfort of his touch.

"Nali, can you hear me?" he said.

There was no response. Cupping her face to force her to make eye contact, he gentled his voice as much as he was able and repeated, "Nali, can you hear me?"

After a couple of blinks, a spark of recognition lit her eyes. "Than?" she croaked.

"Yes, it's me. Have you seen Gilla, Nali? Do you know where she is?"

This time she swallowed and darted her gaze around the room before returning it to his face. "Gilla? I haven't... haven't seen her since..."

The blank mask descended once more over Nali's features, her recent memories evidently too awful to face. Than thought he'd lost her again. Before he could think of something to snap her out of the daze, her lips started moving as if silently working through a difficult problem. He moved closer to catch what she was mumbling but couldn't hear above the discordant uproar in the room. He was about to move her to a stool and call a medic over when her eyes snapped back to his and she gripped his hand tightly between both of her own.

"I haven't seen Gilla since before the warriors came." Nali's eyes held a chasm of pain and suffering that Than longed to close. She looked away from him, and her voice became a robotic monotone as she continued. "They marched into the room and scanned all the children. When they left without saying what they were doing, I followed them. They found a woman with her baby and killed him. Right in front of me. I think Gilla must've left before they arrived, or she'd be here and Elias would be dead too. Just like the rest of them. All dead."

Than pulled her into his chest and stroked her hair with his free hand. She held herself stiffly at first, but she eventually relaxed as he continued to soothe her, whispering nonsense into the top of her head. When her grip eased on his hand, he slid it from between hers, held her gently by both shoulders, and moved back enough to see her face again.

"Oh, Nali. I'm so sorry you had to see that. I wish I could take it away for you. Thank you for telling me about Gilla, though."

Before he could say anything else, she stepped away and lifted her chin a notch. Though the pain was still evident, she appeared more lucid than she had earlier. She surprised him further when she said, "You have to find her and make sure she and little Elias are safe. Go. I need to help clean up in here."

He reached out to her, but she held up a hand and repeated, "You need to find Gilla."

Than's heart broke. What Nali had seen that day would be difficult, if not impossible, to overcome, and he wondered if she would truly be all right. He longed to ease the haunted look from her beautiful eyes, to stay with her until she worked through the trauma. Unfortunately, she was right. He had to resume his search for Gilla. Other eyes, other promises, held him captive to their will. The best he could do for Nali was to ensure someone stayed with her and hope he would be able to return later to offer real comfort.

Nodding his agreement, Than reluctantly let her go but determined not to leave her alone. While scanning the area for an unoccupied medic, Than mulled over what Nali had told him about Gilla. He desperately wanted to believe her supposition that his sister had already departed, but he doubted it. Gilla generally stayed in the Nursery for the majority of the day and was unlikely to have left without him. Besides, Nali wasn't herself and probably didn't know what she was saying.

On the other hand, he'd found no sign of Gilla or the little one, and he'd searched the entire building thoroughly. Maybe she'd been able to escape the warriors and was hiding somewhere outside or running for her life. With nowhere else to look inside, he decided to move on and search the rest of the settlement.

Than snagged a young, tear-streaked trainee who was flitting along the edges of the organised chaos. The poor boy couldn't have been more than seven or eight, and he looked too overwhelmed to be of much use to the qualified medics. Than bent down until he was eye level and said, "I'm Than. What's your name?"

The boy wiped his nose on his sleeve before answering in a whisper. "Nayt... I'm Nayt."

"Well, Nayt, I need you to do something very important for me. You see this lady here?" Than indicated Nali, who was looking around the room and twisting her fingers in the fabric of her jumpsuit.

Nayt nodded profusely and managed to get out, "Yes, sir. That's Miss Menali. She used to be my teacher. She's nice."

"That's right. Well, she's had a bit of a shock today, and I think someone should stay with her until she feels better. Maybe talk to her about something else to take her mind off things. Do you think you can do that for me?"

Slumping in relief, Nayt nodded again and walked over to where Nali had started righting stools that had been knocked over in the melee. Than watched the boy join her in straightening the minimal furniture, saying, "Hi, Miss Menali. Remember me? It's Nayt. I've been training in the med-wing for a few months now, and they've taught me lots of interesting things..."

Than turned away, relieved that they would both have something to focus on other than the chaos surrounding them. He made his way towards the main entrance, eager to resume his search for his sister. As he neared it, however, a guard stepped forwards and blocked his way.

"No one leaves until we give the signal."

"What? Why not?"

The guard didn't answer, merely shoving him back, away from the exit.

Despite Than's question, the Esarelians' strategy began to make sense to him. Of course, this must now be their holding area until their work outside was complete. They wouldn't have let the crowds enter the building otherwise. Even as the thought crossed Than's mind, a handful of humans was thrust through the door behind the guard and ushered to one side, confirming his suspicions.

The need to get to Gilla surged within him, even stronger than before. With the warriors doing a systematic sweep through the shacks, she would need his help to avoid them, or to provide a distraction if they found her. Than took a deep breath to still his mind and slowly rotated, taking in every detail of the atrium and calculating his best route of escape.

A group of large men in the corner by the med-wing corridor caught his attention. They were hefting what looked like folding stretchers under the direction of a couple of medics and a guard. As they prepared to move, Than crossed quickly to them and asked what was happening.

The medic told him that they'd been ordered to bring casualties back from some of the outer areas of the settlement. Thanking God for providing a way out, Than offered his services and fell in line behind a stocky, well-muscled man in red. He remembered to grab one of the makeshift stretchers as the group headed out. They were stopped by a guard—thankfully, a different one to the male Than had already approached—who spoke briefly with the guard leading them, gave him a few directions, and inspected each of their loads before allowing them to leave the confines of the building.

Once outside, Than kept to the back of the group while they passed through two more checkpoints, going through the same process each time. As they entered the warren of shacks through a narrow passage, it became evident they wouldn't be stopped again until they reached their destination. Than gradually dropped back from the others until they rounded a bend and left him behind. Keeping the stretcher as an alibi, Than swiftly made his way towards Gilla's shack, praying he would find her before anyone else did.

He was only a couple of turns from his destination when a strong hand clamped his arm and yanked him from the path down a deeply shadowed gap between two shacks. Than reacted reflexively, raising his arm to throw off his assailant as he shifted his weight to counter-attack. Only a whispered, "It's Aro," stopped him.

As Than's eyes adjusted to the dim light, the form of his leader materialised, along with several other members of the resistance crouched behind him.

"Aro? What are you doing here?" Than relaxed his posture and shuffled farther into the narrow space, keeping his eyes and ears open for signs of Esarelian movement.

Aronin made room for him before answering, "Looking for you. We've been trying to stop this madness, or at least save some of the babies. It's impossible, though. They're systematic and thorough, ready for ambushes and diversions, and we can't get to the weapons we used in the strike. They're using scanners, and most of the boys we've hidden have already been found." He ran his hand over his beard a couple of times and fixed an intense gaze on Than. "Have you seen Gilla and the little one? Are they safe?"

Than slumped. Here was the confirmation that Aronin hadn't found her either. "No," he managed to whisper. "I was hoping you'd know something."

He looked over in time to catch the flicker of a grimace pass Aronin's features, and a sliver of dread wormed its way through Than's stomach. He balled his fists to stop himself from reacting prematurely. "What is it? What's happened?"

The pity shining in Aronin's eyes made Than want to vomit. He watched as the older man signalled along the row of men, causing one of them to squeeze through until he joined them. With regret colouring every word, Aronin said, "I'm sorry, Than. I was hoping it was a mistake. It's best you hear this for yourself." He put a supportive hand on Than's good arm before turning to the newcomer, "Tell Than what you told me when you found us."

The gangly youth sucked in a breath and looked directly at Than. "A squad brought some bodies back to the square outside the Nursery a little while ago, and I managed to hear them report to their commander. One of the drones tagged a woman trying to escape across the wasteland with her son. Apparently, she'd been running from the warriors for more than half a cycle. She fought them when they caught her, so they killed her as well as the baby.

"They don't have a name for her yet, but she was wearing blue ... and she's about your sister's size. I couldn't see or hear any more than that. I'm sorry."

∞

A scream pierced the still, humid air. It sounded like a wounded animal, but Gilla could still picture the scene inside the Nursery and knew it was a woman whose baby boy had just been murdered in front of her. Other cries joined it in a cacophony of misery that Gilla thought couldn't have failed to penetrate the most hardened heart. Unfortunately, they did. Shouted commands and the blasts of weapons, mixed with even more desperate pleas and wails, drifted towards her as they ran between buildings. The search of the settlement for innocents to kill was in full swing. She tried to block it all out. She had to focus.

Tugging a stunned Mirami along when the little girl began to flag, Gilla reassured her that it wasn't much farther and that they could rest soon. She didn't want to let it show, but a niggling feeling that they were being tracked wouldn't leave her alone. She'd doubled back a couple of times to try to shake the sensation, but it persisted in dogging her. They needed to get on with her plan; she could draw off whoever was stalking their movements afterwards.

With all the activity in the main settlement area, getting Mirami into the manufacturing sector was laughably easy. The wall was higher than the one they'd scrambled down earlier but not impossible to scale for one who knew where to look. Gilla was glad she'd listened when Elias had once described the barely visible notches cut into sector walls by the resistance for ease of unseen movement. Additionally, the guard patrols, while more frequent than usual, were simpler to avoid than the better trained warriors had been. She kept Elias strapped to her back for the climb and then carefully hid him in a supply cart once on the other side.

The sector was quiet in comparison with the settlement, eerily so. Many, including several guards, had apparently abandoned their work to see what was happening. A large group had gathered at the check-point. There was a scuffle towards the front of the mob as someone tried to rush through to help their loved ones. His calls for his wife were swiftly cut off by a shock from the rod of the guard on duty.

Gilla took the children quickly to her building and, once inside, directly to her usual work station. She thanked God that the workers of this area had emptied out to join the efforts of those attempting to breach the checkpoint. After settling Mirami in a good position to act as lookout and watch over Elias, she bent to the control panel of the life-pod in front of her and got to work.

As soon as Gilla had pulled open the hatch and ripped out the tracking beacon, she made some adjustments to the settings on the control panel. She had to search for one of the rare palm pads they used for testing systems but eventually found one a few work stations along the line. After waiting impatiently for the systems to sync, she shoved the panel back in its place and closed the access hatch firmly. Tapping on the screen of the pad, she checked the readings and made one or two modifications. A few moments later, she was ready.

It took both of them, pulling together, to wheel the life-pod on its frame to the side entrance of the building. Getting it to the area of the sector where all the completed units sat ready for transport took the last of their strength. At least there, the launch might be taken for a misfire if it were spotted, especially with the note Gilla had entered into the system, logging just such an incident. Hopefully, it wouldn't be noticed at all in the melee. When taking off from a planet, life-pods were fairly quiet until they reached the altitude set for hard burn, and they were small enough to appear, if at all, as a mere shadow on any sensors. Finally, Gilla signalled they were far enough away from the buildings and could stop.

Gently, she pulled Elias around from where he was again strapped to her back. Her throat thickened at what she was about to do. If there were any other choice, she would take it. Unfortunately, this was his best chance to survive the mass murder taking place in the settlement. She blinked back her tears and looked down at his sweet face.

"You changed him while I worked?" She spoke to Mirami but never took her eyes from her son.

"Yes, Mama."

"Good. Thank you." Finally, she dragged her eyes away and turned to her daughter. "Where's the bottle you had? We'll put it in with him."

Mirami pulled a bottle of re-hydrated milk from the waist of her jumpsuit and handed it over. Taking her daughter's hands, Gilla bent her head and prayed. "Lord, you know the danger Elias is in. Please be with him and protect him until we can bring him home." Unable to say more through the lump clogging her throat, she finished with a simple, "Amen."

"I think it worked, Mama. I feel warm all over, and that's got to be God talking back, right?"

Smiling, Gilla tucked the bottle of milk into the folds of Elias's blankets and beckoned Mirami forward to say goodbye. The little girl was subdued as she leaned over Elias and said a few quick words.

"Bye, little one. We'll see you soon. I know we will." She kissed his cheek and moved back, waiting for Gilla at the corner of the row of pods.

Using his blankets as extra cushioning, Gilla strapped Elias into the single support pad. He looked so tiny in the space meant for an adult. *Am I doing the right thing, Lord?* Squashing her doubts, she looked at him one last time and said what was in her heart. "I love you, Elias. Your father loved you too, and Mirami. This will only be for a short time, and then I'll bring you back, when it's safe. God will be with you, and Mirami will be watching on her screen. I'm sorry this is the only thing I can do to protect you. See you soon, little one."

Before she lost her nerve or the tears overwhelmed her, she ducked out and closed the hatch, sealing it from the outside. Jogging the short distance to Mirami, she pulled her daughter away and, without looking back, pressed the remote button that would fire the pod's initial thrusters.

The low rumble and high-pitched whirring that ensued sounded too loud to be missed. A strong gust pushed them a pace forward, covering them in dust as it rolled out in an ever-increasing circle. Gilla feared they had made a grievous mistake, and the pod would be shot down. Thankfully, the other pods broke up the impact of the wind and dissipated the choking dust cloud before it reached open ground. The screaming and weapon blasts coming from the settlement must also have covered the noise made as her son was taken beyond the Esarelians' reach. None she could see as she peered between crates even turned in their direction.

Within moments, the small, bullet-shaped pod lifted into the lower atmosphere at a sharp angle and disappeared from sight. Gilla counted off the time it would take before the pod shot into the upper atmosphere and into space. She saw nothing, despite squinting intently into the sky. *Thank you, Lord.* It looked like he was safe, for now.

Knowing they still had to be careful if they were to pull off their feat, Gilla retrieved the palm pad from her pocket and turned back to Mirami. She checked the data streaming across the screen and, satisfied that the signal from the pod was secure, toggled to the map view and handed it over.

Mirami took it tentatively and also peered at the screen. A crease marred her brow as she concentrated on trying to decipher the confusing information. Gilla wished she had more time to explain properly how it worked, but she would do the best she could before they had to move again.

She squatted next to the little girl and pointed at a white dot moving slowly across the map. "That's your brother. This device is solo-linked to the system in his life-pod. I pulled the beacon, so no one else should be able to track him remotely, and he's too small for regular scanners unless they're really close. That means we're the only ones who can see where he is."

Mirami looked at her with wide eyes, and Gilla nodded in confirmation as she directed her daughter's gaze back to the screen. "I've programmed the pod to fly to a safe place, well out of the way of any spacecraft, and wait there until we recall it or the air in the tanks drops to twenty percent. You can watch what happens to him on the screen and keep an eye on his progress." She pointed out a tab in the corner. "This is the recall button. If you press it, Elias's pod will return to the planet and set down in the wilderness, well beyond sight of the settlement. Only use it if you see something that could be dangerous to him on the screen. You're going to look after him, just like you did for me this morning. All right?"

"You hold it, Mama. You're better at knowing when to press the button." Mirami tried to push the palm pad back into Gilla's hands, seemingly overwhelmed by the responsibility of the task.

"I can't, Kiddo. I have another job to do." When Mirami tried to insist they stay together, Gilla's heart nearly broke. She smoothed her daughter's hair and hushed her, holding her tightly until she calmed slightly. "It's all right, Mirami. God is with us, remember? It won't be long now, and then we'll all be together again. I need you to be brave a little longer and wait for me outside the settlement. You'll be safe there and can watch your brother on the screen to make sure he's safe too. You can do this, Mirami, I know you can. If you need to recall his pod, follow it to the landing site and wait for me there. I'll know where to find you.

"Until then, when we get back over the wall, I want you to run as fast as you can, straight along the edge of this sector and out to the east of the settlement. Find a place to hide in the first group of rocks you come to—somewhere that can't be seen from the edge of the settlement. There are lots of piles of boulders out there from an old dig. It'll be easy to find a safe hideaway without being spotted by the patrols. And don't worry about the drones; they'll be programmed only to identify and tag their targets. Your body mass is much too big for them to take any notice of you if they're only after the babies, and you're too small to be an operational threat."

Gilla knew this with certainty. Her work in the manufacturing sector had included a stint of calibrating the sensors on military drones destined for the new cruiser. She knew their capabilities, as well as their parameters. There was no way she could have smuggled Elias out of the settlement while any were operational, and given the reputation of the Esarelian military, they would undoubtedly have several patrolling the settlement perimeter and securing the surrounding wasteland. Mirami, however, would be safe beyond the border. Besides, it would keep her focused on her brother rather than the chaos surrounding her were she to stay at their home. Gilla finished her instructions with, "Don't stop for anything, and don't come out of hiding for anyone but me."

Mirami's frail shoulders shook slightly, but she sniffled once more and nodded her little head. "Okay, Mama. I can look after Elias for you."

"Good girl. I'm so proud of you." She stroked a few strands of hair from her daughter's forehead and kissed it before standing and checking their gear. She winked to ease Mirami's tension. "Let's go."

It took less time to climb out over the wall than it had to climb in. On the other side, the sounds of slaughter were more distinct. Cries of agony and grief rebounded throughout a large section of the settlement, a harrowing indicator of the progress of the warriors. The horror was not yet over. The rightness of the decision she had made settled in Gilla's gut, and she told herself that she could be brave too.

She scooped Mirami into another swift hug before setting her back on her feet and checking again that she knew what to do and how to use the palm pad. Gilla pointed in the direction she wanted her daughter to go and watched as she ran. Legs and arms pumping in the way of all youngsters, Mirami was soon lost to sight. Gilla stood a few moments longer, sending a prayer flying after her little girl, before turning her mind back to her own task.

Picking up the spare bundle of blankets she had prepared and holding it as if carrying a child, Gilla ran in the opposite direction. If the warrior who had spotted her wanted to ensure they caught the escaped woman in blue, she wouldn't disappoint him. Anything that would throw the death squads off the real trail to Elias was worth trying. When the niggling feeling at the back of her head returned a short while later, she almost smiled in relief as she picked up the pace. Knowing she was leading whoever was behind her away from Mirami and, by extension, Elias, Gilla did the one thing she could do for them.

She ran.

Chapter 14

Day: 17   Month: 07   Year: 6428
Location: Planet U'Du, wilderness outside the main slave settlement

Mirami crouched between two rocks, each the size of several men, resting her back in the nook they created. One was shaped in a way that created a natural overhang and blocked out some of the blazing sunlight. It had taken her some time to run there after she'd left her mama, and Mirami was breathing heavily, her lungs burning through her chest. Her legs felt wobbly as she slumped down to lie against the warm surface of the rocks and pulled her knees up in front of her. Her mouth was dry, but there was nothing she could do about that, so she tried to ignore it.

She'd seen one of the drones her mama had told her about. It had hovered overhead, while Mirami had stood still and tried to ignore it, trusting that it would leave her alone as her mama had claimed. After only a cursory scan, it had flown on, the after-burn of its small engine flaring white in the clear sky. As the low buzzing noise it emitted had faded into the distance, Mirami had understood why these machines were called drones. She'd heaved a sigh of relief. When it had disappeared from sight, and she was sure it wasn't coming back, she'd run on into the wastes towards the massive boulders she now hid between.

The sounds of weapons firing drifted faintly on the still air, the fear and pain of women screaming palpable and suffocating. It scared her. Her mama had told her what was happening, but it didn't make any sense, and she couldn't imagine the scenes taking place back in the settlement. She covered her ears, desperate to block out the noise. When that didn't work, she tried to ignore it by picking up the palm pad she had dropped by her side when she sat. She turned all her attention to the screen she held in trembling fingers. The blips of her brother's life-pod slowly but steadily moving away from the planet helped to calm her racing heart.

A barely human wail echoed between the rocks, making her jump and half rise to run again. She wanted to escape, to find a place where no one would find her and she could block out everything from this awful day. She also wanted to run straight to her mama and wrap both arms around her until the nightmare was over. Trembling violently, Mirami folded herself into as small a ball as she could and told herself to be brave.

She still missed her daddy more than anything, and her whole body ached when she thought about him. She wished he was here and could bundle her up in one of his massive hugs and make her feel safe again. He would have protected them from all the bad things that had happened. She knew he would; he could do anything. But he wasn't here. The Esarelians had taken him away, and it was just her and Mama to look after Elias. A pain stabbed through Mirami's middle at the thought of never seeing her daddy again, and her eyes filled. Blinking away the tears, she knew she couldn't think about that. She had a job to do.

"Your brother needs you to look after him. Mama knows you can do this; just watch the screen and make sure Elias is safe." Saying the words aloud made her feel better. She nodded to the empty wilderness in front of her and looked back at the screen. The blip was slowing. As she watched, it came to a standstill at the edge of an area marked on the map as an asteroid belt.

She breathed out and leaned her head back. He was safe. If only she could relax fully. She wouldn't be able to do that until the warriors had left the planet and her mama had come to push the button to bring Elias back to them. Not wanting to make a mistake or miss anything, Mirami returned her attention to the screen. She wouldn't let her mama or brother down, wouldn't look away until her mama came back. The blip remained in its spot, blinking away as time dragged on.

Mirami's focus began to waver as the heat of the day lulled her towards sleep. Gradually, her eyes closed, her body relaxed, and the palm pad slid between her unresponsive fingers to rest in her lap.

Date: 311.428.149
Location: U'du asteroid belt

The work had been going well. Over the last few cycles, they had been able to set up over three-quarters of a racing lane along the outside edge of the belt. It was going to be a challenging route and one of the most exciting she would ever attempt. Reemah itched to get out there in an arrow and try it out. This had been a great idea. She already felt less claustrophobic and more relaxed than she had since she had been grounded. A small twinge of guilt stabbed her at the reminder that she should be back on the cruiser.

It was not as if she deliberately went out of her way to defy her father, she justified, but when the opportunity presented itself, she also had not given his decree a second thought. Maybe she should make an extra effort to follow the rules when she got back. With this course to look forwards to, she would feel less caged and more able to play the part required of her. There must be something special she could do to show her father that she regretted worrying him so much. As she squirmed in her seat to get more comfortable, she vowed to give it more consideration later. At the moment, she needed to concentrate.

Velay had just finished pulling a giant rock into position with the traction net when Reemah spotted an anomaly on her viewer. She moved closer and tapped the screen in an attempt to make it disappear. Instead, it became a steady blip. She frowned and tapped the screen again before looking up and out of the dura-pane forward window. Sometimes tech developed glitches, but she always trusted her own senses.

A glint of something caught her eye farther along the belt, directly in the centre of her new racing circuit. It could be a piece of debris or metallic ore knocked out of the belt by a larger asteroid. That made no sense, though, as it would not have come to a halt without some counter-force. Whatever the object was, it was small. No wonder it appeared initially as an anomaly on her scanner. They would have missed the thing if it had drifted across their lane at any other point. She sighed. They would have to go back and move whatever it was or risk a collision when they returned to fly for real.

"We're moving, Vel. Something just sat itself down in the middle of our path, so we're going to have to convince it to move on. You'll need to adjust the traction setting; it looks metallic."

"Let's just blast it to nothing. It's much quicker."

"I want to take a look first. All the other scrap metal was farther down the belt."

Velay wrinkled her nose at Reemah's fascination and then huffed out a breath. "Fine, I'm switching net configuration now. How did it get there, anyway? I thought we'd cleared that section pretty thoroughly."

"So did I," Reemah grumbled. This was the downside of flying so close to the belt—a constantly changing environment that could never be fully mapped or controlled. It was why most gave it a wide berth and Buln had not been discovered yet. "Hang on. I may as well have some fun while we back-track. It's not like that thing's going anywhere."

She pulled back on the controls, and Buln responded by gradually dipping under the nearest rotating asteroid and slowly canting to the side to avoid the next two behind it. They could take the scenic route to the metal object a short distance away, she decided. Steering was difficult with such sluggish controls, but she managed to twist and turn the craft on a leisurely weave through the few asteroids at the side of the cleared area instead of flying straight through.

Having fun, she called out, "Isn't this solid? We should have come out days ago."

Velay laughed at Reemah's antics before responding. "I'd concentrate on flying, if I were you. Buln needs all the advance warning for turns you can give him."

"Don't ruin my fun, or I'll tell my father you're corrupting me..." Reemah let her non-threat dangle between them, knowing Velay would never take it seriously.

Her attention was drawn back to the controls when the proximity alert sounded. One of the larger asteroids was heading directly into their current flight path. She slapped off the flashing alarm and searched her screen for a clear, evasive route. Wincing, she realised they might have strayed a little too far into the belt. She spotted an opening. Fitting through the gap was going to be tight, but there was no alternative. She pulled hard to the right and waited for the tub to swing around.

Buln began to make the turn, slow as ever. Keeping one eye on the surrounding area in her viewer for other stray movement, Reemah watched the screen displaying the trajectories of the asteroid and their tub. The lines still intersected, but the angle was becoming smaller with every sweep of the scanners. Unfortunately, so was the distance between them. She muttered under her breath at the control panel, "Come on, you piece of junk, move!" To Velay, Reemah shouted, "We're not going to make it. See if you can move that thing to give us more room."

Velay instantly got to work, scrolling the power up to maximum. When she activated the traction net, the asteroid jerked on Reemah's screen. The net had nudged the huge rock far enough to allow them to scrape past moments later without damage to the tub. Reemah sat back in her chair and let out a long breath.

"Well, that took a few cycles off my life. Can we go back to the cleared area now? Some of these things move occasionally." Velay's tone had *I told you so* stamped all over it. At least she did not say the actual words. Reemah made no reply as she set a safer course back to the cleared area and the mysterious object on her screen.

Day: 17   Month: 07   Year: 6428
Location: Planet U'Du, wilderness outside the main slave settlement

Coming fully awake in an instant, Mirami gripped the palm pad tightly with both hands as she noticed another blip appear at the edge of her screen. She stared at the new, much larger dot. How long had she been asleep, and how long had that dot been so close to her brother? Her heart began to race again. What was it?

For a while, the flashing dot looked as if it would pass her brother's position. Weaving and dodging, it seemed to be moving in an arc some distance from him. She began to relax, thinking it would soon disappear along the other edge of her screen. Instead, it turned and began to head towards the life-pod. Its path became straighter—more direct—with the speed increasing as it neared the previously solitary blip in the centre of the screen.

She didn't know what to do. Should she run back to the settlement for her mama or carry on watching to see what happened? Maybe it would go straight past the pod. Maybe whoever it was wouldn't see him. Didn't Mama say something about no one else being able to track him? Maybe the other dot was just a piece of junk, tossed around by the sea of asteroids up there.

That brought a new fear. What if the object crashed into Elias's pod? What if the pod got damaged and couldn't keep her brother safe any more? He was alone up there with only Mirami to watch over him. Remembering her mama's instructions on what to do if anything got too close, she bit her lip, prayed she was doing the right thing, and pressed the recall button.

At first nothing happened. She held her breath and waited as the two blips came so close together they could be touching. Had she waited too long? Would her brother die? If he did, it would be her fault. Tears bubbled up and fell down her cheeks as she watched, riveted to the screen and what now looked like one large blip instead of two separate ones.

Date: 311.428.149
Location: U'Du asteroid belt

As they made the final approach to the mysterious object on the viewing screen, Reemah got her first good look at it. From close up, she could tell it was not an inanimate lump of metal but a solitary life-pod. Her inner eyelids blinked twice. It had not registered as a pod on her scanners. Where was the beacon? Why had it not activated? Was there anyone inside? The questions dancing through her mind demanded answers. Until she got closer and could investigate, she had none.

Velay had the traction net positioned and was about to engage when the pod surprised them again. It moved. "Come here, you pesky little thing," she muttered. Before she could get another fix, it drifted out of the previously cleared area altogether. Waving her hand in dismissal, she said, "Well, that solves that problem."

Reemah's head jerked up from her instruments to see the unmistakable glow of a power cell at the rear of the pod, propelling it away from them. It shot out of the asteroid belt before she could determine anything more. Without fully thinking through what she was doing, she engaged the thrusters and followed before the vexing pod could disappear from sight.

Velay jumped out of her seat and rushed to the front at the sudden movement. "What are you doing?"

Barely paying her any attention, Reemah corrected course to stay with the pod when it changed direction and sped away. "Following it."

"What? Why?"

"I want to know what it was doing out here with no beacon." She frowned, perplexed by her own reaction. "Someone must be controlling it, must have recalled it. I want to know who and why."

"Then track it from here."

"Can't. It only shows up on the scanners when we're within ten clicks of it. Pods are small; they usually rely on beacons to attract attention. It's already looking like just an anomaly on my screen again. I can only follow it because I can still see the power cell through the window."

Velay looked at the display and then gripped the back of Reemah's chair and spun it around. "Are you crazy? We're heading towards U'du. We can't go planet-side; your father will kill me! Reemah, sneaking out to have some fun flying is one thing, sneaking out and going down to the *planet* is entirely different. You know the rules. What if we get caught? You'll never be allowed out of your suite again, and as for me..."

Gently brushing her friend off, Reemah swung back to the controls. The strongest surge of curiosity she had ever felt was pulling her to that pod. She tried to sound reasonable when she responded. "We're just seeing where it's going, not traipsing around a dirty planet. No one will ever know." Seeing Velay's still uncertain look, Reemah added, "We won't even land."

"You're sure? We won't land?"

"Probably not."

"Probably," Velay repeated. She stood, speechless, blinking her inner eyelids rapidly before capitulating. As she returned to her station, Reemah thought she heard her friend say, "And people think *I'm* the bad influence."

As they followed the pod, its destination became more and more obscure. Instead of heading towards one of the major colonies, it seemed to be aiming for a landing site out in the wilderness, beyond the largest lake on the surface of the planet. Velay had remained quiet since her attempt to change Reemah's mind, seeming to accept the change in their plans well enough. Reemah, however, could not stop her brain from churning with possible reasons for the pod's odd programming.

By the time it touched down in a small, relatively flat spot between heaps of dull grey boulders, her curiosity had reached an all-time high. There was no way she would be able to refrain from getting a closer look. She landed Buln as near as possible to the pod. With rocky terrain throughout the vicinity, that turned out to be a fair distance away in another, larger clearing.

Velay finally rolled her eyes and spoke. "Now what?"

"Now, we investigate." Reemah powered down and turned to her friend. She hoped the twinkle in her eyes and mischievous grin would prove as infectious as always. Bouncing lightly in her chair, the adrenaline of an illicit adventure coursed through her. "Oh, come on. We couldn't find out anything without landing, and now we're too far away. We've got to get closer. Please?" She batted her eyes and tried to maintain her most adorably hopeful expression.

Although her pathetic attempts to garner sympathy or support should not work, given her friend's background, they always did. Velay's eyes shot daggers that Reemah could almost feel, but her friend acquiesced. Pointing a finger at Reemah's still-beaming face, Velay said, "You know I don't like this, but I can't let you go on your own, can I?"

Reemah did a happy wiggle before jumping up. "Let's go."

"Solid." It was the most sarcastic she had heard Velay's tone for quite some time, but Reemah did not care as long as they got a better look at the life-pod.

They gathered together a few bits of gear they might need—water canteens, a med wand (just in case), uduin packs, a scanner, and rods for protection—and attached the items to the utility belts of their jumpsuits. With a final check that they were ready, Reemah punched the panel to open the cargo bay doors.

Chapter 15

Day: 17   Month: 07   Year: 6428
Location: Planet U'Du, wilderness outside the main slave settlement

Was that movement? Mirami wiped her face with her arm, trying to clear the blurring water from her eyes, and looked again, bringing the screen close to her face. The large blip stretched and then gradually became two again as the smaller dot moved slowly away from the other. She cried harder when she realised it had worked and that the life-pod was picking up speed and heading back towards the planet. Fear drained away, and her gasping sobs turned into hiccups.

Trying to hold her breath to get rid of the annoying spasms, she almost missed something flash on the very edge of the screen. Before she could make out what it was, it disappeared. She stared at the spot where it had been and saw it hover again, only half visible, before it once more dropped out of range. Whatever it was, it didn't seem to be getting any closer, and she couldn't do anything about it. Deciding it must be a glitch, she put it out of her mind until she could tell her mama about it later.

As Mirami watched the screen, transfixed, Elias's life-pod re-entered the upper atmosphere and changed direction until it was heading across the wilderness. Her mama had already said it would land in an isolated spot out there somewhere. Unfortunately, that information left Mirami with another difficult decision to make. Was she brave enough to follow the pod over land that most adults said was wild and dangerous? Would she be able to keep her promise to her mama and continue to protect Elias? The prospect of having to go out there alone terrified Mirami beyond all reason.

There wouldn't be much she could do to help him anyway; she was too little. She didn't even have any supplies, other than the palm pad to track the pod's location and a small block of uduin her mama had thrust into her hands as they left their shack. She'd been handed a canteen of water as well but must have left it at the building where her mama worked. It seemed such a long time ago but couldn't have been more than a couple of cycles at most. Maybe Mirami could just stay here until her mama came, and then they could go get Elias together. It couldn't be long before she would arrive; surely, she'd be there any moment. Squeezing one hand into a ball, Mirami watched the blip continue to move slowly farther away.

She wished she wasn't old enough to be a trainee and have to make decisions and be brave and responsible. She wished she was still a little girl and only had to worry about lessons and stupid boys pulling her hair. She wished her mama was here. Mirami rocked back and forth, hugging her knees, until she felt a little better. Thinking about her mama reminded Mirami of what her parents had taught her to do when she felt scared. She should pray.

Folding her hands together, she closed only one eye because she still had to watch the pod and she didn't think God would mind, seeing as she loved her brother. She took a deep, shuddering breath and began. "Dear God, thank you for helping us to save Elias. Please help me to be as brave as my mama. I'm scared, and I don't want to have to go into the wilderness on my own, but I need to so I can look after him until Mama comes for us. Please take the scared feeling away. Thank you for being with us, even on U'du. I love you. Amen."

When Mirami opened her eye and picked up the pad from where she had rested it on her knees, she felt a slight tingling inside. It started in her belly and spread out until even her fingers and toes felt warm and relaxed. Her tears dried, leaving slight smudges across her cheeks and a few damp patches on her yellow jumpsuit. It took a moment to realise that she was confident enough to keep her promise and go into the wilderness to find Elias's pod. The fear hadn't disappeared exactly, just been hidden away behind the new calm feeling and clear head. The questions, doubts, and indecision that had previously been deafening her had become whispers in the back of her mind that she could ignore if she concentrated on the screen instead.

Taking one final look back towards the settlement, just in case her mama was already on her way, and seeing nothing but swirling dust, Mirami turned in the opposite direction and started walking. It was difficult to hold the pad up so she could see both it and the area in front of her. She

Courage

stumbled several times before she found a system that was both comfortable and workable.

Before long, she noticed that the life-pod had slowed and then stopped again. Heading in as straight a line as she could towards the stationary blip on her screen, she clambered over rocks where possible and skirted around them where it wasn't.

She was starting to get hungry and thirsty, her stomach rumbling and her mouth becoming even drier. Figuring she shouldn't take the time to sit down and eat, she slowed her pace as she used her free hand to dig the uduin lump from the pocket where she'd stuffed it earlier that day. After opening the wrapper, she nibbled the lavender-coloured edge while she walked across a relatively flat section of ground and discovered that eating helped keep her mind off her problems almost as well as the nice tingly feeling did.

A clattering of rocks behind Mirami made her jump. Spinning in circles to the left and right like a malfunctioning blender, she searched around her for signs of any malevolent presence. She couldn't see anything, but the sound had unnerved her. She hid for a moment behind a jumbled pile of grey rocks, mottled by whorls of blues and light browns. She'd never really noticed the intricate variance in the colour of the planet's surface rock before. Seen from afar, the colours blended to paint a much duller picture. Picking up a pebble containing a pale, nearly white streak through the blue-grey, she thought it looked pretty in the strong light of the afternoon sun. It reminded her of the stone her mama kept from uncle Than, so Mirami tucked it away in her pocket. It would remind her that God was always with her, no matter what the Esarelians did. The idea calmed her. With renewed strength, she continued on her way, determined to reach her brother as soon as possible.

∞

The hiss of the seal unlocking, and the whoosh of the portal sliding open, preceded a bright, almost unbearable light shining into the bay where they stood. Reemah had never set foot on a planet before and was unprepared for the sudden glare of sunlight refracted through an atmosphere instead of the tinted dura-pane windows she was used to.

Nervous anticipation raced through her body at the thought of what other new experiences she might soon face. The swirling dust that rushed in and wrapped around them was not one of those she had considered—

nor was the intense heat. She blinked her inner eyelids into place, seeing Velay do the same. Tempted as Reemah was to pull the protective bio-suit over her exposed hands and head as well, she settled for letting it regulate the temperature of the rest of her body while those areas soaked up the sun's rays naturally for the first time. It felt strangely good, and she relaxed somewhat.

Velay was sniffing experimentally. Reemah realised, as she watched her friend's nose twitch, that it was because the air *smelled*. Although not necessarily good or bad, it did have a scent. Having only breathed the carefully scrubbed and recycled air of AC units before, it was an unusual sensation. Reemah sniffed as well, trying to place the new fragrance. There was a slightly sour note to the planet's air, but it mostly smelled somehow … earthy. A faint aftertaste of something metallic or burning lingered beyond each indrawn breath.

Looking around, Reemah wondered at the mostly unchanging landscape before them. The rock formations seen from the air were no more impressive from this angle. Drab grey ranged from a light dove colour wherever the sun hit in full force, to a darker charcoal hue in the cracks between rocks and other fully shaded areas. She stepped off the ramp and felt her foot dip into the surface marginally before returning to the expected level. She tested it again by pressing her weight forward and found the same, unexpected give. The ground was not fully solid. What a strange place.

Her thoughts were interrupted by Velay asking which direction they should take and reminding Reemah they must hurry. The expression in Velay's eyes gave away her equal wonder at the differences between planet and cruiser.

Reemah focused on the scanner for a moment and then pointed out beyond the rocks to the rear left of Buln. "That way. It shouldn't take too long to get there."

She was right. Less than a quarter of a cycle later, they rounded a large outcrop to find a small clearing before them. To one side of the centre sat the life-pod, its hatch facing partially away from them and its metallic surface flashing in the sunlight.

"Now what?" Velay whispered from close behind her.

Without responding, Reemah stepped forwards and into the cleared space. She walked slowly towards the hatch of the pod, scanner held out before her to check both pod and immediate area for signs of life. More importantly, the palm-sized tech also checked for weapon signatures. She clutched the rod at her side, ready to draw it if needed.

It was not necessary. Besides her and Velay, still at the edge of the clearing, the only reading on the screen was a small dot inside the pod. Too small for an Esarelian, Reemah wondered what in the universe it could be.

Taking a deep breath, she reattached the scanner to her belt and reached forwards to deactivate the locking mechanism. Nothing happened. She frowned and pressed her PU against it. When that had no impact either, she huffed and set about removing the panel to get to the control circuit board. Someone seemed to have jerry-rigged the hatch to remain shut, a fact that made her even more curious about the contents within.

Eventually, after considerable work inside the control panel, she heard the faint yet familiar click-hiss of the seal disengaging. Not bothering to close the panel, she reached around and opened the hatch. What she saw inside made her freeze.

Shocked beyond anything she had ever previously experienced, she fell backwards and sat heavily. Only the ground's elastic quality saved her rear end from severe bruising. Her eyes locked on the occupant of the pod, and her other senses shut down temporarily; she never even heard Velay approach until she spoke.

"What is it?" Velay asked.

Reemah was still unable to respond, so Velay walked the rest of the way from her position as lookout and peered over Reemah's shoulder through the hatch. Velay blinked her inner eyelids a couple of times and said what was most obvious to them both. "It's a baby."

∞

There were only a few clusters of large boulders between Mirami and the blip of her brother's location when she heard another noise. Stopping to listen more carefully, she heard it again. The scraping, scrabbling, clanking sound that reverberated towards her from the surrounding rocks could only have been made by something against metal. Someone or something was messing with the life-pod.

Panic hit again. Her mind scrambled for a way out—for someone to run to for help. How she wished her parents were here. Her heart pounded faster and faster as she imagined a succession of monsters—each one more horrific than the last—trying to get at Elias. She'd never been anywhere near this far out into the wasteland before and had no idea what could be hiding among the rocks. She stood frozen in a half step forward until her mind finally ceased swirling.

She realised with a whooshing exhale that she couldn't see the pod and therefore couldn't be seen by whatever nightmare was out there. Reminding herself that she didn't know what it was yet, and that it could easily be a piece of scrub tapping against the hull in a slight breeze, she tentatively crept forwards a few paces. When nothing jumped out at her, she took a more confident step and then another, until she reached the safety of a large rock formation.

Deciding that there was less chance of being seen from the ground if she were on top of the rocks, she climbed up the craggy side and prayed she would also be out of reach. It took a while to ease into a position closer to the pod, and by that time the noises had been replaced by what sounded like voices. The conversation itself was too muffled by the rocks to be heard, but she thought she could make out two women speaking in soft tones.

Hope soared inside that her mama had reached the pod first or that some of the other women from the settlement had escaped and found their way to the clearing. Mirami scrambled over the last few humps, knocking pebbles loose and creating a small cloud of dust in the process. Looking up with the expectation of a welcome sight and a small smile of greeting, she had yet another shock.

∞

There was silence for a moment after Velay's redundant announcement that what they were both unable to look away from was a baby. The tiny child broke it with a snuffled yawn. Swamped in thin, plain brown blankets, the tiny face and one hand poked out of the top, near one of the straps that held it securely to the support mat inside the pod. Tufts of dark, downy hair, curling around the edges of the material, indicated the human heritage of the infant. The face was flushed, as if it had been crying recently, which was hardly surprising given the current situation. While the fingers of the visible hand grasped the empty air in front of it, movement lower down indicated unseen legs kicking at the constraints it felt. Wherever the baby came from, it was certainly active.

The baby gave another yawn and opened its eyes. Reemah felt sucker-punched as they locked on hers. They were different from all the humans' she had seen on the cruiser—not that she had ever paid any of them much attention. Regardless, she was sure she had never seen such a colour before. They held her and drew her in, making her feel a strong urge to protect the helpless child. The feeling was so alien to her that she would need time later to process what was happening. Questions and emotions swirled before her in an endless loop of confusion, with only one clear answer. She would try to help the tiny child with the strange eyes and innocent, trusting expression.

Velay interrupted her thoughts. "What's it doing here?"

"It's not an *it*; it's a..." She gingerly released the straps and unwrapped the clothes to find the answer, quickly rewrapping them after peeking inside. "...him. It's a boy. And I have no idea why anyone would put a baby in a pod all alone, but we can't leave him here." She reached into the pod again.

"Are you sure you should pick it ... him up?"

Reemah gave her a bemused look as she pulled back. "What do you think he's going to do? Pull a blast rod on us or explode or something? He's just a baby."

She went back to trying to figure out how to lift the boy out of the seat without damaging him. She had never done this before and was not confident of her ability to hold him properly. Behind her, she thought she heard Velay muttering something about babies often exploding with fluids, but Reemah shoved that image out of her mind.

As she finally managed to gather the cumbersome bundle awkwardly into her arms and started to remove him from the pod, she caught the dull thud of a bottle falling to the edge of the support mat from the folds of one of the scratchy blankets. She asked Velay to retrieve it, moving out of her way while situating the baby more comfortably.

When Velay handed Reemah the bottle, she shook it and, on finding it three-quarters full, decided to see if the baby was hungry.

"Do you even know what you're doing?"

The wariness in Velay's voice made Reemah look up and give a small shrug. "It can't be that hard, can it? The pointy end goes in his mouth, and then we just wait for him to eat." She put action to words and watched as his little mouth puckered before he began to suck greedily at the liquid. He returned her stare as he fed, and she settled in for the duration, captivated and once more feeling a mixture of pity and protectiveness. Velay went back to muttering again.

∞

Two Esarelian women in the cleanest, brightest white jumpsuits Mirami had ever seen were peering into Elias's life-pod with their backs to her. The hatch hung open in front of the one who sat on the ground, while the other leaned over her shoulder. They seemed to be talking about him. It was only as the one standing turned slightly that Mirami saw for the first time that Elias wasn't in the life-pod any longer. He was caught, gripped firmly by the one sitting down.

It was too much. She had arrived too late, and Elias would be taken away. There was nothing she would be able to do to help him. This was one too many devastating events for Mirami. She scrabbled away, back over the rock as fast as she could, her skinned knees unnoticed. A sob tore from her mouth despite her attempt to stifle it. She couldn't help but see the Esarelians spin around as she dropped back down behind the rocks and out of their sight. Bursting into uncontrollable, wrenching cries, she curled into a ball and let her mind go blank.

∞

Reemah's concentration was broken by a small cry and what sounded like pebbles rattling down the side of a rock behind her. Instinct kicked in, and she swung around, already raising her blast rod with one hand as she clutched the baby defensively to her chest with the other. She was just in time to see the top of a small head duck down behind one of the larger boulders at the edge of the clearing.

Velay had also drawn her weapon but looked chagrined at having been too caught up with their discovery to keep an adequate watch on their rear. No one should have been able to get this close to them without being noticed much sooner. Reemah smiled at her friend in an attempt to halt the inevitable self-recrimination she would feel at having missed the intruder.

Looking back at the rocks, Reemah narrowed her eyes and quickly replayed what she had seen in the instant she turned. A small head, covered with brown hair… She released a small "oh" as realisation dawned. A human child had been watching them. That information made this whole situation more intriguing, but she would deal with the potential implications later. For now, she would take one problem at a time, starting with whoever was hiding behind the cluster of boulders in front of them.

She holstered her weapon and gestured for Velay to do the same, transferring the baby into her uncooperative arms the moment she finally, reluctantly, lowered her rod. It took a ridiculous amount of jiggling and awkward manoeuvring before he was settled again. The entire time, Velay glared at Reemah, and she did not need to read minds to know her friend was thinking something along the lines of *Don't you dare leave this child with me! Take it—him—back right now.* She grinned in response, thanking the universe that Velay would not speak and betray their awareness of their audience.

Moments later, Reemah began to edge across the open ground. She raised her hands in a peaceful gesture in case the youngster was watching and needed reassurance that Reemah no longer held a weapon. When she reached the edge of the clearing, she paused to listen. Gut-wrenching moans slipped around the rocks and straight through her already heightened nerves. She dropped her hands, convinced no one was watching her. Taking a breath and looking back at Velay, who was still holding the baby, Reemah stepped silently through a gap in the boulders.

∞

From out of the darkness behind Mirami's closed eyelids, a voice called out to her. The sound was soothing, if the words themselves were not. *Go and talk to them*, it said.

She shook her head. She couldn't speak to the Esarelians who were going to steal her brother away from her. They would probably punish her and take him anyway. There was nothing she could do, or say, to help him. Another sob escaped at the thought.

Go and talk to them, the voice said again. *I will be with you, and everything will be all right.*

Mirami realised the voice was coming from inside her head, but she could almost feel a hand gently brushing her hair as the words formed. The image made her feel safer, calmer, despite her current situation. She tried to stop the trembling that had overtaken her body and found the task suddenly easier than she'd expected.

Still frightened beyond her ability to call back the voice, Mirami slowly uncurled from the ball she'd tucked into earlier. If she followed the first instruction to get up, maybe the voice would speak again and help her feel even better.

She opened her eyes, hoping that whoever the voice belonged to would be standing in front of her, ready to give her a hug and stroke her hair again. Instead, she wished she'd ignored the voice. It was wrong. The being she saw was not comforting at all; it was one of the Esarelians.

∞

At first, all Reemah saw was a ball of dirty yellow smeared with red. Her nostrils picked out the metallic tang of blood. Slowly, the shuddering cloth unfolded enough to reveal the face of a very young girl. Large, terrified eyes caught Reemah's encroaching movement, and the child scrambled backwards until her back was pressed tightly to the rock. Hair was plastered to her forehead, streaming tears formed cleaner streaks down her dusty face, and her mouth was pressed in a tight line. Her chest rose and fell at an alarming pace, making Reemah fear the girl would hyperventilate.

On impulse, Reemah lowered herself to the ground until she was level with the frightened girl and held out empty hands again for inspection. Reemah's encouraging smile was rewarded when the girl's laboured breathing regulated and slowed. Her eyes stayed wary and continued to dart around as if for an escape route, but it was a start.

Reemah needed answers but decided to start with something simple and innocuous. "What's your name?"

There was no response.

She tried again with something more pertinent, given the situation. "My name's Reemah. I'm not going to hurt you; you're safe with me. Why are you out here? Do you know that baby?"

This time she caught a faint whisper. She leaned closer to make out more of the words. "…killing them all … thinks I don't know … have to … safe…"

Most of what Reemah heard was incoherent, and the parts that did make sense did not give her enough information to work with. She clenched one hand in frustration. She could not blame the child for being afraid. As a Ra'hos, Reemah had power of life and death over any human and probably presented an intimidating image to one so young. She was trying to decide what to do next when the little girl surprised her.

Heaving in deep, shuddering breaths and wiping her face with one grimy arm, the poor thing seemed to be making a gargantuan attempt to calm herself. What she said next was still fairly garbled and choppy but was much easier to understand. "I'll go g-get … someone to, to help…"

Reemah smiled again in a way she hoped conveyed her approval of the idea. She kept her tone soft and soothing when she spoke. "Very well, fetch whoever you need to."

Despite the girl's declared intentions, she remained immobile until Reemah realised the problem and moved a substantial distance away. Only then did the little girl spring into action, darting in the direction of what Reemah assumed to be the large planetary colony. Within seconds, she was out of sight, leaving nothing but a small trail of dust dancing in her wake.

Striding back to the clearing and Velay's disgruntled muttering, Reemah began sorting through her options. Maybe she would be able to get some straight answers from whoever returned with the girl. Reemah was not worried about being ambushed; the child was too frightened to be a plant, and they had their weapons if necessary. Leaving the baby with the girl never even entered Reemah's mind. She was too involved in the mystery to turn back just yet. Besides, she felt such pity for the baby, along with a strange sense of kinship, that she was not sure she would be able to leave him with anyone. The revelation shocked and confused her.

Frowning at the direction her thoughts had taken, she cleared her mind and slammed a lid on her emotions. She did not want Velay picking up on them. She might sense more than Reemah was ready to share, even without specifically reading her.

Feeling a sense of relief as she took the infant back into her arms, she filled Velay in on who had been spying on them and what the human child had said before sprinting off. Reemah bounced the baby and paced the clearing to avoid having to make direct eye contact. From the corner of her eye, she could still see Velay watching her as if she was trying to decide whether Reemah was an imposter or simply deranged from the effects of being planet-side for too long. Eventually, it seemed, she decided.

"We should leave. We're already going to be in trouble if we don't get back soon. And if anyone finds out about us being here, it will be beyond imagining." Velay spoke slowly, cautiously, as if to a child who would not follow basic instructions without being reminded of the consequences. In the circumstances, Reemah supposed that was an apt description.

She sighed while deciding how to frame her answer. "I know. But I can't go yet. I can't leave him on his own out here, and I want to find out what's going on." Looking down at the baby, she tickled his chin. His little hand reached out and fastened around her finger, pulling it towards his mouth. She found she liked the unexpected contact.

Once again, Velay interrupted the moment. "There's no knowing who the girl will bring back here. It could turn nasty. Why couldn't we have left him with her? They're the same species. I'm sure she could have taken him to someone who would be able to look after him."

Unable to answer the question, Reemah decided to ignore it. "You go if you want to. I'm staying here. You can pick me up later." She knew it was a ridiculous statement even as she made it, but she could see no other way to divert Velay from discovering the truth—Reemah did not want to give up the baby.

Instead of replying, Velay walked over and peered down at him and then at Reemah as if trying to understand the fascination. After an interminable pause, Velay's face softened and she blew out a breath. Turning back to the boy, she used one finger to pull the edge of his blanket back so she could get a clearer view of his face. She looked directly into his eyes and said, "You'd better be worth all this trouble."

Relieved that she had her friend's support, Reemah also studied his eyes, which were blinking sleepily. She had an inexplicable feeling he would be worth any amount of trouble he caused.

Chapter 16

Day: 17   Month: 07   Year: 6428
Location: Planet U'Du, main slave settlement

Gilla was exhausted. She'd managed to lead the warriors tracking her to the other end of the settlement before being cornered and revealing the bundle was mere blankets. Instead of punishing her as she expected they would, the three huge Esarelians had simply hauled her back to the Nursery and shoved her past the guards stationed at the door, along with everyone else they'd captured.

Since then she'd been helping the medics with the wounded and traumatised, holding woman after woman in her arms while they poured out their grief. Eventually, they each slumped into oblivion, whether from fatigue, shock, or tranquilisers administered by concerned medics. The process left Gilla feeling guilty that she still had a small window of hope for her son and anxious to get back to him as quickly as possible.

Rising from where she had been kneeling to comfort another victim of the massacre, she stretched back muscles cramped from bending over for so long. She thanked God she'd not had to deal with the bodies of the dead, as some of the other untrained detainees had. The injured woman had a large gash along her temple and down to her jaw from crashing into a table while trying to protect her new-born son. It had taken medics a quarter of a cycle and heavy medication to prise the dead baby from her embrace before dealing with her wound.

Gilla punched her thigh in frustration. They were no longer allowed med-wands, and the split flesh, though bandaged and smothered with soothing gel, would leave a nasty scar. It would be one more painful reminder for the young woman of the day she lost her first child.

Resentment and white-hot anger surged once more inside Gilla at the callous treatment and cruel suffering her people had endured throughout the afternoon, and she battled to control the feelings. Once more, awkward shame that she had escaped her share of the agony followed in its wake. It tortured her to feel relief—joy even—that her son still lived.

She shoved the bittersweet feelings to one side and went back to work. Seeing another woman in need of help on the far side of the large, open atrium they were using to gather the overflow from the med-wing, Gilla made her way in that direction. As she neared, the woman reached out both hands, desperate for human contact to stave off the reality she was facing. Bruised, but not broken or bleeding, she huddled on the floor, all mats having been doubled up already for more serious cases. Her grip was fierce as she pulled Gilla down and buried her head in her shoulder. Incoherent murmurs drifted up, but Gilla blocked them out, simply stroking the woman's matted hair and crooning in response.

It was in that position that Menali found Gilla, about half a cycle later. Her young friend was pale and drawn, her face etched with pain. She moved robotically through the common room and came to a stop a few paces away. Gilla heaved herself upright, releasing her charge to pull a stiff Menali into a hug and ask, "How are you doing?"

"I'm … fine. It's fine." Menali's dazed, almost blank features were more worrying than the bland words she muttered.

Gilla looked around them and, seeing a relatively empty space a short distance away from where they stood, guided an unresisting Menali in that direction. "Come on. Why don't we sit for a while? I'm sure you could use a break too."

Menali finally looked up, and a spark of life came back to her face. Before Gilla could tug her friend down to sit on the floor, she blurted, "I saw Than earlier. He was in here looking for you after they started bringing everyone in, but you'd gone. I think he left with a group of the medics." Her face scrunched in confusion. "Where *did* you go, and why would you come back? Where's Elias?"

Clutching Gilla's arm painfully, panic laced Menali's last question. Gilla could tell that her friend would escalate into hysteria with the slightest provocation and sought a way to soothe her nerves. Pulling her into another hug and whispering in her ear so no others nearby could hear, Gilla said, "My son's still alive. Mirami's watching him in a safe place. I'm sorry. I can't say any more with all these Esarelians around."

It worked; she felt Menali's body relax slightly before a shudder wracked it. The sobs started quietly but gave no indication of stopping any time soon. Gilla held on, stroking thick waves of almost black hair that had escaped Menali's work braid and making soft, comforting noises.

Scanning the room over the smaller woman's shoulder, Gilla felt her own world narrow and tilt. Her nonsense words came to an abrupt halt, along with her breathing, as she stared at the last person she was prepared to see coming through the doors—Mirami. She stood in the main entrance, scanning the room frantically before catching sight of Gilla and rushing over. When Gilla saw the tears streaming down her daughter's face, her heart plummeted into a suddenly clenched stomach. Had something happened to Elias? Was this God's punishment for her silent prayers to be different from the rest of her people? She disentangled herself from Menali and moved forwards a pace or two, braced for whatever news had Mirami in such a state. All else swept from Gilla's mind as her daughter approached.

Slamming into Gilla and clinging to the clothes on her back, the little girl nearly bowled her mother over, knocking the air from her lungs. Mirami was visibly traumatised, panting heavily and unable to draw enough breath to speak. Gilla smoothed her daughter's hair back, soothing and calming Mirami as much as possible. When she had calmed enough to let go, Gilla gently sat her daughter down against the wall, where they could talk unheard, and fetched a canteen of water from the supply table in the centre of the room. Helping her to take small sips to replenish her fluids, Gilla waited, maintaining a calm exterior while hiding her tension, until Mirami could say a few words.

She kept trying to communicate between gasps, but at first, whatever she was trying to say sounded broken and unintelligible. Eventually, she managed to get out enough to turn Gilla's blood cold. "Tried ... shack first ... then came here... Elias ... had to press ... pod's come back ... found him ... got to get back... Sorry, Mama ... two of them ... need you... So sorry..."

The urgency and self-doubt in Mirami's voice twisted the knot in Gilla's stomach even further. Any fault was hers. She wished she'd found another option, that she'd done things differently and not put such a heavy burden on such young shoulders. Rubbing her daughter's upper arms, Gilla said, "You have nothing to be sorry for, Mirami. None of this is your fault. You did everything right, you hear me? It is *not* your fault if anything bad happened. I love you, Mirami, very much. You've done very well."

Even as she calmed her daughter, a fog of panic shrouded Gilla's mind and made clear thinking virtually impossible. How would they get out of the building with guards at every entrance? They'd been lucky earlier, but she was sure the vents would be well guarded now. From what Mirami had managed to say, Gilla assumed that she needed to move quickly, but she had no chance of even leaving the Nursery. What was happening to Elias while they were trapped there? How could she get to him? Had they risked so much, faced so many dangers, to fail now, stuck with all the other women she had pitied less than a cycle ago? *Oh God, please no.* A thought broke through the thick layers of panic, and she asked her daughter, "How did you get in here?"

Mirami looked at her blankly, her fear momentarily forgotten, before saying, "Through the main door."

Gilla rushed to the window at the front of the common room and saw guards and warriors standing in small groups outside, talking amongst themselves. Their demeanour was more relaxed than it had been when she was marched past them earlier, and none were watching the main entrance. It seemed the nightmare was coming to an end, and she would be able to leave freely. She sagged with relief, the panic instantly receding.

Still peering through the window, she saw the reflection of Mirami approach wearily. The sobs had dwindled, but she was still winded, and her breathing was loud. She tugged on Gilla's arm, getting her attention the way she had as a toddler. "Mama. We have to go… Now!"

Unable to talk while they ran, Gilla had discovered nothing more during their trek from the Nursery to the clearing in the wilderness. She still hadn't been able to get Mirami to tell her what had gone wrong, and was frantic with worry. Walking out of the central building after Mirami's plea without even stopping to tell anyone, including Menali, had been nerve-wracking. However, the guards had mostly ignored them as she and Mirami made their way through the main entrance and across the expanse outside. Moving quickly, they had navigated the warren of shacks to the edge of the settlement and not looked back once. No one had followed them, as far as Gilla could tell.

They cautiously approached the clearing where Elias's life-pod had landed, Gilla wondering what she would be facing, and Mirami trembling like a leaf in strong wind. The first thing Gilla saw when she rounded the last of the rocks was the pod. Before she could run the last few spans to retrieve her son, her endeavour was halted by a most frightening sight.

Two Esarelians stood to the side, their backs to her. Unlike the guards stationed on the planet, these wore bright white jumpsuits, with the faint glimmer of their bio-suits peeking out at cuff and collar. Utility belts at their waists held rods that swung with each slight movement they made.

Gilla's first coherent thought was to find a way to get them away from the pod and her son before he was discovered and killed. Futile or not, she searched for any means of distracting them from him. It was only when one turned that she realised it was too late.

The long, almost delicate face was decidedly female with a soft expression. Eyes of bright violet gazed at the bundle she cradled in her arms. Gilla started. Eyes of *royal* violet looked down at Gilla's precious son, still wrapped in the blankets she had used to cushion him from the harness of the pod. The eyes of an Esarelian Ra'hos were fixed on *her* child.

Gilla sank to her knees and bowed low, trembling as much as Mirami had earlier and finally understanding why. Pulling her down as well, Gilla wrapped an arm protectively around her little girl's shoulders. The wait to find out what the Ra'hos would do with them seemed interminable to a mind blank with shock and fear.

"Rise and come forwards. I have been waiting for your arrival for some time and would have answers now." The voice was smooth and clear, demanding but not imperious or angry as far as Gilla could tell. It settled her somewhat, and she did as requested, still gripping Mirami firmly by the hand.

On closer inspection, the royalty before her showed no signs of hostility, and Gilla determined to stay calm and do as bid until she knew more about the situation. It would do her son no good to act rashly, no matter how much her insides screamed for her to grab him and run as far and as fast as she could. She sent a quick prayer heavenward for direction as she pulled herself together, and with her typical quiet resolve, she stepped forwards to meet her fate. She came to a stop several paces in front of the woman who still gently rocked Elias.

"It seems this child has been abandoned in a most peculiar manner." The Ra'hos paused as if to gauge Gilla's reaction to the statement. While her heart tore at the use of the word abandoned and her mind screamed a protest, she managed to keep her face void of expression, not knowing the implications for her small family. Seemingly satisfied with what she saw, the Ra'hos continued. "When we landed, I heard screaming and weapons firing from that direction," she pointed towards the settlement with one finger. "What is going on?"

They were so far out in the wilderness, with so many rock formations and hillocks between them and the settlement, that Gilla could hear nothing. She reminded herself that Esarelian hearing, like so many other things, was far superior to that of any human ability.

Not knowing what Esarelian royalty would want to hear about the atrocities Gilla had witnessed that afternoon and still fearful of the consequences for Elias, she avoided answering at first. *What should I say, Lord?* Though she wanted to shout that Elias was hers and demand that the Esarelian hand him over and leave them alone, something held Gilla back. A strong urge to wait came out of nowhere and blindsided her with its force. Following it, a small breeze ruffled the fine hairs around her temples and brought a calm sense of purpose, which washed through to her bones. She knew what she had to say.

Taking a steadying breath and squeezing Mirami's hand in reassurance, Gilla turned and asked her daughter to wait on the other side of the rocks, outside the clearing. It was plain from Mirami's widened eyes and suddenly much tighter grip that she didn't want to go, but Gilla didn't have time to argue. The last thing she needed was for the seven-year-old to hear that, in reality, the babies were being murdered rather than taken away, or to speak guilelessly about her brother and accidentally reveal to the Esarelians their relationship. More firmly, Gilla said, "You have to trust me. Go and wait in the little nook we passed just before the clearing, and I'll come and get you as soon as I can. I promise. Go on now, Mirami."

Mirami reluctantly started walking in the direction they had come from, looking over her shoulder at nearly every pace until she reached the edge of the clearing.

As soon as she was out of hearing range, Gilla launched into the truth. She told them about her visit from Amina, how it had been interrupted, and the sickening death of her friend. She told them about watching the warriors kill every baby boy they came across, and of them searching the building systematically for any hidden infants. She even told them about the massacre in the settlement, and how her people were herded into the Nursery after each shack had been searched, and how the new ban on technology for humans made treating the injured difficult or, in some cases, impossible.

What she did not tell them was anything about her personal trials during that time. Something told her she needed to find out their intentions before revealing that the baby the Ra'hos held was Gilla's own son. She finished her account with being found and brought back to the clearing by Mirami with no idea what awaited them.

The Esarelians were silent throughout her recitation. They shared occasional looks, and both frowned at the details of the murders, but they said nothing, not to question Gilla or defend their people. When she finished, the silence lasted for a long time. She could see the Ra'hos's hands tighten fractionally, but there was no other reaction until she spoke.

"It seems that, rather than abandon him, this child's mother aimed to save his life. She must love him very much," Reemah stated.

"I'm sure she does," Gilla agreed. *So very much! He is loved beyond reason*, she added in her head.

"However, she cannot know whether his life is still in danger. I will help her in this."

Gilla was about to fall at her feet once more and thank her with every fibre of her being, but the next words out of the Ra'hos stilled Gilla before she could move. She sucked in a silent gasp of agony. Blackness threatened the edges of her vision, and she clamped her lips together until they were numb. A physical blow could not have caused as much pain. She thought she must have misheard, but when she forced her eyes to look up, the expression on the other woman's face confirmed that she had indeed said, "I will adopt him."

∞

Never, when Velay woke up that morning and decided to bust Reemah out of confinement for the day, did she think she would be standing on the disconcertingly soft rock of a planet, breathing sour, unclean air, and witnessing her best—sometimes only—friend essentially decide to commit suicide. Yet there she was. If Velay could go back and start the day again, she would have taken Selah's offer of a trip to the garden suite and happily wandered the flowerbeds for as many cycles as was deemed appropriate. Better that tedium than this sheer lunacy.

The Ra'hon had occasionally balked at their friendship and the situations they got into together but had always been talked down with enough grovelling. This was different, though. This would break so many rules and taboos that it would not just be their association at stake. Velay genuinely feared what would become of them both if news of the day's escapades and Reemah's intended motherhood came out. Velay needed to do something to stop her friend, and fast.

Tempted for the first time ever to break the one sacred vow she had made as a child, Velay reached out with her emotional senses. Before she established a link, she pulled back and slammed a lid on that option. Reemah would never forgive a betrayal of that nature, and Velay feared her friend's reaction even more than the Ra'hon's punishment. Reemah had always been a true friend, no matter how bad things got with the other Hos. There had to be a way to reason with her.

Velay stepped forwards and cleared her throat. She flicked a glance at the human and decided formality was the best way to proceed. "May I speak with you, Ra'hos?" When Reemah turned to her, Velay added more quietly, "In private."

Reemah allowed herself to be half guided, half pulled to the far edge of the clearing, but Velay knew she still needed to tread carefully. She saw the way Reemah held the child and the minute signs in her face, only noticeable to someone who knew her extremely well, that showed how smitten she already was with him.

With another quick visual sweep of the area and a small frown for the human, Velay began. "Do you know what you're doing, Reemah?"

When Reemah kept her eyes on the baby as she opened her mouth to answer, Velay knew that whatever her friend was about to say would be solely based on what she wanted to do next, and not on any of the many possible consequences. Velay hated going against her friend, and very rarely did, but she needed to intervene before it was too late. Holding up a hand to stave off the inevitable plea for help, she plunged ahead with her own viewpoint.

"I know what you want, and I can see how much you want it. But think about what you're saying, Reemah. Someone wants these humans dead, and whatever we think of the decision, we're in no position to overrule that—either of us." She added a pointed look with those words and held it until she was sure she had Reemah's full attention. "We're not supposed to be here or know anything about this. According to internal sensors, you're still in your suite with Selah. How would you explain this? And how do you expect everyone to react? You see how they treat me, and my father's a member of the Hos. This baby is *fully human* and you want to adopt him as your *son*, your *first* son. Think about this; you're not stealing an arrow or consorting with halves and low-born this time. Adopting a baby is a huge commitment, which there's no coming back from. You won't ever be free again. Are you sure you're ready for that?

"It's too much, Reemah. I love you as a sister, and I've been right next to you through every major event in your life, but you can't do this. It's wrong for so many reasons. Your father will never allow it, and I dread to think of what he'll do to both of us if he ever finds out. Can't you leave the baby with the female so we can go home? She obviously has feelings for him, and I'm sure she'll know how to look after him properly. We can find a way for you to visit occasionally and keep an eye on him if you really need to."

Reemah seemed to consider for a moment, while pacing and bouncing the baby. She stopped when she had made a decision, and Velay held her breath while she waited to discover their fate. It would be theirs. Despite what she had said, she would support Reemah with whatever she decided. Their friendship had always worked that way.

"If she'd said the baby was hers, I'd have given him to her. I would never interfere with a mother's rights. But what chance would he have then, given what she's just told us?"

"If it's true," Velay interrupted. She had felt the emotions flow from the human as she related the events of her day and knew them to be genuine, but Velay was out of her comfort zone and suspicious of everything and everyone on the planet. Besides, would Reemah's father really have ordered the wholesale slaughter of innocent babies? That is what would be needed for the warriors to be used on any planet, and it did not bear thinking about.

"If it's true," Reemah conceded. "I believe her, though, and that's something we'll have to talk about later. For now, we need to focus on the baby, and she wouldn't be able to hide him forever. I'm sure there will be a close watch kept for any they missed today, especially if the military were involved. They don't leave loose ends.

"More importantly, she didn't claim him. For all we know, he could be an orphan, and I can help keep him safe. My position and privileges extend to all in my household. They wouldn't be able to touch him if I claim him as my son. I know you think I'm not ready for this—no one will—but I am. Since the explosion, I've been feeling restless and adrift." She huffed and locked eyes with Velay before continuing. "You know I've been feeling that way for a long time, even before that. When I opened that hatch and saw this baby inside, something clicked into place, and I felt like I knew what I had to do and where I had to be. This isn't about proving a point or getting my independence. I've been holding him for the past half cycle, and I've connected with him. I know it makes no sense."

She huffed again and half turned away to stare blindly into the distance. Turning back moments later, she squared her shoulders in a move so familiar that Velay began to realise their reality was, indeed, about to change. She felt Reemah open her emotions, revealing the truth of her next words. "I'm making the right decision, but I won't be able to pull it off alone. Help me do this, please?"

Velay looked down at the baby and tried to decide not if, for that was inevitable, but how soon this would blow up in their faces. Mentally telling him again that he had better be worth it, she gave Reemah the only answer she could. "Oh, blast me now! What do you need me to do?"

∞

Gilla had barely paid any attention to the second Esarelian before she pulled the first away, having eyes only for the one carrying her son. She watched the other more closely as the two whispered together at the opposite side of the clearing. Slightly shorter, yet more lithe and graceful in her movements, she was not so dissimilar to the Ra'hos, apart from the striking green and wide tilt of her eyes.

Straining unsuccessfully to hear what they were discussing while each looked down occasionally at Elias, Gilla still reeled at the Ra'hos's earlier declaration. Her heart was breaking at the same time that hope bloomed. While she felt sick to her core and hated the very thought of her son being raised by an Esarelian, Gilla was aware enough of the implications of the day's massacre to understand that this might be Elias's one chance to live free of constant fear for his life. For that, she would suffer through anything.

With no other recourse in the circumstances, she prayed for the strength and courage to do what must be done. She also thanked God for giving her the foresight to insist Mirami stay away while she talked to the intimidating pair. Watching this would devastate the girl who doted on her young brother. Unable to follow the subtleties of the conversation, Mirami could have easily blurted the truth and unknowingly ruined Elias's opportunity for a much better life than they could provide. Gilla knew intuitively that if the Ra'hos became aware of his parentage for certain, she would not make such a generous offer.

Interrupting Gilla's musings, the two Esarelians approached her once more, and the Ra'hos spoke again. "I am Reemah, first daughter of the

Ra'hon of Esarel, Ashal. I am able to protect this child and have decided that I will do so. My decision stands."

Gilla bowed a more formal acknowledgement and gave her own name in return. Now that Reemah's status as a Ra'hos was confirmed, there was no other option for a slave being addressed by one so far above her. Apart from the occasional glance up, Gilla kept her eyes lowered.

"He must have an Esarelian name if he is to live and thrive among us," Ra'hos Reemah said in a voice that held both warning and compassion. She seemed to be watching Gilla carefully.

"What will you choose, Ra'hos?" Gilla was proud she didn't stumble over the words.

"I will call him Mahsan."

Gilla's universal translator told her that the name meant found, claimed, or wanted, depending on the context. Her heart clutched. He should be none of those things to the Esarelian woman, and he was already all of them to Gilla. She managed to grate out a response around the pain in her chest. "It sounds perfect."

"I will need someone to look after my son here on the planet for a while. There are things that must be taken care of before I can take him home with me. It may take some time. Do you know of anyone…"

Gilla jumped at the dangled opportunity to spend more time with her son, genuinely grateful for the generosity bestowed on her. Having been willing to give him up in order to save his life, she suddenly found she had been given him back. Only for a short while, she reminded herself. It did not matter. Any time with him would be cherished.

Thank you, Lord, for your unfailing love and kindness, for giving me this second chance. I will always be your humble servant. Hiding her sudden shift in emotions, she answered as calmly as she could. "I would be able to do that for you, Ra'hos Reemah."

A smile flickered across the face gazing down at her. "Good. I will pay you for your trouble."

"Oh, there is no need—"

The gaze turned intense, and a frown crossed Ra'hos Reemah's features before they cleared again. Gilla instantly regretted her interruption and bowed her head again in submission.

"I will pay for your services and appoint a guard to protect you both. It is uncertain how long the killing you spoke of will be in effect, and I would not wish Mahsan to become an accidental victim while he remains here on U'du."

Ra'hos Reemah glanced to the other Esarelian and then brought Elias—Gilla couldn't yet think of him by any other name—forward and placed him in her care. After trailing one long finger gently down his soft cheek, the Ra'hos pierced Gilla with another intense look, nodded once, and turned swiftly away.

"Wait here with Velay until I return," the departing figure called out over her shoulder.

Mere moments later, she had moved beyond sight, leaving only an awkward stillness and a rising trail of dust in her wake. A short time after that, a cumbersome transport tub could be seen hovering a short distance away, above the undulating, rock-strewn wasteland, and then shooting skyward in a direction Gilla could only presume would lead to the space cruiser where the Ra'hos lived ... and that would soon be Elias' home.

Shaking the heart-breaking thought, Gilla concentrated on the present and was finally able to enjoy the weight of her son in her arms once more. His eyes were open, and his hand was grasping in the familiar action she wanted to burn into her memory forever. She stayed that way, content simply to gaze down at him, until reality intruded once more.

Her temporary high crashed with the realisation that Mirami still waited beyond the rocks and would probably be terrified for them, especially as the sun was close to setting. Unsure of Velay's intentions or her instructions from Ra'hos Reemah, Gilla peered across at the quiet Esarelian from beneath her lashes. Velay was leaning against a rock, directly in the sun's path, as if bathing in the lengthening rays. Her eyes were closed, and she seemed relaxed enough.

Gilla decided to be over-cautious in her still precarious position and approached on soft feet. Although she had made little noise, Velay's eyes snapped open when Gilla came within two arm's lengths. A small, begrudgingly amused smile lifted the corners of the Esarelian's mouth. She seemed willing to wait for Gilla to speak first.

Clearing her throat, Gilla took one more step forward, bowed her head, and said, "My daughter is waiting for me, and it will be dark soon. May I go to explain the situation and send her home for the night? I won't take long and will return immediately. She's just beyond those rocks."

Velay assessed Gilla for long moments, nodded, and returned to her previous position. Gilla no longer thought the Esarelian relaxed, however. She was more like a hunting animal, very aware of her surroundings and waiting to pounce as soon as her unwitting prey made a wrong move. It unnerved Gilla, and she hurried away, wrapping her arms more tightly around Elias and tucking him under her chin.

She found Mirami huddled exactly where she'd been told to wait when they first arrived at the clearing. The little girl looked exhausted, as if the weight of two worlds sat on her shoulders. Gilla felt a spasm of guilt at all she'd been forced to ask of her daughter that day and vowed to protect her as much as possible from further pain.

To that end, Gilla needed to get Mirami back to the settlement before Ra'hos Reemah returned. The bargain they had struck would be hard enough to handle without having to console Mirami. Gilla also wanted her daughter isolated from any danger should the Esarelians prove false and bring warriors down on them. After all, the Ra'hos *had* left a guard of sorts to watch Gilla while she waited.

Shifting Elias to one hip and crouching down, Gilla reached out and gently shook Mirami's knee. "Wake up, Mirami. It's me. Time to go home, Kiddo."

Mirami jerked awake and instantly shot up to look around them. Gilla smiled and drew her daughter's attention to Elias, knowing it would settle her to see him. It did. Mirami exclaimed and threw herself at his bundle, pressing her cheek as close to his as she could. Enjoying the tender moment, and not wanting to break it, Gilla extricated one hand and hugged both her children.

Reluctantly, she finally moved back and pulled Mirami's face up. Knowing she was about to burst with questions, Gilla forestalled them with a look and spoke first, quietly so Velay couldn't hear them. "It's all right. I've got Elias, and he's safe. The Esarelians back there who found him are from the royal family, and they're going to help us. I think they feel sorry for everything that's happening here. Anyway, they're bringing someone to guard us so the warriors can't get to your brother. I have to stay here and wait for them, but I don't know how long that's going to take. I need you to go and tell your uncle Than what's happened and let him know we're all safe. Stay with him until I come for you, and try not to worry; it's all over now, and I'll be home soon."

Gilla would never actually lie to her daughter but knew that hadn't been the complete truth either. Mirami was at the end of her endurance, though, and there would be time for the rest later. Gilla watched a range of emotions cross Mirami's small face as she processed the news.

One thing became instantly clear: she did not want to leave them. "No, Mama, please don't make me. I want to stay here with you. I don't mind waiting, really, and I can help with Elias."

"Shhh, not so loud." Gilla couldn't think of a valid reason she could give for why they should keep their voices down but was saved from having to as Mirami ducked her head and clung to her mother in a silent request.

Gilla whispered her next words. "It's going to be dark soon, Mirami, and you're tired. Please go back to the settlement; you need to get some rest. Besides, Uncle Than will be worried about us. Won't you help me by telling him we're safe and not hurt?"

After a moment, the sensation of a head nodding against her chest brought the first moment of true relief since she saw Mirami appear in the Nursery building earlier, crying and desolate. Gilla kissed the section of hair she could reach and squeezed her approval before helping her eldest child stand and, for what seemed the millionth time that day, watching her run away as fast as she could.

With resolution, Gilla turned and trudged back to the clearing, to a waiting Velay, and to an uncertain future.

Chapter 17

Day: 17   Month: 07   Year: 6428
Location: Planet U'Du, main slave settlement

It had taken more than a cycle after joining forces with Aronin and the others for Than to discover the identity of the woman killed by the warriors. It hadn't been Gilla, and the relief that had flooded him upon hearing the news had had him dropping to his knees in thanks to God. Guilt had followed quickly on its heels for feeling such elation at another innocent woman's death. Helplessness had trailed that thought, and it had been all Than could do to keep going with his search for Gilla.

With no sign of her *or* Mirami over the ensuing cycles, he'd finally allowed himself to believe there was a possibility his nephew had somehow escaped the slaughter. If the little one had been killed, his mother would have been caught, and word would surely have reached Than. What worried him now was where Gilla was and how long she could remain hidden.

He had to acknowledge one thing about the warriors: they'd been ruthlessly systematic in their search of the wider settlement. It had become more and more difficult for him and his friends to remain undetected. In fact, had it not been for the secret rooms carved deep into the rock beneath several shacks, where they'd waited for patrols to pass, Than's group would have been found more than a cycle before the incursion ended and the warriors withdrew to the flight centre. How Gilla had managed it—if indeed she had—Than had no idea.

Having deployed most of their men to assist in other areas early on, Aronin, Willan, and Pinna remained with Than. They checked Gilla's home several times, setting a local boy to watch the shack in case she returned, and then spread out to search Damaya's shack, the prep rooms, and anywhere else he could think of that she might have gone. He would have tried the wilderness, where they'd played together as children and where he still trained as part of the resistance, but he knew she wouldn't have been able to get Elias past the perimeter drones he'd heard. The bodies outside the Nursery had been proof of that.

The work sectors had remained on lockdown throughout the day, with both guards and warriors posted at all checkpoints. Huge crowds of workers had gathered there, attempting to get back into the settlement to aid their families. While they hadn't been forced to return to their work, they hadn't been allowed past the sector borders either. It made Than grateful that he'd left his post as soon as he heard rumours of the murders and that he knew how to get out of his sector unseen.

He didn't think there was much chance Gilla would have gone to her work place, or that she'd have been able to hide a baby inside if she had, but they'd run out of places to look. Than and Aronin managed to sneak into the manufacturing sector and check her building to be certain. Fearful of discovery, Than quickly moved away from a heated argument between a worker and his team leader over whether a misfiring life-pod would be counted against the tally for the day. Otherwise, there was nothing out of the ordinary and no sign of Gilla there either.

When the encroaching darkness made it difficult to continue searching, they regrouped at Gilla's shack to decide what, if anything, to do next. Though it seemed the warriors had finished their grisly task and were preparing to leave, chaos still reigned throughout the settlement, and there were many areas where the resistance leaders were needed. However reluctantly, Than could see the wisdom of focusing their efforts elsewhere.

He just couldn't bring himself to give up. Not yet. He owed it to his sister, and Elias, to keep looking until they were discovered, even if it took all night. Than was about to say as much when he heard a commotion outside. When his name was shouted in apparent desperation moments later, he rushed to the door.

∞

It felt to Mirami as if she'd been running for five days straight. Her legs were rubber, and her lungs burned. Both sensations were becoming extremely familiar to her. Pushing through the discomfort, knowing if she stopped she was unlikely to start again, she closed the gap between herself and the settlement she could now see in the distance.

At her current speed, she thought she would just reach her destination before the freezing cold of full night fell. She would need to. The prospect of being stranded, on her own, in the wastelands, after dark was too terrifying even to think about. Keeping her eyes on the scattering of shacks at the nearest edge of the settlement, she blocked out everything except reaching them.

The colours cast by the setting sun both astonished and awed her. She'd never really paid it any attention before and was surprised at the rich hues created by the low angle of the rays. The sky held slashes of red, orange, and gold while the rocks around her were awash with a rosy blush that warmed her soul even as the dropping temperature cooled her skin. Farther away, at the point where the molten globe sank into the horizon, the surface of the planet came alive with deeper shades of magenta and plum. It was beautiful. Had she not needed to reach home before dark overtook her, she would have stopped and stared in wonder. However, that need pressed down on her, and she turned her eyes to the approaching settlement once again.

Eventually, as the sun was disappearing below the horizon and a chill chased her across the ground, she stumbled to a halt beside the first shack she came to, bracing her arm against the wall and heaving in gasping breaths. It took some time to reach a point where she could once more hold her weight on her legs unaided and even longer before she could move again. By the time she dragged herself along the twisting passages and into the settlement proper, darkness had shrouded the last of the light, and she shivered with the cold.

She made her way to the shack she and her mama had been sharing with Uncle Than since the Selection. Not knowing whether he would be there after the day they'd just experienced, it still seemed the best place to start. Besides, Mirami was so tired she needed her sleeping mat. Jogging through the tunnel-like passages, she tried to ignore the feeling that she should have stayed with her mama and that something very bad would happen while she was alone.

It took longer than usual for Mirami to get to her family's shack, as she had to skirt several clusters of mourners blocking her route, but she made it without her legs giving out. Sitting outside, wrapped in a blanket and chewing on a small piece of uduin, was Damaya's son, Gerom. Mirami was startled to see him there but didn't have the energy to question it. Instead, she raised a hand to him in a mini-wave as she passed on her way to the door.

He jumped up and barred her entry. Blinking in surprise and too tired to play silly games, she moved to go around him. "Get out of my way, Gerom."

Again, he put himself in front of her, this time folding his arms and puffing up his chest in an attempt at intimidation. She stamped her foot and told him to move, but he stayed where he was.

"You can't go in there. They're talking." He said it as if he'd been given the most important job in the world and those sentences explained everything they needed to.

"Who are? You know what, I don't care. That's *my* shack, and you can't stop me going home."

"Can't I? Watch me." He grabbed her around the middle and lifted her off her feet to swing her away from the door. Three years separated them, and he was much taller than her. Limbs that used to be spindly had started to strengthen with the work he now did in the processing sector. The only difference her struggling made was to twist her uniform and knock his messy curls into his eyes. Normally a little jealous of his lovely hair, right then she just wanted to tug on it in frustration.

"Let me go! Let me go! I need to see my uncle. Uncle Than! Uncle Than!"

By the time she screeched the last demand for her uncle, the man himself stood before them. Half the neighbours watched too, some from doorways and windows, others from the street where they had come running on hearing her cries. Feeling guilty for causing any distress after the day they'd all had, she lowered her eyes as they filled, and her cheeks heated with shame. She could see her uncle frowning but couldn't tell whether it was at her for yelling or at Gerom for hauling her around like a sack of laundry. Uncle Than's low voice, when he did speak, sounded more worried than angry. "What's going on here?"

"She was about to interrupt your meeting—"

"He wouldn't let me through—"

They both spluttered their explanations at the same time, and her uncle held up a hand for silence. As he stalked towards them, they arranged themselves into a more presentable tableau. Gerom let her go and smoothed the mop of hair off his face, while she righted her clothing and stepped out of his reach, just in case he got any more ideas about manhandling her. He still had an infuriatingly superior look on his face, which, if she was a little younger and not in training, she would wish she could splatter with a handful of grey mud.

Expecting a lecture on creating so much noise and disturbing the neighbourhood, Mirami was surprised when her uncle kneeled down in front of her and pulled her into a tight hug. She wrapped her arms around his neck in an automatic response, being careful not to knock his healing shoulder. He was warm and smelled like home. Tempted to cry with relief at the feel of an adult who loved her offering comfort, she reminded herself that Gerom still stood beside them and sniffed away the tears.

Uncle Than must have heard the snuffling, because he pulled back and looked intently at her face. Still ignoring everyone else on the path between shacks, he brushed a few strands of hair off her forehead and gave her a quick wink with the grin he wore like a comfortable blanket across his face. "Come inside, Kiddo. You're freezing, and I'll bet you could do with some food before you sleep."

"I need to tell you what happened to me and Mama today," she blurted, her main purpose for racing back to the settlement hitting her with its urgency once more.

"That too. I want to hear everything, but let's get you warm first. All right?"

She nodded and rubbed her arms.

Uncle Than stood and put his hand around her shoulder, guiding her towards the shack. She couldn't resist turning her head to stick her tongue out at Gerom as they passed him on their way inside. Who did he think he was to keep her out of her own home? His face scrunched up and darkened like a thundercloud as silent reply, their longstanding feud still going strong. She was too tired to worry about how he would pay her back for winning this round, so she ignored him and stepped into the warmth of the only home she had ever known.

It felt different. At first she couldn't understand why, but then her gaze landed on several figures hunched over the table and leaning against the far wall. Her forward momentum came to an abrupt halt. With effort, her overloaded brain sifted through some of Gerom's earlier words and picked out "they're" and "meeting". Unable to fit those pieces together in a way that adequately explained the sudden presence of these strange adults *here*, in her mama's space, and with nothing else to go on, Mirami let her uncle usher her to a stool hastily vacated by a much smaller man.

He was thin and had a scruffy beard that he kept pulling. He stood next to a larger man with a scar half hidden behind a short beard, looking askance at her every so often and making her uncomfortable. She turned her attention to the next man, who had gentle eyes and a soft smile as he watched her slowly chew the uduin Uncle Than placed before her. Huddling further into the blanket he had also provided, she waited nervously for one of them to tell her who they were and why they were in her shack.

Uncle Than introduced the men to her as friends of his and her daddy, calling the older, smaller man Willan and the large one, who looked powerful enough to take down a Baketag but made her feel less self-conscious, Aronin. The third man, lost in the shadows of the corner, was Pinna. Uncle Than told her they were there because they'd been helping him look for her and her mama, but that they would be gone soon; they just wanted to hear her news first, if she was brave enough to tell them. The details of his words washed over her. Only his comforting presence as he pulled the second stool close and tucked her into his side penetrated the fog of exhaustion lulling her eyelids closed.

She ducked her head and bit off another piece of uduin while the warmth of the blanket seeped through her skin and into her bones. As her thoughts drifted, they snagged on the message from her mama, and Mirami jerked upright again.

Turning to look up at her uncle and block out the others filling the small room, Mirami relayed the events of the extremely long day. She stumbled over her words at some points, and at other times, his face blurred in front of her as she cried. When she couldn't look him in the eye, she absently tugged at a frayed end of lilac bark twine that was poking out from where it had been tied off underneath the edge of the crudely constructed table. Occasionally, as she told her story, she glanced at the three strange men looming in the background and trembled uncontrollably with nerves. At one point, the large man, Aronin, had to restrain the smaller man, whose name she had already forgotten. Mirami moved closer to her uncle then, not understanding what had caused the anger in the room but wanting to get away from the other men's fearsome expressions.

Eventually, she finished with her mama talking to the Ra'hos who would help them and then sending her back to the settlement to tell Uncle Than what had happened. Since Mirami had started speaking, he hadn't said a word. She looked up at him as her words trailed off and tried to make out what he was thinking from his expression in the dim light of the globe. The silence pressed in on her, making her feel as if her ears were about to pop.

"You should get some rest for what's left of the night, Kiddo. Thank you for telling me what happened. I think you did great, and I'm so proud of you." He squeezed her for long moments and tilted her face up to make sure she'd heard him before unwrapping her blanket cocoon and ushering her to the back room and the sleeping mat that was calling her name.

As she got ready for bed with sluggish, robotic movements, she accepted that having to return home had been a good thing. She was glad to be in her own corner with her own blankets and her uncle next door to protect her. The one thing that would have made it better would have been for the rest of her family to be next to her. That and for the raised voices in the main room to be quiet, although even the angry shouts and harsh, half-whispered replies soon sounded muddled and far away as sleep claimed her.

∞

Seeing Mirami caught up in Gerom's grasping, tangled arms outside Gilla's shack had momentarily stunned Than. He'd walked towards her, half afraid she was a figment of his fevered imagination and would disintegrate into the atmosphere at any time. When he'd hugged her, he'd been shocked at how cold she was and had realised that wherever she'd been, it would take some telling and was probably still affecting her. He'd vowed to be gentle with her, no matter how desperate he was for news of Gilla and Elias.

Shutting the door to the small sleeping chamber after making sure Mirami was settled for the remainder of the night, Than walked over to the stool he'd sat on while listening to her recount her experiences and sank back down onto it. He stared at his open hands before him, silently wondering at the extraordinary events of the day. His thigh bounced, drawing his excess energy, as his mind processed everything they had been told. His nephew was alive. For that alone he would forever be grateful to God; his desperate prayers since he'd first heard of the slaughter had been answered.

While he was lost in thought, Aronin dropped onto the second stool like a giant onto a matchstick. The wood creaked as he settled but held firm. Clasping Than's good shoulder in support, Aronin ran his other hand through his short hair.

Predictably, Willan was the first to break the silence. He'd been bursting with whatever was on his mind since halfway through Mirami's tale, pulling on his beard and tapping his fingers, and could contain himself no longer. He stepped towards the table and into the light, his face a mask of fury as he spat, "We can't trust the Esarelian. We have to get Gilla and Elias back here before it's too late."

Looking up at him, Than shrugged his shoulders, wincing slightly at the tug of healing muscles the unconscious gesture had caused. "We can't. It's the middle of the night, and we don't even know where she is."

"Then we need to ask Mirami. She must rem—"

"Not going to happen, Willan." Than interrupted before the incensed man could go any further down that track of inquiry. "She needs to sleep; she's only seven years old. She's exhausted, half frozen, and she's had a horrendous day by anyone's standards. Didn't you hear what she's been through?"

"Yes," Aronin joined in. "It's a miracle little Elias is still alive. We need to do all we can to help them, but morning will be soon enough to figure things out."

Willan leaned over the table with both hands flat on the surface, providing stability to a man on the edge. "Miracle you say. Huh! One baby left alive out of more than a hundred. They were killed for *nothing*, and there's only *one* left, thanks to the quick thinking of his mother." He raised one finger close to their faces in emphasis for a long moment and then waved the hand in a disdainful gesture with his next angry words. "Yes, God's surely looking after His favourite people with this mighty miracle of His. I keep telling you—we're on our own!" Folding his arms across his chest, he glared defiance at them, challenging them to dispute his statement.

Than spoke just as fiercely, although in a forced whisper. "Keep your voice down. Mirami's sleeping next door, and I do *not* want her disturbed. Besides, this wasn't God's doing." His voice became softer and even quieter as he said, "Maybe it was ours. We thought we got away with the attack. Nothing happened for days afterwards while we worried and laid low. But we should have known they wouldn't let something that major go unpunished. Maybe this was it. Maybe this was their revenge on the whole settlement because they couldn't find *us*." To himself, he added, *maybe Nali's right, and we shouldn't make them angry at all.*

Aronin turned to Than, trying to make eye contact, but he kept his head down, not wanting the others to see his pain and self-recrimination. The things he'd seen when he finally got inside the Nursery... the bodies. He shuddered and closed his eyes on the images that haunted him.

"This wasn't God's doing, *or ours*. It was the Esarelians. They are cold and heartless, and one day they'll have to answer for it. And if not in this life, then in the next." Aronin's voice was clear and resonated with conviction. It helped bolster Than, until Willan brought the conversation back to reality.

"Then we definitely can't trust one with the only boy we have left," Willan said. "There's no way she actually wants to *help* them."

Saving Than from having to, Aronin answered. "Well, there's nothing we can do about it now. We'll have to wait and see what Gilla says when she gets back."

Willan huffed again before throwing his hands in the air and storming out of the shack, leaving the door swinging behind him. Than stood to close it, needing the movement to help settle him again. He watched Willan's shadowy form stalk between two shacks and disappear around a bend in the path. From behind, Than heard Aronin tell Pinna to let Willan go, saying he needed to cool off and clear his head on his own. Than returned to the others, sighing and wishing he had the same option to walk away.

"I'll keep a close eye on Mirami—make sure she's coping with everything."

"Poor kid," Pinna said, looking towards the door to the back room. "She's been through so much."

Than completely agreed, though all he said was, "She's tough, just like her mother. And her father."

"We'll all watch out for her, Than. It's the least we can do for Elias." Aronin rose, stretched his back, and tilted his head towards the main door, catching Pinna's eye. "We'll see you tomorrow, Than. Don't worry about your shift; I'm sure we can get someone to cover it until we find out what's going on with Gilla and the little one. The news will be good, I know it. God's been watching over him so far, and He won't let anything happen to him now. Not after everything today."

"You're right. I know it too. Are you sure about the shift? I can manage fairly well now, and you know I'm not on the double shifts yet. I only escaped from the med-wing the day before yesterday."

At Aronin's determined nod, Than nodded appreciatively in reply and added his thanks for their support.

Before they could say anything more or take their leave, there was a knock on the door. Than spun around, surprised at the sound so late at night and wondering if Willan had returned. When he pulled the door open, however, causing the bark strip hinges to twist and creak at the sudden movement, his mind ground to an abrupt halt, and his mouth fell agape.

∞

Menali was devastated. Looking after the children in the Nursery was her life, and spending time with the babies had been her greatest pleasure. They were the only extended family she'd allowed herself for more years than she could remember, and now half of them were gone. All those boys, such precious children, gone in the space of a single day. The horror washed over her in waves that threatened to drown her with each rising swell. The serviceable braid she wove her hair into before each shift had worked loose, and straggly tendrils refused to stay tucked behind her ears. Her face, drenched with tears, was blotchy and puffy, and her body felt weighed down so that each step dragged.

She was in no state to complete her current errand and had no wish to either, but as always, when someone asked for help, she responded. Cursing her obliging nature, she reached forwards and knocked as confidently as she could in the circumstances. It sounded a timid tapping in her ears, and she was startled when the door swung wide only a moment later.

Looking handsome, if a little rumpled after his frantic day-long search for his sister and nephew, Than stood just inside the entrance. The comparison between the two of them could hardly have been more profound. Again, she regretted agreeing to come here this evening instead of waiting for morning, when Damaya could have come herself.

Damaya had exploded into the Nursery earlier that evening looking for Gilla. On finding her and little Elias missing, with no clue as to their whereabouts, she'd invited Menali home for a quiet chat and to get her away from the horrors of the day. They must have been plainly written across her face from the look Damaya had given her. Menali had readily accepted the offer and had allowed herself to be ushered out with the briefest nod to her supervisor. Her body had felt as if it belonged to someone else and she was merely a spectator, watching as it had responded to Damaya's prompts to sit, eat, and finally drink. Menali had been slowly regaining control of her senses and releasing the stress through a long bout of blubbering when they were interrupted by Gerom.

When he'd flown into Damaya's shack a half cycle ago, he'd been flustered about Mirami's return to the settlement. He'd babbled something about a job going wrong and never being trusted again, and it had been obvious that Damaya would need to calm him before she could investigate his wild ramblings. Recognising her desperate need for news of Gilla, Menali had volunteered to find out what was going on. Now, she wished she'd stayed quiet.

Admittedly, Damaya could hardly have left her son in such an agitated state, and neither of them would have slept a wink while waiting until morning for news. Why did it have to be Menali, though? Why couldn't she have left Damaya's before Gerom returned, or have bumped into someone else on the way, who could have then talked to the unsettlingly roguish man holding the door open?

Than still hadn't said anything, and Menali paused, uncertain. Did she look that bad? *At least he won't try to toy with me again*, she thought, trying to look on the bright side. She began to grow more and more uncomfortable, standing on the path in front of the shack, and wondered whether she should retreat and send Damaya in the morning after all. As Menali finally began to step away, he seemed to come back to himself with a shake. He reached towards her with one arm while sweeping the other back in a gesture of welcome. She thought she heard a quiet strangled sound come out of his mouth before he cleared his throat and said, "Nali! What are you doing here? Come in, please."

Stepping past Than into the dim interior of the shack—nearly identical to every other hastily built dwelling—Menali had a sudden impression of a family of her own sitting around the table, in a place where they could have a small piece of privacy together. It was gone before she fully grasped it, but it left her with a sense of loss that twisted her already shredded heart.

As she blinked away the last vestiges of the image, she realised they were not alone. That was good. She'd be able to handle talking to Than with others present. All she needed to do was ask a few questions, find out the basic details, and get out again. After returning to Damaya's to pass on the information, Menali could trudge back to her dormitory in peace. Then she would sink into her sleeping mat with a blanket wrapped around her head to block out the world for a few cycles.

Her safety in numbers vanished as the two other men said their goodbyes and slid out the door. She didn't miss the wink the taller, familiar-looking man gave Than on leaving, and her confidence plummeted even further. Twisting her fingers together in the silence that followed their departure, she avoided Than's gaze and thought of how to start. In the end, they spoke together.

"How are you?"

"How are you?"

Blinking at their identical wording, Than's face relaxed into a wide smile, and he leaned casually against the far wall, giving her plenty of room to feel comfortable. It was an insightful gesture, which she appreciated even as she wondered why he would think to do such a thing. Warming to him despite her internal warnings, she peered more closely and noticed the compassion in his eyes. Rather than address it, she focused on her task and asked about Mirami.

"She's asleep next door," Than replied. "She was on her last legs when she made it home, but she told us what happened to them. Gilla and Elias are safe. It's a bit of a long story, and you probably won't believe half of it—I'm not sure I can, really—but the important thing is that he's alive, and they're staying outside the settlement for the night."

After hearing they were both safe, Menali sagged with relief. Her friend had escaped a second time, and Menali finally had something to be thankful for this day. Her eyes closed, and she said a quick prayer under her breath for the woman who had been more sister than friend over the last few years. Although surprised and concerned when Than went on to mention an Esarelian being involved, after the shocks of that day, Menali didn't have the emotional energy to do more than scrunch her eyebrows to show her confusion.

She was saved from having to formulate a verbal response when Than spoke again. It seemed he hadn't been distracted from his earlier concern after all. "What about you, Nali? Today must have been terrible for you. Gilla always said when we were growing up that everything looked better after a hug, and you look like you could use one..."

The way he said it, so like his sister, sounded innocent, with no ulterior motive other than to support a friend in need. His body language, when Menali peeked over, suggested the same. Not knowing what to say to such an unexpected offer, and only having vague and distant memories of what it felt like to be held by a protective man, she stumbled over her answer. Feeling flustered yet again in his presence, the truth tumbled from her lips before anything else. "I probably need a hug more than anything right about now. It's been so... Today just... I can't..."

There were no words, but it turned out that none were needed. He cautiously approached and wrapped his strong arms around her. She'd not been hugged by a man since her father, too many years before to count, and hadn't realised how much she missed it. It felt comforting; more so than any embrace from Damaya or Gilla, and Menali absently wondered why that was. His body was lean and warm, the worn fabric of his jumpsuit faded and soft under her cheek. Why those things equated to a sense of complete peace, she couldn't bring herself to examine too closely. Instinct warned her that this was too easy, too natural, and too good. She pulled back.

As she did so, she noticed his shoulder flinch. Worried that she'd accidentally hurt him, she uncharacteristically spoke without thinking through the consequences or implications. "Oh, your shoulder! Do you need help with it?"

His eyes jumped to hers and assessed her as heat crept up her neck and cheeks. His words, when they came, were careful and deliberate. "Thank you, but you don't have to do that. Gilla's been helping me change the dressings at night, but after today..." He trailed off, the worry for his sister etched on his face. Visibly pulling himself together, he continued in a more cheerful tone. "It completely slipped my mind. I can leave it till the morning this once. Maybe I'll ask Dee to help until we find out what's happening with the little one. She *can* be a bit rough, but I can handle it."

Feeling that retreat would be more humiliating at this point than anything else, Menali swallowed her doubts and forged ahead. "Don't be silly. It's still healing, and I can help you with it. It's not a problem."

They both knew that it *was* a problem. She was sure he could hear her heart trying to jump out of her chest, and even without its incessant pounding, the blush across her face gave her true feelings away. Sternly telling herself it was no different than being in the Nursery, dealing with Petran's many scrapes and cuts, she gathered her courage and gave Than a determined nudge towards the cupboard containing his clean bandages and salve.

After gathering the supplies she would need, Than sat on the stool closest to the globe. He undid the front of his jumpsuit and gently pulled it just far enough down his shoulder for her to reach the edge of the dressing. He then sat perfectly still, angled slightly away from her so she could get to work.

She moved quickly and efficiently, removing the old covering before cleansing and applying an even layer of the thick healing gel. Without looking anywhere other than at the table or his wound, she managed to wrap the bandage around the affected area and secure it in place. The whole process took no time at all, and she didn't once notice the warmth of his skin or the softness of his hair where her hand touched it in passing. She was soon tidying up while he re-dressed behind her.

Again grateful to him, this time that he had not spoken during her ministrations and made the whole procedure more awkward, she let her guard down and smiled as she turned to face him once more. His hands stilled on the fastening of his jumpsuit, and his eyes did the melting thing they occasionally did when he stared at her so intently. A gamut of emotions swept across his face before he whispered, "Nali…"

Seemingly as startled as she by his reaction to her, he threw on his customary grin and casually said, "So, you want to see me semi-naked again tomorrow? You're much gentler than Dee and cuter too." He followed the request with a wink.

It was the reminder of his true character that she needed. He was playing with her again, as he would with any female paying him attention. Feeling foolish for not following her own rules and allowing him to get to her so easily, she crossed her arms over her chest to shore up her defences. She ruthlessly squashed the recollection of his hands rubbing her back less than half a cycle earlier and pulled up to her full height. Knowing not to look directly at his eyes for fear of what she might encounter, she focused her gaze at the wall over his left shoulder as she spoke in clipped sentences.

"I don't think that would be a good idea. I'll tell Dee what Mirami said about Gilla and Elias; she's been worried sick all evening. I'll also ask her to help with your wound in the morning. Although, if she's too rough, I'm sure there are any number of women who would gladly take her place as your medic. It's late, and I should go. Good night."

He tried to interrupt her, but she ignored whatever it was he was saying. It would no doubt be something charming that aimed to draw her in until she was putty in his hands. Then he would grow bored and move on to the next target of his flighty affections. No, she was better on her own. As resolutely as she could, she walked to the door, pulled it open, and stepped out into the bracing cold, the last remnants of her fragile feelings blowing away as she went.

∞

Than watched Menali walk away and felt like punching the wall. Frustration gnawed at him. He'd been doing so well. Remembering Gilla's advice after his last encounter alone with Menali, he'd been giving her space and not pushing or flirting too much. When would he learn? She wasn't like the other women he'd been around; she was sweet, caring, generous, supportive, hardworking, innocent, and shy. Everything he finally knew he wanted in a life partner. But that was the problem. She was so shy and uncertain of him that he had to take baby steps each time they were together.

Running his hand through his short hair, he pinpointed the exact moment he'd lost her. It was the wink. He'd had to hold his breath while she worked on his shoulder. Her nearness had spiked his nerves and heightened his awareness of her every move. Her slender fingers had been sure and warm on his shoulder, and the fact that she'd willingly tended to him after the day she'd had floored him.

When she'd smiled at him as he covered up, the horror that had ravaged her earlier expression had fallen away, and all he could see was the beautiful young woman he first met on the day of the Selection. His heart had burst from his body and sat squarely under her little heel, ready for her to crush or pick up as she wished. He'd never felt this way about anyone before, not even family. He'd panicked. Falling back on the familiar had given him much-needed moments to gather himself and coax his heart back under his own control once more. Unfortunately, the flirty comment had had the opposite effect on her, and the wink had clinched it. She'd shut down and run, and he couldn't blame her.

He'd tried to explain that he didn't mean it, that it had come out wrong, even that she made him so nervous that he couldn't think straight around her. Thankfully, by that point she hadn't been listening to anything he said, or he would have been mentally kicking himself for a different reason. Knowing there was no way to make things worse, he called after her a promise he intended to keep.

"You're wrong about me, and I'm going to prove it to you, you hear me? I'm not giving up on you, Nali. I won't." He quietly added to himself, "I can't; I'm falling for you."

Chapter 18

Date: 311.428.150
Location: Esarelian Primary Space Cruiser, transport hangar bay

Lorith stepped off the large military tub and onto the solid metal floor of the cruiser's hangar with a sense of weary relief. Stretching tight muscles, he paused to one side of the ramp while his elite squadrons marched past him to the cramped quarters of the warrior sector. He had debriefed them on the flight up from the planet, and most were more than ready for a cleansing cubicle and as many uninterrupted cycles of rest as they could get. As they had just completed a difficult yet important mission, he could not blame them. Absently noting that they were not creating as much noise as they typically would on their return home, he decided to push up their training schedule to prevent them overthinking the events of the previous day.

As the last squad disembarked, one of his seconds, Merin, approached. "It is good to see you, Na'hor. How did it go?"

Merin tossed Lorith some uduin, knowing his bizarre penchant for the tasteless but nutrient-rich blocks after planet-side or difficult missions. Lorith shot his closest friend a look in return, which was all that was needed for the other male to know how the mission had fared—and that he appreciated the snack.

Taking a moment to unwrap and bite into his favourite post-work rations, Lorith drifted back to the times as a child when he had accompanied his father on survival expeditions to various planets. Upon their return to the cruiser, they had always shared a portion of uduin to bulk up and counter any hunger experienced while away. Those trips were some of only a few precious memories Lorith had of his father before his untimely assassination. Lorith shook off the recollection before it took him too far down a path towards yet another round of futile investigations aimed at restitution.

Instead, he turned his attention back to the present and Merin patiently standing at the base of the ramp. Eyes the colour of storm clouds surveyed the hangar before them. They were quick, indicative of a sharp intelligence that had ferreted out their hidden enemies and saved their lives on more than one occasion. Lorith trusted his friend more than anyone in the known universe. They had been inseparable since early childhood, joining the military together and rising through the ranks. Lorith was all but safe from plots with Merin at his back.

All too aware that they could not speak freely in front of the labourers dotted around the hangar, Lorith used the hand signals they had developed as young boys together to ask what he had missed while on U'du. Aloud, he requested an official report from his subordinate.

The report was mundane, as expected, but Merin's hands indicated there was more that needed to be said once they were alone. When he had finished, Lorith said, "Very good. I have some data files in my office that I need to update before I meet with the inner tier. I also want you to look at the schedule for the third roster of warriors; they need to rotate back into training as quickly as possible."

Merin was about to reply when something caught Lorith's eye at the far end of the hangar. He held up a hand to forestall the other male and narrowed his eyes in the direction he had seen the flash of white. He had not been mistaken. There, in the farthest corner of the enormous, double-height space, next to a smaller multi-compartment capable tub, stood Ra'hos Reemah. He knew of her grounding, as did all in positions of authority with access to certain cruiser systems. What in the universe was she doing there? He moved towards her, intending to find out.

As he did so, he watched her movements closely for any clue to her intentions, knowing she would be reticent when directly addressed. She was talking to one of the workers, but he could not determine which class as she blocked his view of the male's chest insignia. Unfortunately, he scurried away when Lorith was still only halfway across the open space at the centre of the hangar. Moments later, Reemah looked up and saw him.

Her eyes locked on his for an instant, before she narrowed them in... Disapproval? Annoyance? Contempt? He never could read her micro-expressions well from a distance. Before he could get close enough to be sure, Reemah had whirled away from him.

His eyes narrowed on her back, and he picked up his pace, reaching her before she had a chance to dart out of sight.

"You have some dirt on the back of your jumpsuit, Ra'hos."

"Oh!" She jumped, apparently surprised by his voice so close behind her, and spun towards him while covering her rear with both hands. He thought she did well to cover the embarrassment on her face. He almost did not catch it and wondered whether it was from being dirty or getting caught. "I fell over earlier and must have landed in something. I will sort it out when I get to my suite. Thank you for informing me." Her tone was imperious and icy. She nodded imperceptibly and began to turn away again.

"It's *grey* dirt."

Her inner eyelids blinked, and she faced him once more. "I fell near some crates they just brought up from the planet. Those stupid slaves never cleanse them properly before they are loaded."

Not quite so haughty this time, he thought. *Interesting*. He did not believe her in the slightest but, without incontrovertible proof, could say nothing against one of the Ra'hos. Changing tack, he decided to address the more pressing concern. He moved closer and looked down, directly into her eyes, to gauge her reaction to his next question. "May I ask what you are doing all the way down here, Ra'hos?"

For the second time, she blinked once before speaking. It was telling, and he anticipated her answer as one would the latest play in the entertainment suite. She did not disappoint.

"My father wishes me to take my position more seriously. I have been touring the entire cruiser in an attempt to get to know the needs of my people more personally. As there may be a security concern with some of the areas I wish to visit, I decided to keep my visits informal and confidential. I am sure you understand and will not feel the need to interfere or inform my father. I wish to surprise him with my more extensive understanding of the workings of the cruiser during our next meeting."

He would have questioned her further had his attention not been called away by Merin, reminding Lorith of the meeting he must attend imminently and the *work* they needed to get to first.

Reemah took the opportunity to stride out of one of the small, auxiliary portals behind the tub she had been pointing at earlier. Her back was straight and her gait confident, presenting the image she had deftly painted for him and hiding the universe-knew-what. If not for the untimely reminder of his more pressing responsibilities, he might have followed her. Instead, he decided to store the fascinating details of their encounter away for later perusal and chase her down the next day if necessary. After all, his race traded in information, and it might prove useful at a later date.

With one last glance in the direction the Ra'hos had taken to escape him, he set his mind to the tasks ahead and jogged back across the hangar to Merin. There would be more than enough to occupy Lorith's thoughts on their way to the office adjoining his more-spacious-than-average military quarters. Jerking his head in the direction of the main, double-width portal, he said, "We should go."

Less than a cycle later, with a head full of mildly worrying—yet so far disjointed—information that had been gathered during his absence, he entered the throne room where he would give his report of the mission on U'du to the Ra'hon and the rest of the inner tier. While he mentally reviewed the details of his debrief one last time, he strode confidently towards the large throne at the end of the room and gave his customary respectful bow before Ashal. Low and formal, it was also genuine for the male who had been a friend to Lorith's father and a mentor to him, even after his decision to enter the military.

When asked to rise and take a seat with the others, he did so, glancing at the expressions of each. Sunath looked detached as ever, but he would soak up every detail of the discussion to come. He was intelligent, efficient, and ruthless—without resorting to assassinations—a combination that Lorith had come to respect and that had amassed the other male a fortune to rival the Ra'hos family. He acknowledged Lorith with a slight nod of the head and resumed reading the display of a databloc.

Nishaf, on the other hand, was much harder to read—a fact which had led to Lorith ordering covert surveillance and data gathering on him over the last decade. Nothing concrete had been found to date, but the beginnings of a pattern danced on the edge of Lorith's awareness. Though Nishaf's face remained entirely neutral, he sat straighter in his chair now than he had when Lorith first walked into the room.

As soon as Lorith was comfortably seated and had placed his databloc on the obsidian table in front of him, Ashal brought them to order. "Now that we are all present, we will dispense with the usual preamble and get straight to the matter at hand. I wish to know how the culling progressed. Did all go as planned, Lorith?"

In order to clear his mind and ensure his own expression would remain as blank as those around him while he spoke, Lorith took his time linking his databloc to the main display before launching into a dispassionate yet clear recounting of the mission on U'du. He kept the details brief and clinical, focusing on the way his warriors worked together as a well-coordinated team and making a point of mentioning individuals who had impressed him and might deserve advancement. It took more than half a cycle to cover the entire events of the day from take-off to landing, and by the time he was finished, the others around the table were as informed about the operation as he was.

Nishaf, a gleam in his eyes that Lorith was sure the other male was unaware of—or he would have masked it—leaned forwards slightly and asked, "So, it is done?"

Lorith sighed internally. He hated to have to repeat himself but had become used to their need to review certain aspects of his operations more than once. Sometimes he wondered why they did not just skip directly to their questions rather than sit through his initial report. However, knowing it was part of his role of Na'hor, and enjoying the position on balance, he curbed his irritation and answered as thoroughly as possible.

"Yes. We did a house by house search of the entire colony to ensure complete success." An image of a human female hidden in shadows and clutching a bundle flashed in his mind, but he pushed it away. He should probably have personally checked whether she had been captured, but the search had been thorough. There was no way his warriors would have missed her. He refocused on the present and what he had been saying. "One female tried swimming out into the lake to avoid the culling, but she was caught by a perimeter drone and her child terminated by the nearest squad. Two more attempted to escape into the wilderness with the same result.

"The drones picked up several larger life signs fleeing towards the north and east during the course of the day. However, as they did not scan as targets, they were allowed to pass. With no food or water, I have been assured by the new Head Guard, Lamesh, that they will eventually return, or die. All human males from new-born to the age of five have been culled. The slaves are so busy mourning, patching the wounded who tried to interfere with the process, and burying the dead that I doubt they will think of rebelling again for a long time to come."

Sunath broke the silence that followed to ask, "What about casualties?"

"There is no need for concern on that count. Some of the warriors incurred minor wounds, but all of those were taken care of by med-wands before we even left the planet surface. One of the younger males, new to the squadron, was ambushed by a group of humans and was more severely hurt. He was transferred to a med-pod immediately on our arrival back at the cruiser. He will be out in eight cycles and is expected to be fully rejuvenated at that time. I will check on his progress one cycle after that and add the information from the medics to my final mission log."

"And the colony itself?" This enquiry came from Ashal, keen as always to maintain progress on his new cruiser.

"As per our orders, damage was kept to a minimum. A few pieces of furniture were broken here and there, some buildings sustained blast marks—nothing structural—and the walls of one shack had to be pulled apart to get to a female trying to hide her child in a small gap between them." Knowing what Ashal was really asking, Lorith added, "There was nothing that will interfere with work in any of the sectors."

"Good. Good! Lorith, you have another unmitigated triumph on your record. Your military career will be added to the Ancestral Canon if you keep going like this. Esarelians in the distant future, especially those joining the ranks of our warriors, will be able to study all your greatest accomplishments, and your name will live long beyond your lifespan. It pleases me to be your Ra'hon."

The speech was the highest praise Ashal could give, short of conferring the status mentioned, and Lorith should have been extremely proud of himself in that moment. However, it felt wrong to win such esteem through a one-sided massacre, where the foe was unarmed and innocent. His personal honour rebelled at the over-zealous response from his superior, but he could not snub the male who had acted as a sometime surrogate father. Lorith humbly accepted the accolade by rising to bow and remained silent.

As he sat back down, he noticed a flash of pure fury cross Nishaf's face. Gone before it fully formed, only Lorith's keen observational skills and honed instincts assured him that it had been real. He pondered the implications of such an emotion in his civilian counterpart while the meeting wound down, contributing only when addressed and paying only half his attention to what was said.

By the time the meeting broke up, Lorith was keen to return to his office and go over, once more, the intelligence Merin had stored in the hidden compartment for him. The tickling along the base of Lorith's skull, which had always served him well as an early warning system for danger ahead, had intensified recently and would no longer be ignored. He wanted to know what it signified, and the sooner the better. A familiar feeling told him he would be watching Nishaf closely in the coming days.

Lorith also needed to check on Ra'hos Reemah at some point in the near future. As he ran a frustrated hand over his scalp, he decided it would be better to get some rest before tackling that particular problem. Taking time to unwind and catch up on some much-needed sleep would put him in a better mood to deal with the unruly Ra'hos. He found keeping track of any member of Ashal's immediate family distasteful, however necessary and prudent it proved to be, and dreaded to think what the spoiled first daughter had mixed herself up in this time. It did not matter. Whatever her latest disastrous scheme was, it would wait until the next day.

It would have to.

Chapter 19

Date: 311.428.150
Location: Esarelian Primary Space Cruiser

Fuming, Reemah stalked down one of the side corridors from the hangar to the storage bays. Thanks to Na'hor Lorith, she had been forced to go the long way around, walking towards her private suite and only doubling back when she was sure he had not followed her. It had taken up time that she needed to gather the necessary supplies, commandeer a guard for her new son, and get off the cruiser again before anyone else spotted her somewhere other than the suite. She made a mental note to see whether Velay could change the internal sensor records to include a trip down to the hangar bay and along to the engine rooms or guard stations.

If she was honest with herself, she would admit that finding Lorith in the hangar earlier had spooked her more than a little. It had been a close call that had left her heart pounding harder than usual. His intense look had drilled down into her defences, stripping them away in an attempt to reach the truth behind both her presence there and her dishevelled appearance. The entire encounter had left her feeling exposed. She knew he had not believed a word she had said and berated herself for not cleansing the back of her jumpsuit before landing.

She also knew that, fortunately, her status meant he would not question her explanation without hard evidence to the contrary. Still, she had to weigh the very real likelihood that he would investigate further against the overriding need to complete her mission and leave the cruiser. She feared he would expose her before she finished making all the arrangements necessary to protect Mahsan until she could find a more permanent solution.

Determined to hurry, in case Lorith did mention her whereabouts to her father, Reemah strode faster down the utilitarian passageway. She barely noticed the metallic black flooring and dingy off-white wall panels as she ran through the list of what she needed to accomplish and the time frame she now considered likely in which to do it. It would be tight, but she thought she should be able to get off the cruiser without running into the cold, odious Na'hor again.

She recalled the way he had stood in front of her, a marble statue of icy superiority. Internally shivering in response to his hard stare, she had managed to answer his questions without an outward flinch. Even the way he had paused long enough to make her uncomfortable between statements made her loathe him. He was so calculated in everything he did. Even so, she could not understand her innate reaction to him.

Once again attempting to focus on her current goal, she thought instead of Mahsan. Within just a few cycles, he had given her a sense of purpose she had been lacking for more than a century. It was difficult to believe that such a tiny *human* child could have such a profound effect on her. Nevertheless, the image of his innocent, unusual eyes brought a smile to her face and lightness to her step. She had to quash the impulse, difficult as that was, for she was nearing the storage bay and had to present a regal bearing to those stationed inside.

As she rounded the last corner and approached the work station just inside the enormous bay, she forced her features into the blank mask she had perfected as a youngster. Having only been in the vast space on a handful of previous occasions, she was still awed by its immense size and the sheer amount of supplies stored there. If necessary, the cruiser could last several decades in space with no need to restock.

Time being in short supply, she wasted none in ordering the head worker to requisition and immediately load a prepared list of items onto the tub she had acquired for her personal use. The tone she used forestalled any questions the deferentially bowing male might have had, and she was on her way to her next destination before he had even risen upright.

Buoyed by the ease with which she had completed her first task, she quickly made her way to the primary guard station. It would be trickier to have a guard removed from the roster, but her status as Ra'hos should ensure complete cooperation with no report to her father. She was counting on it.

Again taking secondary corridors that were not likely to be used regularly by others, it took less than a quarter of a cycle to reach the hub for all on-board guards. Some were from the underclasses, trying to improve their station in life one rung at a time. Others had attempted the prestigious yet arduous warrior training and dropped out for some reason. Be it injury, poor aptitude, or something entirely different, many ultimately joined the guards instead. It made for a somewhat disparate group of males responsible for internal security throughout the cruiser. The only exception to their jurisdiction was the throne room and the Ra'hos' private suites on the uppermost decks. Those were guarded exclusively by an elite force of warriors hand-picked by her father and the Na'hor.

The guard behind the outer counter appeared at first glance to be a failed warrior. His expression and posture suggested a false sense of importance often exhibited by those hiding a weakness of character that would have seen him removed from the military training programme. His snapped demands to a subordinate a moment later confirmed her suspicions. She would need to put him in his place as swiftly as possible.

She was about to cover the last few strides to the counter when something, or someone, caught her attention in a smaller anteroom. Without further thought, she changed direction and walked through the arch and into the dim space.

The human slave was tall for his species and looked strong. Transferring bulky equipment containers from a hover-transport to the shelves along the side wall, he moved with ease and hardly seemed to notice the weight of each item as he swung it up and across, before smoothly sliding it into place. He did not pause between lifts, stretch his back and arms occasionally, or even look up. He just kept steadily and rhythmically unloading the goods until the pile before him was gone.

An idea began to uncoil in Reemah's mind, and she pushed up from the wall she had been leaning against while watching him and strode forwards. "You," she snapped more forcefully than intended. "Follow me."

He slowly unfolded himself from where he had been crouched to push the last crate into position on the lowest shelf. He was almost as tall as some of the underclass Esarelians, which both surprised and pleased her. Obviously new, he warily brought his eyes up to meet hers. As soon as she looked at them, she knew she had made the right choice. The intelligence she saw there had not yet been wiped out by the harsh treatment especially common towards slaves in this sector. Adding that to his impressive physique, she was sure he would be perfect for what she had in mind.

She turned and was pleased when, however cautiously, he followed as instructed. With at least two paces kept between them, he shadowed her path back into the main area and towards the counter.

Reemah did not wait for the Esarelian to turn from where he was poring over the display of a databloc and face her. She stood to her full height and said, "I will be taking this slave for the foreseeable future. You will need to remove him from your roster."

Without moving or even looking up, the guard asked what she wanted him for. His disrespect irritated her, and she lowered her voice to a more menacing tone when she spoke her next words. "How dare you question your superiors! Do as I have commanded at once."

He finally glanced in her direction, and she saw his eyes take in the creased and dusty jumpsuit she wore. His gaze never rose any higher before returning to the data display, and he dismissed her once more. "Superior? Right..."

As his last word trailed off in overt disdain, another guard came out of one of the portals at the side of the counter. In a position to witness the entire situation, he looked across at Reemah and froze. It was evident that *he* noticed more than her otherwise admittedly dishevelled appearance, as he bowed a formal greeting and hissed to his compatriot, "She is Ra'hos, you fool. Look at her eyes."

The first guard swivelled so fast that Reemah expected him to keep going in a full circle. Opening her eyes wide, she allowed him a good, long look at the violet irises denoting her unquestionable rank among all Esarelians. His eyes likewise widened, although she knew it was for a much different reason. He spluttered an immediate apology and fell to his knees in submission before one who could take even his life in retribution if it pleased her.

It was more difficult to see him while he cowered behind the counter. Unwilling to lean forwards to peer over the top, thus negating some of the commanding presence she held, Reemah wearily told him to regain his feet. He wisely kept his head lowered as he scrambled to obey.

"Now that our relative positions have been established, you will sign this slave over to me immediately. I should punish you for your insolence..." Reemah paused as if in thought and watched him squirm under her scrutiny as he tapped a screen to carry out her command. Unfortunately, she knew she needed to leave before she was found by Lorith or her father.

"However, I shall think on it before deciding your fate. You will be dealt with later."

As the newly cowed guard confirmed the transfer with her personal code, the human decided to speak for the first time. He had barely finished saying, "Where are you taking me?" when the Esarelian male lunged across the counter and back-handed him with a lightning fast strike across the face. The human staggered to the side with the force of the blow and crumpled against the wall with a sickening thud and a thin trail of bright red blood oozing from the corner of his mouth. The guard, still leaning half across the counter, snarled, "Never speak unless spoken to, *human*."

Reemah was amazed the slave was still conscious and further impressed when he wiped gently at his face with the back of his hand and slowly regained his feet. She could see him tamp down the anger at his mistreatment, before he once more bowed his head and stood motionless. When she noticed his feet braced apart, ready for any further contact, and his hands loosely fisted at his sides, she again congratulated herself on her choice of guard for Mahsan.

"You presume to touch my property?" She whirled on the guard for, she hoped, the last time. "You go too far. For this, I will have your freedom. Take him away and add him to the slave roster in place of this one."

The second guard, who had, until this moment, stayed to the side, jumped forwards to do her bidding. By the time she had moved to the entry portal, she could hear the struggles of the male she had just condemned as he was cuffed and dragged away for processing. His hapless, wailing protests followed her retreating back down the corridor until she turned into a side passage.

After she had shaken off the unfortunate series of events, Reemah glanced at the human. He appeared none the worse for the encounter, barring his already swelling jaw. He trailed along in her wake, now staying less than two paces from her as she navigated the cruiser corridors back to the transport hangar.

Rather than continue to refer to him as the human or the slave, she asked his name. He mumbled something incoherent around the jaw that she suspected was broken. She watched him surreptitiously for the length of a passageway, but he showed no signs of being in pain as he walked soundlessly to the side and slightly behind her. Making a mental note to ensure an additional med-wand was included in their supplies, she left him alone. She would find out his name, and the extent of his injuries, soon enough. Indeed, she intended to find out a lot more than that about the human she assigned to watch over her son.

Her son! The concept still surprised her with how good it felt.

Mahsan would be safe with both of the humans she had employed to look after him. She knew it instinctively. They would each do their best to protect what was possibly the only male baby left on the planet. All she needed to do was provide the necessary supplies and ensure he had a home to come to on the cruiser as quickly as possible.

She hoped Buln would be ready to fly by the time they reached the bay. Having left orders with the crew should be enough for a Ra'hos to get her way, however inconvenient to those around them, but her earlier run in with Lorith had her on edge. She rarely traded on her status but would do anything to get back to Mahsan before she was reported to her father.

When they entered the hangar bay, she strode directly to her somewhat affectionately nicknamed tub and checked the cargo hold. Relieved to find it fully loaded, she quickly ushered the human on board and scanned the area as soon as he was out of sight. It would not be prudent to let him discover that her acquisition of him was anything less than above board. As there appeared to be no sign of any warriors sent by Lorith to watch or detain her, she sealed the side hatch and made her way to the main cabin.

On her way there, Reemah passed the human, who was buckling himself into one of the passenger seats. A throwaway glance at him reminded her that he had been injured and needed medical attention. With an abrupt change in direction, she headed to the stack of supplies along the left side of the cargo bay. She rummaged through one of the packs until she found what she was looking for. Pulling it out, she tossed the fully charged med-wand to the human. At the last possible moment, he shot out a large, strong hand and grabbed it from the air like a toddler sneaking treats from a plate.

"You would do well to take care of your face. Once we are underway, I am going to explain what I want you to do, and I am sure you will have some questions."

One perfunctory pre-flight check later, she was activating Velay's cloned PU to sail past the force field and into the comforting blackness of space. Flying through the empty expanse before her was the only place Reemah truly felt alive and unfettered by the demands of her position. Finally back in her element, her body relaxed into the pilot's chair. She set the tub on a circuitous course for U'du, avoiding scrutiny from larger craft and the arrows patrolling the main supply route. At last satisfied they would remain undetected, she settled back to wait until she could reunite with her precious new baby boy. There would be many ramifications to come from her decision to adopt Mahsan, but for the time being, she would simply enjoy the anticipation of being a new mother.

Chapter 20

Day: 18   Month: 07   Year: 6428
Location: Planet U'Du, wilderness outside the main slave settlement

Gilla woke to her shoulder being roughly shaken. Taking a moment to process where she was and what had happened, she stretched cramped muscles and sat up, causing Velay to back away and make room. They had slept in the wasteland, waiting for Ra'hos Reemah's return. After cycles of alternately sitting on one of the smaller boulders and pacing with Elias, Gilla had found a large rock with a slight overhang to bed down next to. Up close, the surface had been riddled with veins of bluer and whiter shades where, from a distance, it merged into a solid dull grey. She had stared at the patterns as she shivered and tried to sleep. It had been freezing in the exposed open space overnight, and the Esarelian had eventually huddled close to share body heat and protect them from the worst of the biting wind.

Though she was half Oeal, which warmed her cold Esarelian blood somewhat, and the bio-suit she wore like a second skin regulated her body temperature, Velay still had not looked entirely comfortable with the intense cold of night. Sleeping on the bare ground with no mat or blankets had also been, from what Gilla could ascertain, a new experience for the Hos-born woman.

They had spent the remainder of the night crowded together under the slight lip of rock, trying to get some sleep. Gilla had curled around Elias, sheltering him from the cold and ensuring he was secure as he slept. She, herself, had been less comfortable. The surface of the planet, while having a slight give, was not the most relaxing place to spend a night, and it had taken a long time for exhaustion to overtake her.

Seeming to have quickly acclimatised to the harsh conditions, her sleeping partner was already up and moving around the clearing. Checking for what, Gilla had no clue. She had attempted several times the evening before to start a conversation with the surly Esarelian but had received minimal responses each time. Unsure whether her reticence to speak was due to worry over the Ra'hos, a dislike for Gilla's species, or something else entirely, Gilla had finally joined her in silent contemplation before succumbing to sleep.

This morning she had to focus on Elias. He needed feeding and changing. While feeding would not be a problem, finding cloths to replace those she suspected were heavy by now would provide more of a challenge. As if reading her mind and agreeing with the assessment, Elias began to snuffle and then let out a piercing wail.

Velay flinched at the sound and hurried over to see what the noise was about. For the first time since their initial meeting, she initiated conversation. "What's wrong with him? Why is he crying like that?"

Gilla could have smiled at the innocence of the questions, but she held it in check, not knowing how Velay would react. "He just needs feeding and changing, that's all. There's nothing to worry about."

"Oh." Velay sat on her haunches and stared at the scrunched up face of a baby in full crying mode. She looked fascinated by the change in him.

"Um, we do have one small problem, though." When Velay's attention instantly shifted from Elias, and intense green eyes bore into Gilla, she hesitated before explaining, "I can feed him easily, but we have no more cloths. I used the one we found with the pod last night and the other is wet."

Comprehension transformed the expression of those eyes, mere hand breadths from her own, into something softer, almost friendly, before they narrowed in thought. Muttering under her breath, Velay stood and fiddled with something on her utility belt, producing a large square of fabric. It was the softest material Gilla had ever touched, and the notion of ruining it as a baby's cloth gave her a moment's pause. She asked tentatively, "Are you sure we can use this?"

Velay waved a hand in a dismissive gesture and said, "Of course. It is nothing."

With that assurance, Gilla got to work. She decided to remove Elias's dirty cloth first to make him more comfortable. She would then let him air while she fed him, and hopefully, he would empty his bladder before she put the new cloth around him. If she was lucky, he wouldn't need to be changed again until the Ra'hos returned.

Before Gilla had done more than unwrap a side of his old cloth, Velay jumped back and put a hand up to her face. "What is that smell?" she mumbled around fingers clamped to her nose and mouth.

Gilla couldn't help herself. She took one look at the Esarelian's stricken face and burst into laughter. The kind that came from the gut and would not stop, it sent tears streaming down her face every time she glanced back at the big bad Velay bested by a child's dirty cloth. It took some time, and a determined effort not to peek at Velay, to regain control and stop the crying. She wiped her face with a corner of the baby's blanket and sat back, feeling better at the release.

Instantly realising what she'd just done, Gilla froze. Chagrined by her outburst at a superior's expense, and half expecting a pain punishment in retaliation, she awaited Velay's reaction with bowed head and baited breath. Luckily, the Esarelian merely grunted and waved for her to proceed. Gilla felt her entire body relax at Velay's apparent tolerance of her humour and risked a glance to see her suppressing a smile of her own.

Not knowing how to answer the question still hanging between them other than to point out the obvious, Gilla turned her attention back to the dirty cloth. From behind her, she heard Velay shift, but whether to see more clearly or avoid the sight entirely, Gilla had no clue until the woman asked another question.

"Ugh! How can you touch that stuff? It's disgusting."

Angling her head to be able to observe Velay while continuing with her task, Gilla did answer this time. "He's just a baby. He can't help himself, and he'll get sick if he stays like this. Won't you, little one?" She tickled his tummy, eliciting a gurgle and double fist pump from him, before continuing. "What choice do I have?"

Silence and, from what she could make out, a thoughtful expression greeted her pronouncement.

A few moments later, Velay cautiously approached. She watched with barely disguised trepidation, wide-eyed and breath held, from behind the safety of Gilla's back as she worked. Gilla completely removed the old cloth and cleaned Elias as much as she could in the circumstances. The woman peeking over her shoulder, as if at a terrifying enemy, must have realised what she needed and handed over a canteen of water without comment. Gilla thanked her and finished cleaning her son.

When she was satisfied, she picked him up and cooed to him, humming an old lullaby and rocking from side to side. Settled from his earlier bout of screaming, Elias looked up at her and pumped his legs and fists. She waited for Velay to move away, wanting to feed him in private, but she didn't move. She still stared at Elias with an expression Gilla couldn't interpret.

Needing to get on with his meal and feeling awkward, she cleared her throat and reached up to fumble with the opening of her jumpsuit. Velay finally took the hint and, waking from her trance, jumped up to scan the clearing again. She had periodically been sweeping the area for signs of the Ra'hos's return or other, more unwelcome intrusions. What she would do about any such activity was a mystery to Gilla, though she noticed the rod strapped to Velay's utility belt was within easy reach.

Images of those rods in use and the damage they inflicted were still too fresh, and Gilla had to force them from her mind. To distract her, and make the most of their time together, she turned her eyes back to her son and watched him take his fill. She assessed him from head to toe and thanked God that his time in the life-pod seemed to have had no adverse effects. Things could have gone quite differently.

In fact, the series of events she had experienced in a single day sent her thoughts along a different tangent, and she soon found herself pondering the bargain she had made with Ra'hos Reemah. Her mind told her that it was the best, possibly the only, way to ensure her son's survival and safety. In reality, his future would be much better with the Ra'hos than if he stayed on the planet to become a slave with the rest of his people. In that regard, she thanked God that she had stayed quiet and been willing to give him up. Her heart told her something entirely different, though: that it would break when he was taken to the cruiser to live with his new *mother* and that it wouldn't matter how long she had with him first.

Unwilling to allow herself to dwell on that aspect of their deal, she quickly redid her jumpsuit when the little one was done, boosted him up to her shoulder, and settled in to wait for signs of Ra'hos Reemah's return. Slowly rubbing circles on her son's tiny back, she soothed them both with the motion, as the sun climbed higher in the sky.

Some time later, but before the sun hit its peak, Velay pointed out a dark spot in the distance that gradually materialised into what Gilla presumed was the same tub Ra'hos Reemah had flown away in yesterday. The low hum of its engines reached them soon after the bulky transport tub came into view, and Gilla hoped no one from the settlement could hear it. Her hypothesis as to the pilot was confirmed when the tub passed overhead and circled their clearing, Ra'hos Reemah peering at them through the front window. The Esarelian angled the tub away and then slowed and sank behind several clusters of rocks to set down in a clearing some distance away.

After only one glance at each other, Gilla and Velay both set off in that direction. Gilla was certain Velay's sense of urgency stemmed from a vastly different cause than her own wish to meet the inevitable head on. Whatever their personal motivation, both women moved quickly in the direction they had seen the tub land.

As they approached, the curtain of dust kicked up by the landing thrusters enveloped them in its choking clutches before moving on to work its way around clusters of boulders and through crevices between larger rock formations. It left a haze in its wake that, like an overtired child at bedtime, refused to settle. They turned their heads aside and covered their faces, Gilla also ensuring that Elias was tucked against her neck with his blankets blocking out the particles. In that manner, they covered the final stretch between themselves and the powering-down tub.

She thought she heard a muttered, "Good to see you again, Buln," before her attention was drawn to the tub. A thin strip of light was slowly widening into the rear cargo doorway as Ra'hos Reemah lowered the ramp to the ground.

Through the still-swirling dust, a shape formed in the centre of the cargo bay. It took on the proportions of a well-built human as whoever it was stepped forwards. Gilla realised this was the guard Ra'hos Reemah had said she'd provide for them. Anticipation mixed with fear of the unknown man until something about the way he moved struck her.

Although it couldn't be true—was impossible, even—she recognised the gait, the size and shape of the shoulders. Her heart faltered, her mind scrambling to provide some explanation that wouldn't shatter her soul if it proved false. The truth could not be denied, though. Before her disbelieving eyes, bringing hope back to life with every step he took, Elias strode through the opening doors and down the ramp, stopping at the bottom to look around in incomprehension as the dust finally settled.

Gilla took one involuntary step towards her beloved husband and whispered his name on little more than a sigh. Her eyes filled with moisture, but she blinked it away, not allowing anything to blur her vision of the man she loved. Scanning him from head to toe, she checked for injuries or other signs of abuse at the hands of his captors. Her arm began to rise of its own accord to reach his precious face. And at that moment, Ra'hos Reemah appeared behind him, shattering the illusion of their perfect reunion and slamming Gilla back to reality with a force that sent her back a pace.

It was a few heartbeats more before Elias's gaze swung in her direction as he methodically scanned his surroundings. When he saw her, a brief flash of confusion crossed his face and then his eyes lit. She knew he would have moved, would have called out to her, if not for the sounds of the Ra'hos behind him and Gilla's warning look and minute shake of her head.

She was relieved when Velay took the Ra'hos's attention away from them. The woman with whom Gilla had called a truce of sorts threw herself at Ra'hos Reemah in a giant hug that shocked Gilla with its emotional intensity. Though she had begun building a begrudging friendship with the green-eyed Esarelian through their shared discomfort overnight and the brief conversation regarding the changing of a dirty cloth, Gilla would not have guessed at Velay's capacity to care so much about another. She had remained, on the whole, aloof and closed off around her human companion.

Whatever the depth of kinship between the two women, it was plain to Gilla that they were extremely close. She began to hope that her son would feel the same warmth from them when the time came... She once more prayed for courage and then added thanks for the miracle of Elias's return.

Neither she nor Elias had moved since their eyes met for the first time. Gilla smiled and began to edge closer to him. She was halfway around the edge of the clearing when the words being exchanged by the two Esarelian women registered.

"...we have to hurry," Ra'hos Reemah was saying. "Lorith saw me in the transport hangar, and we'll both be missed if we don't get back soon."

"Does he suspect where you are?"

"Not yet, but he will soon enough. I'm sure he knows I've already been here once." Ra'hos Reemah stopped abruptly, as if remembering they were not alone. She turned to face Gilla and Elias, who now stood less than two arm lengths apart.

"Ah, Gilla! Let me introduce the man I have chosen as guard for you and my son." Gilla noticed absently that the Ra'hos used a more clipped, nasal tone with them than she did when she addressed Velay and thought no one else was near enough to hear. She returned her attention to what was being said, though, before she missed something important. "This is Elias. He will act as your protector until I return, and he has been provided with one of my personal codes as authority for his actions. As a human, he will be able to blend in with the others of your race, posing as husband and father if necessary, in order to avoid detection or confrontation with the planetary forces. I am sure this will be a needless precaution but find it an acceptable ruse should it prove too arduous for you to remain beyond range of the colony."

Gilla nearly choked at the very real relationships the Ra'hos unwittingly described but managed not to look across at Elias. Although the strategy was hardly worded or spoken as anything requiring a decision on her part, Gilla nodded her agreement. She felt almost guilty for letting the Esarelian continue without informing her of all the pertinent facts. Almost. Her son's future was worth any guilt she might incur.

Ra'hos Reemah went on to explain how to use a locator chip that only she would be able to track and that they were to keep with them at all times. Having an inbuilt dedicated-communication system, it was much more sophisticated than the simple device Gilla had rigged to follow the movements of Elias's life-pod only a day earlier.

The Esarelian told them that she had scanned the surface of the planet on her way back to the clearing and that there were some promising-looking caverns and caves no more than a day's walk from their current location. Those should be far enough away from the settled areas for them to remain hidden in relative comfort while they awaited her return. The provisions she had requisitioned would last far longer than she anticipated they would need to remain in the wilderness. She had included various pieces of technology they might need, as well as more basic supplies such as food, water, and a heat source.

The only point at which she stumbled in her instructions was when she described the necessities she had gathered for *Mahsan*. There, she had relied on pure conjecture, having had no previous experience with young children. Again, Gilla felt a pang of sympathy for the other woman and stepped forwards to assure her that what she had given them would be more than sufficient for his needs. A look of understanding passed between them before Gilla stepped back once more.

"It may be some time before I am able to return, but I will be in touch at regular intervals in the meantime." Finally satisfied that they had all the information they would need, the Ra'hos turned to Elias and told him to begin unloading the supply crates.

While he did so, she took Mahsan from Gilla and walked over to Velay, where the pair went back to whispering. Gilla felt the separation from her son keenly, even though she knew it would be brief. She got to work helping Elias organise their huge store of supplies. They remained silent in the presence of the others, but their fingers occasionally brushed in passing, and Gilla felt a frisson of excitement at his proximity.

By the time they finished, there were several distinct piles around the far edge of the clearing from the tub. Gilla stood, hands on hips, surveying the scene in amazement. She had no idea what they would do with it all—until Elias spoke from directly behind her, making her jump.

"Here. Fill these bags with what we'll need for the next few days. We'll store the rest over there until we need it."

Still recovering from him sneaking up behind her, but appreciating his enduring ability to read her mind, she squinted in the direction he was pointing. A short distance away, she could just make out a small crevice between two outcroppings of rock. It would be hard to spot from any other angle and was far outside the range of activity from the settlement. Elias pointed out a boulder that he would use to block the entrance and secure what they left there.

With everything sorted, there was no more reason to delay. Ra'hos Reemah wandered over with Elias in her arms and Velay in tow a pace behind. Whatever they had been discussing so animatedly was evidently resolved, and the two moved in sync once more.

The Ra'hos seemed almost distressed at the prospect of leaving them alone. She hugged Mahsan to her tightly and whispered in his ear for a long time. Waiting patiently to the side, Velay watched Gilla and Elias closely. It unnerved Gilla, and she fought to prevent herself from stepping closer to the comforting presence of her husband.

Eventually, Ra'hos Reemah ran out of words for her son and, somewhat reluctantly, transferred him to Gilla. As she did so, the Esarelian made eye contact and said, "Look after him for me. I will come for him as soon as I can."

Giving the hand that still clutched her middle finger a small shake and then a kiss, she turned on her heel and walked quickly to the transport tub. It was not until that moment that Gilla truly believed the Ra'hos would stand by her word and allow Gilla to keep the little one, however temporarily. The level of relief she felt surprised her, although it shouldn't have after the events of the past month.

She held her breath as Velay approached.

"I know you will take good care of Mahsan. You are a good woman. Just remember, Reemah *will* return for him."

Velay squeezed Gilla's arm in what she could only suppose was a sign of support and farewell. The unexpected action stunned her more than anything else. When Velay turned and strode after her friend, she left Gilla confused and with an uneasy suspicion that the Esarelian knew the truth.

Moments later, the cargo bay doors of the tub clanged closed, distracting Gilla's thoughts from the implications of Velay's words and gesture. The clink of the external locking mechanism signalled the Esarelians' imminent departure. Gilla and Elias moved out of the clearing to give the tub room to take off and protect themselves, as much as they were able, from the noise and dust-laden wash.

It didn't take long for the tub to rise, or for the too-familiar dust cloud to expand from the point of take-off. What had been a low hum when Gilla had been farther away during the tub's landing was a loud roar as it passed overhead and disappeared into the sky above them. The dust settled slowly around the clearing, and silence descended with it. They were finally alone.

Within the blink of an eye, Elias was in front of her. His arms came around her waist, and were it not for the complication of the little one she was holding, he would have lifted her off her feet and swung her around in a wide arc before kissing her senseless. She could see the desire to do just that in his face. Instead, he squeezed gently and held her in a tender, if awkward, embrace. How long it lasted, Gilla couldn't say and didn't care. He was here, he was really here and holding her. His distinctive scent of fresh sweat was just as she remembered it, and the tears she had been holding back for so long ran down her face unchecked.

"I've missed you," he said into the hair on top of her head.

She managed to choke out, "I've missed you too."

"Thank God we're together again. I've prayed for it every day since they took me."

Gilla couldn't respond past the lump blocking her throat, but her tears intensified and she clung to him more tightly. Elias pulled back and, tilting her head up with one hand, used the forefinger of his other to dry her face with butterfly soft sweeps. He kissed each eye, then the tip of her nose and finally her lips. It was like coming home, and Gilla sank into him, wedging their son between them.

The sensation of baby Elias's wriggling brought her back to reality and she reluctantly stepped back. Carefully turning the little one in her embrace until he was upright and facing his father, she tugged on his blankets until his head was free.

"Elias, I'd like you to meet your son. I named him for you, but given what's happened, we can't really use that now. I know you heard Ra'hos Reemah call him Mahsan, and I'll explain everything soon. I promise. We have a lot to talk about—"

"And we will. We have all the time we need to talk." He smiled wide at her before looking down at the squirming infant she held. "For now, let me just get to know my son awhile."

He reached forwards and lifted his child from her arms for the first time. Clearly emotional, Elias inspected every visible part of the little boy cradled in his large muscled forearms. He sat down heavily on the ground without even checking beneath him, still staring at the miracle he held. When eyes the exact replica of his own looked up and locked with his, Gilla heard his indrawn breath and then a whispered, "His eyes…"

She said nothing, knowing what he meant and content to let him work through the emotions in his own way and at his own pace.

"When…" He managed to push the single word out while tickling the baby's neck and watching him wriggle in response.

"The night after the Selection." Gilla couldn't stand even the short distance between them any longer. When she sat down next to him, he automatically wrapped one arm around her.

As if shaking himself free of a dream, he lifted his head, if not his eyes, and asked, "And Mirami?"

Gilla leaned into his side and reassured him as best she could. "She's fine. She's so brave and strong, Elias. I sent her back to the settlement to wait for me with Than." She clutched him as a thought occurred to her. "We'll have to go back for her."

He pondered for a moment before firming his jaw—the way he always did when deciding something difficult. "Is she safe?"

She nodded.

"We'll have to leave her where she is for now. I can't wait to see her, but we must stay hidden. We need to find somewhere away from the guard patrols and work details until the Ra'hos returns. She'll be checking our location, and I won't leave you alone until you're completely safe. I'll go back for Mirami after that, probably in a few days, all right?"

Though she hated to leave her daughter, Gilla knew Elias was right and that Than would do his best in their absence. She nodded again.

Elias changed the subject, bouncing his son in his lap. "So what *will* we call him?"

An idea struck Gilla, and she almost laughed at what her brother would think. "Than's been calling him 'little one' since he was born, and it's become quite popular…"

"That sounds typical of him. How is my reprobate of a brother-in-law?" He became serious as he added, "Is he all right after the Selection?"

"He will be. You know Than; he bounces back quickly. In fact, if I'm not mistaken, I think he might have just met his match." She looked up into her husband's face and grinned. "Why don't we swap stories as we walk?"

Gilla blew out a breath of frustration. She was trying to sling one of the packs they'd finally finished packing onto her back while still clutching the little one safely to her chest. With only one hand, she couldn't get the leverage she needed, and the heavy bag kept sliding back down her arm to the floor. It didn't help that she caught Elias grinning at her struggles from where he stood, already loaded with the largest pack on his back.

"Here, let me help you." He took his son, holding him up high in the air before plopping him down in the crook of his arm. His every action with the little boy was as gentle as it had been with Mirami at that age. A look of wonder came over Elias's face, and the sight of father and son together brought tears to Gilla's eyes and a lump to her throat.

As she positioned the straps of the pack comfortably on her shoulders and settled it into place, she whispered, "I don't know what I would do without you, Elias."

He smiled at her, a beautiful smile that she'd missed so much since he was taken. As she watched, mesmerized by his presence after so long alone, his face changed. He sniffed the little one's cloth, and his nose wrinkled at the smell emanating from within. Gilla laughed, carefree, and took the child back. After all, it had been many years since Elias had helped her change a baby's cloth.

Elias put his arm around her shoulders, pulling her close to his strong, warm body, and laughed along with her. "Neither do I, beautiful wife. Neither do I."

She moved away to quickly change the little one. When she finished, he tugged her gently back into his side. Picking up their remaining bags in his other hand, he guided her around a precarious looking group of boulders, and they set off into the wastelands and an unknown yet suddenly brighter future, together.

Epilogue

Date: 311.428.155
Location: Esarelian Primary Space Cruiser, Hos private suites

Nishaf lounged in one of his elegantly carved and upholstered danta wood chairs. He was enjoying a glass of the highly prized Oeal wine he had had imported last season, letting the velvety heat of the liquid soothe his throat and settle in his stomach, spreading warmth through his entire body. It was their best vintage yet and well worth the exorbitant amount he had paid for it. Just one more means with which to impress his guest, the choice of wine was as calculated as everything else in the room.

Ordered, impeccably clean, and opulent—without being gaudy or maudlin—the wealth and prestige on show through each choice of furnishing brought him great pride. Abstract artwork from the most highly acclaimed holo-painters was projected onto walls covered with priceless silk hangings. Tamolut ivory figurines, in intimate yet tasteful poses, created pleasing breaks in the display. The suite was spacious and light, the furniture minimalistic but costly. He had even arranged for scented air to be circulated. After all, this meeting was critical to his plans and needed to progress smoothly.

"Would you like some more? It truly is an excellent year and best enjoyed fresh." Nishaf half rose to pour but settled back when a hand was raised in refusal. Internally thanking the universe that their mutual need to remain clear headed meant he would part with less of his favourite wine than originally anticipated, Nishaf also recognised the flip side of that decision: he would have to be at his persuasive best to achieve his aims for this particular alliance.

"Now that you have suitably impressed me with your stock of drink and delicious canapés, why not tell me why I am really here?"

The low, musical voice contrasted with Nishaf's own damaged tone in a way that nearly made him wince. He kept his face neutral, also concealing his annoyance at the overt reference to his attempts at creating a favourable setting.

"To discuss a mutually beneficial arrangement, of course," he replied.

Nishaf noted the spark of interest in eyes normally devoid of expression or emotion and knew he had contacted the right person. Relaxing back into his seat, he outlined his proposal.

Fingertips pressed together above a linen-clad stomach, and a wide, full mouth pursed in contemplation. "It will take time, decades even…"

"And what of that?" he asked. "Our lives are long, and we can be patient."

With a resolute exhale, his counterpart asked, "What do you want for your part in this … endeavour?"

Prepared for this, Nishaf paused to sip his wine before responding, not wanting to sound too eager. He carefully set the glass down on the side table and perused the selection of sweets with an air of nonchalance. There would be no going back from his next statement, but Nishaf already knew it would be worth the small risk of exposure. He fought to keep his hand from rising to his neck. "I want the humans completely exterminated." He paused. "And I want Ra'hos Reemah for a mate."

Silence was the only reply, until Nishaf began to wonder whether he had, indeed, made a mistake. He was about to launch into damage control when the response finally came. "I see. And what do you imagine I will get in return?"

Suddenly, this was proceeding even more smoothly than he had envisaged. He leaned back against the comfortable cushions and let a smile steal over his face before saying, "What I know you have always wanted."

His guest smiled in return and held up the crystal glass for Nishaf to pour more wine. As he did so, Nishaf began to anticipate the years ahead as he had not done in a long time, and a shiver of excitement ran down his spine.

He would finally have his due.

AUTHOR'S NOTE

While this story is based on passages in the Bible and I have strived to remain true to the essence of the events and people described there, it is a work of fiction. The bulk of this novel has been created from supposition and conjecture based on pure imagination and my own limited understanding of human nature. I hope the reader will forgive any variances from how they perceive these critical moments in Exodus.

I would like to address the two main discrepancies from the Biblical account. Firstly, despite popular opinion and myriad modern interpretations, it was not the work of soldiers in a single enterprise to kill the Israelite baby boys. Exodus 1v22 tells us that all Egyptians (as in the general population, or at least those who owned slaves) were instructed to kill them when born, and it is implied that this mandate lasted several years. Jochabed hid her son for three months after his birth to protect him from this fate and only put him in the river when she could no longer conceal his presence. To hide him for so long shows great determination, as well as ingenuity. Given the logistics for the setting I chose, I decided to focus on these characteristics rather than the exact course of events. I apologise to those who would have preferred a narrative more closely aligned with the original.

Secondly, and rather surprisingly to me when I read it, it appears from modern translations of the Bible that Miriam was not set to watch over and protect her brother. Rather, as Exodus 2v4 tells us, she was sent only to observe what happened to him. This confused me for some time. How could a mother who had spent the previous three months protecting her child against great odds suddenly appear to toss him to the elements with so little regard for the outcome?

Two possibilities came to me. The wording of her request to her daughter could have been misinterpreted by either the son who eventually wrote the account of her deeds, and wasn't present at the time, or by those who translated the text into modern English. Otherwise, she could have seen no alternative other than certain death at the hands of the Egyptians and entirely trusted her son into God's care, knowing her daughter would be powerless to help but wanting to know God's will in the situation. Whether her son lived or died in that river was down to God and God alone. I chose to believe that her faith was so strong that she trusted God enough to let her son go and, again, used this rather than the exact Biblical account to guide my retelling. Once more, I offer apologies to any who have drawn a different conclusion or would have liked to have seen the original wording.

On the matter of slave conditions, I feel that most modern conceptions of slavery are driven by our more recent knowledge of prison camps and the brutality of various regimes aimed at the subjugation or annihilation of a particular race. The process by which the Israelites became slaves to the Egyptians was gradual, with requirements and expectations slowly changing from being prized citizens and respected workers to overworked slaves whose numbers were feared by their masters. Even when Moses returned to free them, it was only the leaders who were beaten for their people failing to meet targets (Exodus 5v14), rather than every individual being worked to an early death.

My research into slavery in Egypt, while brief, supported this interpretation. Owning slaves was not a common practice at that time, and most individuals were more like indentured servants paying off a debt than true slaves as we view the term today. Slaves were given considerable freedoms in ancient Egypt, allowed to marry whomever they chose, wander at will within reason, and even own property and land. They were often given positions of authority, as documented in the Biblical account of Joseph.

With this in mind, I created a world where certain, crucial freedoms were denied the humans, but in other respects, they were initially treated well enough to be productive over a lifetime, in line with my understanding of ancient slavery in several different cultures.

The resistance was a movement I thought would be realistic in those circumstances and a possible cause for Pharaoh's fear of outright rebellion or collusion with his foreign enemies. Apologies, again, to those who see these things in a different light and are confused or frustrated with my version of events.

In general, I have always been fascinated by the characters surrounding Moses. The faith and courage his mother displayed in saving his life, not only by putting him in a basket on a dangerous river, but also by giving him up to another to raise, have been an inspiration to me. So little is said of her in the Bible, yet she had such a powerful role to play in Moses' survival. I have always wanted to tell her story, to figure her out, and I look forwards to one day meeting her and asking the thousand questions I have regarding her life.

I would love to discuss my interpretation of her character with you. My contact details can be found at the bottom of this note, and I will always respond to anyone willing to take the time to write to me.

Finally, thank you for reading this book. Writing has been a dream of mine for longer than I can remember, but I've only recently found my own courage and given it a go. Having others read my work is a tremendous compliment. I hope you enjoyed the results and will read the next instalment of The Legacy Chronicles. I would also be most grateful for an honest review of Courage on whichever site, app, or social media platform with which you are most comfortable.

Visit Lauren at:

www.laurenhsalisbury.com

www.facebook.com/gillascourage

Contact Lauren at:

laurenhsalisbury@gmail.com

DISCUSSION QUESTIONS

1. What are the similarities and differences between Gilla and Jochabed, whose story can be found in Exodus 2?

2. In Courage there are many characters, all in different places spiritually. Which did you most connect with and why?

3. Has there been a time in your life when you faced a situation that tested your faith? How did you navigate that challenge?

4. Which character do you think had the most courage and why?

5. In what ways did the characters develop courage throughout the book? How can you become more courageous in everyday life?

6. Imagine what it must be like to live in a time or place where your family is not safe, as many still do today. What would you be willing to do to protect them, and how would your faith impact that decision?

COMING SOON

Can two people with opposing principles overcome their differences to be together?

Than has spent his life ostensibly having fun while secretly fighting for his people's freedom. A member of the underground resistance, he is only ever serious around his comrades and his family. When an injury forces him to step down from active duty and his reluctant nurse sparks his interest, Than finds himself in uncharted territory. The fascinating woman will have nothing to do with him.

Menali's past has taught her to keep her head down and trust that God has a reason for allowing the human race to suffer on U'du. When Than explodes into her life, he refuses to take no for an answer and challenges all of her preconceptions. He soon has her re-evaluating her priorities and wondering what life with someone like him would be like.

For a sneak peek of Conviction, go to my website:
www.laurenhsalisbury.com/conviction

Printed in Great Britain
by Amazon